REPORTER ON THE RUN

Carlene Miller

New Victoria Publishers
Norwich, Vermont

Published by New Victoria Publishers Inc., PO Box 27 Norwich, Vt. 05055
A Feminist Literary and Cultural Organization founded in 1976

Cover Design Claudia McKay

Printed and bound in Canada
1 2   3   4   2004   2003   2002 2001

Library of Congress Cataloging-in-Publication Data

Miller Carlene, 1935-
      Reporter on the run : a Lexy Hyatt mystery / Carlene Miller.
      p. cm.
      ISBN 1-892281-14-7
      1. Hyatt, Lexy (Fictitious character)--Fiction. 2. Women journalists--Fiction. 3. Lesbians--Fiction. I. Title.

PS3563.I3763 R46 2001
813' 54--dc21

                                       2001030571

For Dottie
—may you keep the ball in play somewhere

ONE

"Go get 'em, my Ninja warrior."

I glared at Wren only half meaning it. From the top of my short auburn hair to the soles of my feet, I was uncomfortable. I would never feel at home in the coarse white jacket that drooped about my torso and pants that didn't quite reach my ankles. I transferred my glare to the youths trooping into the Martial Arts Academy. Several twirled their colored belts of gold and green and blue. I toyed with my own plain white one.

Wren chuckled. "You're taller than they are, have broader shoulders and I can attest to the strength of your hips."

I grinned in spite of my desire to continue pouting. Grudgingly I admitted, "I know this is good for me and I'm learning worthwhile stuff, but I'll probably never need it."

The setting sun, still quite early in January, burnished Wren's blonde hair with a copper glow as she leaned toward me and reached to grip my wrist lightly. "I hope you won't—but a black eye, concussion, and a broken arm in less than six months do not bode well. Nor does your practice of sharing territory with murdered bodies. Somehow you missed the lesson on reporters covering the news, not being part of it." She tightened her grip. "We are trying to look out for you, Lexy."

The "we" was herself, Marilyn Neff, owner of the lesbian bar the Cat, Detective Roberta Exline, and Charlie and Meg, two friends of contrasting ages I had acquired over the summer. As a Christmas gift they had presented me with the outfit and a paid-up series of lessons in self-defense, knowing I couldn't refuse.

I covered Wren's hand with my free one. "I like the other ways you look out for me better." I was pleased to excite a flash of desire in her green eyes. "Maybe I'll learn some new moves to try out on you later." I left the car but bent down before closing the door. "Don't drive off

5

feeling too smug, Miss Carlyle. I know perfectly well that you drop me off and pick me up to make certain that I go in and do my duty."

I straightened and closed the door feeling a bit smug myself. Wren and I had been lovers for less than a year—homeowners together for only two months. Our relationship was still a work in progress, one of testing and discovery. Finding our way around each other was a challenge and a delight I could live with forever.

At least we were able to do so in relative quiet and calm now. Our agreement to commit to each other had been only the beginning. I hadn't been prepared for the whirlwind of decision-making and activities that followed. Finding a house, supervising changes, making purchases, moving in—everything accompanied by legal and financial meetings and mountains of paperwork. It hadn't been easy arranging all that around our jobs. Sometimes I had felt permanently out of breath.

I reached the entrance door at the same time as my nemesis, an eleven-year-old of straight lines and severe demeanor. I had heard her called Kelleen, not a name that fit her dark coloring and somber guise. She never slouched. The top of her head didn't quite reach my shoulders. Her walnut-brown hair curved from a center part to just below her ears. Severe bangs touched thick straight brows above eyes that were always slightly hooded. Even when she spoke, the thin lines of her lips moved little.

She asked, "Have you practiced your stances?"

There have been times in my life when I would have paid a fortune for her flat, authoritarian tone. I tried for a neutral, "I have."

Without further comment she entered ahead of me and went immediately to a space in the front line. I chose an end position in the third line and began limbering exercises. Monday night we had been put through a number of weight-shifting stances and forced to maintain them for long periods to increase our balance and concentration. The cat stance, weight back and front heel off the floor, had been my downfall—literally. I had pitched forward into Kelleen, clunking my chin on the top of her head and grabbing her hips for support. She hadn't flinched or lost her balance—merely lowered a hand to straighten her blue belt.

The preceding week I had collapsed sideways, destroyed by the pain of a charley horse. Standing next to me that time, Kelleen had not broken the rhythm of her moves as she said with exaggerated patience, "Point with your heel, not your toe." Had she watched me,

I don't think I would have taken her advice. As she had stared complacently ahead, I stretched my leg, pointed with my heel, and achieved immediate relief.

Now the instructor said, "Palms flat on the floor, Lexy. And begin your rise from the abdomen." She watched me as I flattened my hands and then lifted my torso. She stared at my thighs knowing that I had used them to straighten up. The concept of the abdomen as the center of force was eluding me. But I liked her instructional methods. She favored no one and delivered commands without threat or intimidation. She modified the Asian rituals of respect with American directness but omitted the cloying friendliness that lately pervaded business and service transactions. We addressed her as Major, her rank after twenty years in the army. Her most distinctive feature was a high flattop—what I described to Wren as porcupine hair.

After individual stretching, she put us through partner stretches and then the various stances we had learned. Next she paired us novices with more experienced partners. She commanded us to open our minds to perceive our opponent's intentions, to visualize our own bodies as a collection of pliant limbs easily and quickly moved. For the first time I became fully involved. It excited me to see my opponent's movement coming in time to defeat it.

Until I was paired with Kelleen.

She faced me squarely, unmoving. Her very stillness became a distraction. I began focusing on different parts of her. Then I shifted my weight from one leg to the other. Shifting my stance, I took a kick to my abdomen and landed hard on my rump. It felt like an eternity before I could inhale again.

Kelleen returned to her position and waited. I scrambled to my feet and faced her. This time I centered my gaze and held it. When I spotted her drawing a deeper breath, a slight rise of her tunic, I stepped back and to the side. Her foot merely brushed the strands of my belt.

Her lips moved in a fraction of a smile. "You are beginning to learn."

Shortly after eight o'clock Kelleen and I stood outside waiting for our rides. Her mother arrived first. One look at the woman framed in the car window and I understood the daughter's name. She was a bushy-haired carrot-top complete with white skin and freckles. There was even a hint of Boston Irish in the voice apologizing to her daughter for being a little late.

She looked me up and down and said, "Would this be the famous Lexy Hyatt?"

I stepped forward. "I'm Lexy."

She responded, "Brie O'Mara. I've been wanting to meet you. I don't get a crack at the *Ledger* in the mornings any more until Kelleen has scanned for your byline."

I didn't look at the girl but I sensed her discomfort at having that revealed. "It's nice to know she sees me functioning more skillfully than I do in there."

The gleam in Brie O'Mara's eyes told me she had heard the stories. I added, "Though I'm not always happy with what has to be covered." I was thinking of yesterday's coverage of a dead newborn in a dumpster and the arrest of a fourteen-year-old for assisting friends in killing her parents.

"I can believe that. But you do it effectively." She brushed at her hair. "May we give you a ride?"

"Thank you, but mine's coming across the lot now."

Kelleen walked around to get in her mother's car without a word to me, but I saw her give Wren the once over as Wren's car pulled up behind.

Soon Wren's contralto laughter filled the car as I related my latest humiliation. "But I'm beginning to find the flow, as the Major says. And I'm beginning to enjoy my Christmas present." I touched my hand to my abdomen. "But I'm going to have a whopper of a bruise."

"It's a good thing I'll know where it came from," Wren teased. "Wouldn't want to think you were practicing take-downs with some mysterious beauty nearer your age."

"Watch out, woman. I may do some bruising of my own when we get home."

Wren smirked, then said, "Not until you call Joe Worthington. He called earlier. Something going on at the paper?"

"More than I have a handle on. I never used to pay any attention to the powers-that-be outside my own department. I was too busy learning the game. Struggling to get off the puff-and-fluff detail. The Standishes were little more than names to me when they died in October. I've seldom exchanged words with Andrea. I've only seen the back of Andrew's head a couple of times."

"Cutesy names for twins."

"There's nothing cutesy about her that I've seen. Don't know much about him."

I fell silent and thought about the unease that had been permeating the corridors and cubicles of the *Ledger* since the death of the elder Standishes. When I started at the newspaper proofing and editing, I concentrated mostly on surviving in the trenches, learning how to work with the level of hierarchy immediately above me, and progressing to reporter. Here and there I acquired background on the *Ledger* itself.

Originally it was a community weekly, established by John Iberson in the 1880s and concerned more with social and cultural events than hard news. Around 1900 the Orange County *Chronicle* was launched by William Standish, who had been covering the Spanish-American War for Hearst and decided to stay in Florida. The *Chronicle* concentrated on promoting the area in terms of business opportunities, climate and growth potential. Eventually it became a daily. The two papers were merged in the early 1950s by the marriage of Rose Iberson and Lyndall Standish.

I spoke aloud to Wren. "Did I tell you how the paper got its name? I heard it during the flood of reminiscing after the funerals."

She hummed a negative as she sliced through traffic towards an exit lane.

"The story is that Rose Iberson insisted on a contest before their wedding to determine which name the paper would keep. As the challenged, Standish got to choose the contest. They were members of the Laurel Oak Country Club and known for their tennis, but supposedly she was gambling on his being gentleman enough, or concerned enough about his public image, not to choose something where his male strength would be too obvious an advantage. He proposed a badminton game."

"Badminton!"

"Yep. When I told my mother the story, she said it was quite the rage as a game for mixed doubles at social gatherings back then. That made me remember something one of my history teachers said." I grinned. "She was the first teacher I had a crush on and I hung on her every word. She said that the 1950s worked hard at reminding women they were the weaker sex after they had been building planes and ships, managing alone or going off to war themselves. But I played badminton a few times. It took a lot of quickness and finesse."

"Which Rose must have had," Wren interjected, "since *Ledger* is the name that survived. I trust Standish took it gracefully."

"Must have. I heard she kept a shuttlecock under glass on her desk." We laughed together at that.

Our togetherness was still a thing of wonder to me. I had worried that it would be too binding, too stifling. But Wren had shown her understanding, or maybe just acceptance, of my need for space as well. I hadn't asked her to attend the martial arts classes nor had she requested it. When she was deep into creating a design, I would sometimes go off somewhere alone. She never objected.

I looked out into darkness broken by slashes of light and thought about the vitality of Rose Iberson who had been killed along with her husband when their Cessna crashed in rough terrain near Macon, Georgia. Both had semi-retired before I arrived at the paper and both being pilots often flew to various cities on business or pleasure. In October they had been on their way to Atlanta for a convention of newspaper publishers when a line of heavy weather sweeping though Alabama had hurled unexpected mini-tornadoes halfway into Georgia.

The deaths of the Standishes hadn't touched me personally, except to make me value a note from Rose expressing her pleasure at a series I had done on small airports in the area. Well before their deaths, their daughter, Andrea, was already running things from her second-floor suite. Apparently she preferred working through upper-level management rather than employing the hands-on approach that came naturally to her parents, especially her mother. True, I had seen her more often lately in the first-floor environs. And I had noticed guarded conversations starting up or stopping abruptly at her appearance. Also there was an unusual degree of prickliness on the part of my immediate boss, Joe Worthington.

As though reading my mind, Wren asked, "Did the Standishes dying so suddenly affect things at the paper?"

"Not in any specific way that I can see, but there is a general…disquiet everywhere. I heard somebody wonder if there was some kind of problem with their wills. People get antsy about their jobs whenever change appears on the horizon."

"Surely they'd leave the paper to the daughter who has been running it," Wren said emphatically.

"Things don't always get done right."

We were getting close to home and the traffic had thinned. Wren gave me a searching look. "Do I hear a little rancor in that voice? Old wounds perchance?"

"You caught me. There's an air gun, a BB rifle, that will forever stick in my craw."

"Tell me."

I told her. "I spent a couple of weeks at my great-uncle's farm when I was around nine. I was there with my mother for a reunion and the chance to get to know some of my Midwestern relatives better. We kids nosed into everything and one of our discoveries was this neat air rifle with fancy scrollwork on the stock. Uncle Ernie let us target shoot tin cans and such. Said that the best shot would get to take it home."

Wren said knowingly, "And you were the best shot."

"Sure was. But he gave it to one of the boys. Said guns weren't for girls. Now that I'm older and wiser I don't think guns are for anyone." I added with vehemence, "But that one was mine! I earned it. Twin or not, I hope Andrew hasn't been given some kind of edge over Andrea because he's male."

A moment later I forgot my irritation with past and present situations as Wren turned into our driveway and pressed the garage-door opener. After so many years of dorm and apartment living, arriving home to a house I owned with the person I loved was heaven. I felt grounded without being immobilized, joined without loss of self. The Lexy of a year ago would not have thought that possible.

The door rumbled down behind us as I released my seat belt. Wren stopped me from getting out of the car with fingers lightly spread over the back of my neck. I scarcely had time to draw a breath before her mouth covered mine, first sweetly soft, then hard and hungry. Her lips skimmed my face, pausing at my closed eyelids, tracing my nose, sliding to suck gently at the hollow of my throat.

She murmured huskily, "Did you learn any new moves to try out on me?"

I nibbled at her ear. "You keep wondering about that while I call Worthington."

She thrust away. "You bully!"

I lowered my voice theatrically. "Not yet, my pretty."

We entered the kitchen just as the garage light clicked off. I plucked the cordless phone from its cradle and moved into my office area. It was the short leg of an L that turned a corner to widen into Wren's workroom, complete with skylight and wide windows for good light. I punched in Worthington's number and sat at my desk.

He answered on the second ring and started rattling off orders before I could identify myself. I hated caller ID which announced me before I could even speak. "Need you in the office good and early

11

tomorrow morning, Lexy. Ms. Standish will be meeting mid-morning with a representative from every department concerning Sunday, but earlier than that she wants—"

Something in his tone got under my skin. "I'm participating Sunday, Joe, but I don't have any official..."

"The boss lady said she wanted Lexy Hyatt there by six-thirty. So Lexy Hyatt will be there. Got that!?"

"Yes, sir!" I was just as curt as he had been.

"Ah, I'm sorry." He sounded honestly regretful. "I just got off the phone with one of Chris Cross's henchmen. Left a bad taste in my mouth. I'm just an old newshound who wants to die in harness, but those guys have got me chasing my tail. Right now I'm just being the messenger, so don't shoot me. Okay?"

He hung up leaving me with questions. What did Andrea Standish want with me? Who was Chris Cross? Why was Joe upset?

I looked at the pictures tacked to the wall above my desk—family that came with the territory and friends who had become part of who I am. I touched my fingers to the faces of those dead—two grandparents, the pitcher on our state championship team in high school, and my Uncle Kurt. My mother's fraternal twin, he had died in Vietnam before I was born but his features and hairstyle lived on in me. "Good night, guys," I whispered in the semi-darkness.

I went in search of Wren.

TWO

I found Wren—or rather heard her—in the bathroom brushing her teeth. Wearing only underwear, she stood leaning over the sink which emphasized the long curve from shoulder to waist and over a hip. My fingers tingled with the anticipation of stroking that flow of skin.

Our eyes met in the mirror. "Ready to play the bully?" she challenged.

Something in me wanted to put her off balance, override her control. I countered her provocative question with an unrelated one of my own. "Do you know anything about a Chris Cross? Doesn't sound like a real name."

Somewhat perplexed, she lounged across the bed, her blonde loveliness framed by the dark green spread. I sat on the edge. She said, "Oh, it's real all right. Christopher Cross, actually. He's the head of Chris Cross Communications. I submitted a logo design for the radio station they bought recently, assuming their application for new call letters come through—WCXC."

"Know anything about the company image?"

"Some. It's a company on the move. Started out in pagers. Expanded to cell phones. They've bought into some AM and FM radio stations. And I think I've seen the name in connection with WCOL-TV. Buying stock or bidding on it outright. Don't remember which."

"Are they into newspapers?"

"I don't know. Is this connected with the call from Worthington?"

"Only because he made an offhand reference to Chris Cross. He called to pull me in early in the morning for a meeting on Sunday's activities. It seems the boss lady requires my attendance." At Wren's quizzically raised brows, I added, "I have no idea why. Guess I'm a little out of sorts about it. You know how I hate organizational stuff. I just want to do my work without stubbing my toes on the higher-ups."

"Well, its a good thing some of us are into the organizational stuff.

Sunday should be quite a day. Everything is on 'go'. Publicity and involvement are peaking. I'm looking forward to it."

I agreed. A variety of women's groups had combined to organize fund-raising activities for Women's Health Week. The Sunday morning walk/jog/run would be one of the major activities. Hundreds of people were expected to gather wat an old train station and railyard which had been turned into a mini-park. The old track and rail bed had been removed, then renovated into wide paths for walkers, joggers, skaters, and bicyclists, cutting through undeveloped woodlands.

Many walkers, joggers and runners would be survivors of major illnesses. Others would be wearing pictures of loved ones, friends, or celebrities who had died or were invalids. Many businesses and groups had been generous in sponsoring participants or contributing money and services. I could have run under the sponsorship of the Cat or *Ledger* but chose to pay my own entry fee. I was running in the name of my third grade teacher who died of an aneurysm the summer following my year in her class. It had been my first experience at losing someone important in my life.

I asked Wren, "Are you still planning to work one of the stands along the track?"

"Yes. The Art League is going to give away water and juice. And I plan to have my sketchpad with me. I've been commissioned by the Women's Forum to do a cover for their next publication."

"Great!" I stretched out alongside her. "That calls for some celebrating." I drew her to me in a passionate kiss, unhooking her bra at the same time. I stroked her back as my tongue probed the sweet recesses of her mouth, tasting the mint of her toothpaste. "Still want me to bully you?"

Uncharacteristically, Wren giggled. "You wouldn't know how to be a bully."

I tugged her upright and tossed the bra toward a chair. Then I stood up pulling her with me. Quickly I shrugged out of my tunic top and whipped it around her shoulders. Before she could react, I had tied the belt in a half-hitch, pinning her arms at her sides. A slight shove tumbled her back on the bed.

She cried out a surprised, "Lexy!"

I peeled her panties over her hips and down her firm thighs. I ruffled my fingers in her thick blonde pubic hair and her thighs slackened. This time she moaned my name. I bent to smooth my cheek against her golden mound and she mewed a cry of desire.

I stood upright and looked down on her.

Her eyes were wide and bright, her moist lips parted for deep breathing. "Untie me, Lexy." The command was tentative.

"Not until I've drunk my fill. Bullies are like that."

She gasped, her breathing deepening even more. I knelt on the floor and spread her legs wider. I laughed softly as she shifted closer and one leg went over my back. I parted her with my fingers, exposing the satiny inner flesh. I breathed hot breath on the moist cleft.

She begged, "Again." I did it twice more and she strained to lift herself closer to my mouth.

I stroked the pulsating flesh slowly with my full tongue, soon increasing my speed. I could feel Wren's struggle to free her arms, see her hands trying to reach me. I enjoyed a control I seldom exerted over her.

Her voice rough with need, she pleaded, "In me! In me, Lexy! In...me—"

I thrust my tongue as deep as possible. She groaned her satisfaction and dug her heel into the small of my back. As her body began to lift and thrash, I sought the engorged bud and sucked it between my lips. Lightly I tongued the very tip of it until pleasure rocketed her body from my grasp.

I nearly climaxed myself and could feel the gathering of my own hot juices. Hurriedly I removed the rest of my clothes. Wren had managed to sit up. A simple tug at one end of the belt and I freed her. She pulled the tunic off and patted it. She said in a breathy voice, "Not the use for which this was intended—but I'm not objecting."

We scrambled under the covers, seeking each other's warmth. I stretched a bare arm to turn off the bedside lamp.

Wren teased, "After what you did to me, you want to hide in the dark?"

"I'm not hiding—just preserving electricity." I snuggled close, breathing the vanilla scent of her.

"Oh, Lexy. What a tangle of complexities you are. Will I ever unravel all of them?"

"I hope not," I mumbled into her neck. "Wouldn't want you to get bored with me."

Wren lifted herself on an elbow. She brushed at my hair. "Never...not ever."

She settled her head on my shoulder and began stroking me with the backs of her fingers. I willed myself to relax and enjoy the sensations. In a moment she said, "Why are you smiling?"

"I've discovered another bonus of my martial arts classes. I'm more aware of my body as an instrument—in this case an instrument of pleasure."

She ducked her head under the covers and her voice came as though from a distance. "An instrument for me to play."

My nipples hardened for her mouth. I felt the gentle draw that sent waves of heat coursing down my torso to flare hottest between my legs. I gave myself up to her—to the mouth that seemed to be everywhere at once, to the fingers moistening my throbbing crevice before entering me, to the rhythmed thrust of her hand driving me toward explosion.

I skipped up the steps to the *Ledger* entrance, my body still vibrating with the physical memories of the previous night. Sooner or later, I knew, Wren and I would begin to slip from the honeymoon that now plunged us often and fiercely into each others arms. Robert Frost was right when he said "Nothing gold can stay." But I wasn't ready to relinquish our golden time yet.

It was only a little past six o'clock and few day people were present, but I heard the clack of computer keys coming from Barbara MacFadden's cubicle. I detoured into it before Joe Worthington could spot me from his glass enclosure. Dubbed the Iron Maiden for her gray hair and severe demeanor. she was known for her relentless pursuit of information with skills honed long ago in Army Intelligence. She had been a surprising ally when I found myself involved as an amateur in two murder investigations. I patiently waited for her attention, knowing she would not turn from her work until she had completed the task at hand.

"Yes, Miss Hyatt?" She never used first names at work.

I could never tell how she knew who I was without looking. I asked bluntly, "Do you know why Ms. Standish wants to see me?"

She turned, her deep blue eyes registering neither interest nor concern and replied. "Recently she gathered personnel folders of which yours was one. Also she called up files of special activities and accomplishments of staff members. Whatever the cause, I do not suggest you keep her waiting."

I said a weak "Yes, ma'am" to the back of her head as she returned to her work. At such times it was difficult for me to remember that at the Billet I was permitted to call her Barbara and see her warm and amused among veteran friends.

Standing in his doorway, Worthington snapped his fingers at me the moment I stepped into the hallway. He jerked a thumb toward a private hallway as I approached him. "Take the steps back there to Ms. Standish's. Your meeting's upstairs."

"My meeting?"

"Right. The department reps will be in distribution later this morning getting instructions and shirts and caps for their sign-ups for Sunday." He peered at me over the glasses that rode low on his nose. "Don't keep her waiting. The others are already there."

I felt like there was a conspiracy to throw me, ignorant and unprepared, into some predicament. At the top of the stairs the door to the owner's suite was open. The large room was as sleek as Andrea Standish—all light grays and mauve, the lines of the furnishings clean and smooth, few frills. The lady herself was at a silver and glass desk. She wore a charcoal gray pantsuit relieved by a white satin blouse and pewter jewelry. Her hair was a pale lemon, relatively short, swept back and up in a stylish salon cut. The eyes she turned to me were a surprisingly soft blue, much like clean lake water shielded by mist.

"Please join us, Ms. Hyatt."

I was waved to a chair and a cup of coffee handed to me. It was a dark roast with a hint of almond. The "us" was Tamara Gantt, a young African-American woman who had recently escaped editing to take my place as rookie reporter, and a man I recognized from printing. He had assisted me when I had done my turn as guide for a school class being shown the working areas of the newspaper.

"I appreciate the three of you being here so early." Andrea's voice was moderate, carefully nonconfrontational. "I know you are all participating in the Women's Health Week activities this Sunday—and that each of you is essentially sponsoring yourself—for worthwhile personal reasons, I am certain."

Was she going to twist our arms to participate under the *Ledger* banner? I felt my inner hackles rising, but her next words soothed them.

"I have no intention of interfering with that. I would, however, like to persuade you to change the nature of your participation. Specifically, the orienteering event."

I had considered that event before deciding on joining the groups of runners and joggers. I had enjoyed my two encounters with orienteering, drawn by the hiking elements, the challenge of conquering unknown terrain, the out-of-doors adventure. Armed with only a topographical map and a compass, you sought markers in their proper sequence to take you from start to finish in one to three hours. Not nearly as simple as it sounded. Courses were generally set up to cover two to five miles of varying terrain. Finding markers clearly designated on a map was far easier than finding them in the natural setting itself.

I was reclaimed from my thoughts by a change in Andrea's tone. "Forgive the elements of Mission Impossible intrigue, but I am going to ask you to pretend that this meeting never occurred—whether you accept my proposal or not. I need a team in the field to protect the *Ledger*. You three have the qualifications and, I think, a predilection for responding to challenge." She definitely had our attention. "The *Ledger* is sponsoring the orienteering event and will be contributing a large sum in the name of my parents. Of course that disqualifies me, and my brother Andrew, but I insisted that *Ledger* employees be allowed to participate."

She sipped coffee, intentionally making us wait for more information, I thought. "My brother has informed me that he intends to race 'for fun' and not as an official participant."

Her disapproval was obvious. Was she expecting us to waylay him in the woods and tie him to a tree to preserve the good name of the Standish family? What was wrong with him competing for the fun of it? I could imagine his mother choosing to do the same thing. I blinked my eyes and ducked my head over the delicate coffee cup as I felt her gaze probing my eyes for my thoughts.

Looking away from me, she continued, "I am concerned that my brother is going to try to manipulate the outcome of the event. I don't want that to happen."

Tamara interrupted, "How could he do that?"

The man from printing explained, "Easy. Send people off in the wrong direction claiming it is a faster or easier way. Hide or move markers."

Andrea nodded. "Those are the kinds of things I want people out there trying to guard against." She looked my way again. "You may be wondering why I don't just keep Andrew off the course. Our being twins increases the natural friction that sometimes develops between siblings." Her eyes became a frozen blue. "But more, or perhaps it should be less, to the point there are private issues that prevent me from dealing with my suspicions openly. I'm not asking you to put yourselves at risk in any way. Just attempt to be where necessary to keep the contest clean by your mere presence. I know that all three of you have experience in orienteering and are resourceful and intelligent people. Will you help me? Help the *Ledger*?"

Tamara and the man agreed without hesitation. I only nodded my head slightly. I didn't like the idea of being used but I liked less the idea of a fixed outcome. Also, I was intrigued.

Andrea added, "I will see to it that you are registered and go off at different times. Since you can run singly or in pairs, I'll trust you to select a companion to aid you if you so wish. Just make certain I get the name by the end of the day."

She turned around a picture frame and we saw a fairly recent photograph of the four Standishes taken underneath the plaque on the front of the building. Andrew was a handsome male version of his twin except that his form was muscled and his face soft with an affected nonchalance.

Andrea thanked us sincerely and we rose in unison, but she added, "Ms. Hyatt, a word more with you, please."

When the others left, we remained standing. Removing a folder from a drawer, she said, "Ms. MacFadden speaks highly of you. She says you know how to function by your instincts." She drew a picture from a folder and handed it to me. "That is Nelda Cross. She will be in the race. My instincts say Andrew may want to maneuver a win for her."

I looked intently at the picture. The woman was petite, raven-haired, sharp-featured. I could not guess her age. She could be young, well preserved near middle age, or anything in between. My concentration still on the picture, I said, "And you want me to…?"

"Stick to her like a sandspur. But make certain you beat her at the end." Her voice was flint striking a response in me—awakening the slumbering athlete who thrived on competition. Even as I resisted being her pawn, I was assessing my fitness for competition.

I said only, "I'll try." Her nod was both an acceptance and a dismissal.

Worthington was haranguing a computer technician so I quickened my stride past his office. I passed my own area as well and again sought out Barbara MacFadden. It was as though she were waiting for me. Two folders were passed to me with an admonition.

"Andrew Standish and Nelda Cross. Read them off grounds on your own time."

I risked a request. "Is there anything you can add that could be of help?"

She did not hesitate. "Andrew is a playboy in the most literal sense of the word, but do not let that put you off guard. He is as intelligent and driven as his sister but chooses to operate in a very different arena. Nelda Cross has a ruthless husband. And she may be equally ruthless. Your workday is at hand."

I accepted this second dismissal and went to work.

THREE

"Hey, Lexy!"

Halfway down the steps, I turned to see Tamara Gantt. She waved me toward the stone ledge bordering the steps and joined me there, asking as she sat, "What did you think of this morning?"

As I sat down I shoved the folders I carried part way under me. "I'm not sure we got the whole story but I'm willing to go along and see how it plays out."

"Paul Jared thinks she was telling it like it is. Just wants to keep her twin brother from making a mess that might make the paper look bad."

"Paul Jared? Is that the guy who was up there with us?"

Tamara nodded as a sudden wind tried to lift her shiny black hair free of the gold combs that held it back from her face. Her skin was a cocoa brown and the late afternoon sun highlighted her round cheeks. "He's a nice man. Single father. His wife died of ovarian cancer a few years ago." She shook off the sad thought. "Anyway he said he heard that Andrea had to follow after her brother and clean up messes he made one summer down in the bowels." She used the staff word for the underground rooms where the paper was printed and distributed.

I said, "I didn't know he ever worked here. In five plus years, I've only seen him passing through a few times. Most of those since the Standishes died."

"Paul said the old-timers down below told him Andrea was the one with ink in her veins. Worked her way through every department, starting with delivery when she was a teenager. That's probably why I got my job."

"Explain."

Tamara said, "In a minute. They said every so often Mr. Standish would drag Andrew in and try to get him involved. Nothing ever took. They thought he made the messes on purpose as a way to get out."

21

I considered that. Could the same thing be going on again? Was he trying to make a mess of the orienteering event to get out of some involvement arranged by his sister? But I didn't buy my own supposition. I had seen enough of her to know she was unlikely to share her power—especially with someone unconcerned and inept. Still, family factored into equations differently...

Tamara was saying, "I started out in delivery just like our highly motivated boss—though I didn't know it at the time. I had come home from Spelman with degrees in English and journalism. Knew better than to bloody my knuckles on doors that weren't going to open to me, so I made a real nuisance of myself in the Trees."

The Trees was the name of a large African-American community so called because all the streets were named for trees.

"I begged, browbeat, and bullied people into signing up for *Ledger* delivery," Tamara explained. "I used every trick I could think of, from getting your kids into college to having easy access to the lottery numbers. I knew the Trees would be a blank area on the distribution maps. When I plunked down fistfuls of subscriptions, the white folks let me in."

Despite the mild tone, I saw her eyes dim for a second. I asked, "How long did you throw papers?"

Tamara's easy manner returned. "For nearly a year. I did a good job, too. Increased subscriptions. Made some decent money. Then one day I parked my butt right here and waited for Ms. Andrea. Met her at the bottom of these steps. Told her who I was and what I had done in the Trees. Told her where I had gone to school and what degrees I had. Said I had a nephew who could take over my route and keep it going." She grinned broadly. "I asked her if there was any place for me inside."

"What did she say?"

"Very little. Just said to report to editing Monday morning. And I did. Had to work two jobs for awhile till I got my nephew trained. Now I'm a reporter. You watch out, Lexy Hyatt. You just might be working for me someday."

I laughed. "As long as you don't try to take me off the beat and stick me in an office permanently."

"Deal." She held out a hand. I slapped it lightly. She said, "Can't be sure how long I can hold on here, though, if Cross Communications has a foot in the door."

Did everyone know about that organization but me? "What does that mean?"

Tamara waited until a group of people leaving the building passed us. "What little I know comes mostly from an ad salesman I've been dating who just left a radio station Cross bought out. There were major changes right away. All new management does that, but Davonne said that some of the new people Cross brought in are right-wing crazies. The kind who know how to behave in the parlor but what they do in the back room is something else. They made big changes in commercial and program content at the radio station. Then they herded the liberals and moderates toward the door. All done very politely—and legally. Davonne is big on conspiracy theories. Thinks its part of the takeover of Florida by the deep-pocket conservatives running the Republican Party.

"You said they have a foot in our door. Have they bought into the *Ledger* already?"

"Not that I know of. But there's a woman in advertising and a man in promotion who seem to be on Joe Worthington's tail a disproportionate amount of time for the positions they hold. Davonne said Cross manages to plant people before he gets officially or financially involved. Gets the lay of the land that way." Tamara became more intense. "There's been a buzz in the office about Worthington pressuring reporters to make changes in their copy. He's hit on me a couple of times that way. Most think its coming from upstairs but I'd vote for Cross after what I heard from Davonne. Hope we're all wrong and Worthington's just going through male menopause."

Silently I agreed, thinking of some of my own recent confrontations with the news editor over copy. Maybe it was time I tuned into the buzz. My private life and work schedule had made me keep my head lower than usual lately.

Tamara said offhandedly, "I would hate to buy into a conspiracy theory, but..." She shrugged. "I'm genetically predisposed to smell sell-outs."

I didn't want to consider Worthington in that context so I said only, "Maybe we should make the *Ledger* part of our beat for awhile. Quietly, of course." I shifted and felt the folder on Nelda Cross under my thigh. I was anxious to get to it.

Tamara agreed. "If we manage to keep the orienteering race clean, that may give us some leverage with the boss. Can't believe she would want the paper tarnished by special interests any more than she does by her brother. It looks to me like she's been letting things run themselves since her parents died. Giving people time to adjust to their being gone. Got a feeling that's all about to change."

I nodded my agreement, started to get up, then settled back down. "How did you get into orienteering, Tamara?"

"My boyfriend again. Just jogging was getting boring. Two weeks ago we came in third in a field laid out through a section of Ocala forest."

I asked, "Are you going to have him run with you Sunday?"

"No. I'm not sure he wouldn't get too caught up in the competition and forget what we were there for." She wrinkled her nose. "The truth is he probably wouldn't go along anyway. He's lighter skinned than I am but blacker on the inside. He'd probably accuse me of being a good house-nigger."

The term made me uncomfortable. "Not fair to catch it from both sides," I commented.

Her smile was a shade cynical. "I imagine you run into that, too. You're too fair and balanced not to." The smile broadened into a teasing grin. "Though seeing you march with the bare-breasted Avengers would be a hoot."

This was the first time she had ever directly addressed my being a lesbian. Some other time I would enjoy dissecting the similarities and differences of our situations. By unspoken mutual agreement we shifted to a short discussion of our plans for Sunday before going our separate ways.

It took me longer than usual to reach the Cat's parking lot due to the heavy Friday traffic. On the way I thought about Andrea's request and expectations, Worthington's unusual behavior and the possible threat of Chris Cross to the policies of the *Ledger*. I didn't need them thrown into the mix of my life right now. Happy as I was merging my life with Wren's, it required time and concentration. And I was working hard on the job pursuing satisfaction and security.

I didn't see Wren's car anywhere around the Cat, so I pulled into the small side lot and opened the folder on Nelda Cross. On top was a page from a media trade magazine. Above a short article on the expansion of Cross Communications into radio was a picture of husband and wife at a party, well dressed, drinks in hand. She was smiling coyly at the camera but his smile was lost in bulldog jowls. Despite the expensive suit and well-groomed look, the ruthlessness referred to by the Iron Maiden radiated from the picture. Cross didn't look like the kind of man who would tolerate his wife playing games with Andrew Standish. Immediately another thought surfaced. He did look like a man who might make his wife a partner in manipulations to gain a foothold at the *Ledger*.

A short article from a Women's Forum *Bulletin* included information that Nelda Cross had been a gymnast in high school and college. She continued to maintain a fitness regimen with the assistance of a personal trainer. I was offended by the quotes attributed to her, stressing the coexistence of fitness and femininity and attacking out-of-shape women as a blight on the social landscape. I realized that my own fitness and athleticism would not give me an edge in the orienteering event.

I gleaned a few vital statistics from the contents of the folder. Surprisingly Nelda Cross was forty-five. She had been a television personality in Jacksonville when she married Christopher Cross ten years ago—after he divorced his first wife. So much for conservative family values, but then that put him in sync with many politicians and businessmen. It was also her second marriage, her first having been to a sports announcer. She and Cross had moved to Orlando four years ago and she had recently been elected to the Women's Forum. I was familiar with the Forum as a high-powered group of social, business, and political women beginning to make themselves felt in city and county concerns. I wondered if Nelda Cross was representing herself or her husband's interests.

Though the light was fading rapidly, I exchanged her folder for Andrew's. His contained much more and I plucked a piece from the top group. It was a newspaper article dated Alaska two months ago and covered the death of six snowmobilers in an avalanche. Dozens of snowmobilers had taken to the mountain slopes following a ten-foot fall of new snow. They were high-marking, a dangerous practice of speeding up a slope to see who could leave the highest track. The U.S. Forest Service continually tried to discourage the activity and had warned that a sudden decrease in temperature heightened the possibility of avalanches.

Seven had been in the lead when a small avalanche rumbled down a gully. The lead man had angled toward the edge of the group and narrowly missed being hit by a larger fall some minutes later. That fall killed the other six in the lead. Many further below had been tumbled under snow or swept furiously downward. They had all survived though many were seriously injured.

The lead man who escaped both injury and death was Andrew Standish.

I jumped at a hard rap on the top of the car. Wren said, "Didn't anyone ever tell you you could go blind reading in the dark?"

"I heard it would improve your eyesight," I retorted. "I don't have any trouble finding you in the dark, do I?"

Wren lowered her voice. "After last night, I may put you on restriction. This martial arts bravado is going to your head."

"I rather thought it went to other places."

She opened the car door. "Get out of there, bully. I've been bending over a drawing board all day." She pointed to the folder in my hand. "And leave your work here. I want to be taken dancing."

Inside the Cat it was still early—only two customers at the bar, a few at tables, one couple tossing darts. The small band was setting up. Melody, large and graceful, waved from behind the bar, her blonde hair reflecting the colored bar lights. She set out two napkins where she knew we would sit and moved to prepare our drinks. Despite my having become a homeowner, the Cat was still home as well.

We sipped our bourbon and Scotch, bantering with Melody and asking after her partner Victoria, an energetic young woman as diminutive as Melody was large. When the sound of the band tuning up melted into real music, we went to the dance floor. I chose to lead and drew Wren tight against me. I let a hand ride her hip and she nibbled an ear. We spoke little.

Back at the bar she asked me about the morning meeting with my boss. I gave her a very sketchy version, pausing whenever anyone was near enough to hear. Her brow furrowed in a mild frown.

I hurried to forestall her objections. "Now don't give me that look. We're not being asked to do anything except be in the field—spread out so that maybe one of us can have Andrew in sight and complicate any wrong moves he might want to make. He doesn't know any of us and will think we are just other competitors." I did not tell her about Nelda Cross and my specific assignment to beat her to the finish line.

Eventually we went to our reserved table in the plusher, quieter dining room. By unspoken agreement we avoided any more discussion of the *Ledger* and Sunday. Mostly we discussed the planting of trees and shrubs in our bare backyard come spring, as well as a day trip to Mossville and Lake Arrow to visit with friends sometime in February.

As the server was removing our plates, Wren glanced around the room. She called my attention to a table on the other side. "See the two over there. The tall brunette is Linda Dorsey. She's an attorney. Quietly out. Helped the Art League when we had to battle city hall.

They actually wanted to tear down our building."

"I know. And just for parking! I wrote a feature on the building itself—how old it was, how unique the brickwork designs were, all the different uses of the building in the past. Tried to make it sound like it would be an historical travesty to destroy it just to give some bankers easier access to their own oversize building."

"You wrote that story! I always thought it helped save the day. And I didn't even know you then. I'll have to plan a special way to say thank you." Her eyes were bright and playful.

I tried for a sultry tone. "Does that mean you are going to bully defenseless me?"

Wren said cavalierly, "You worry about it for a few nights."

I was aghast. "A few nights!"

"You heard me. You're in training for Sunday. No more fancy food, alcohol…or sex…until afterwards."

Before I could retort, she spoke again of the women at the far table. "The strawberry blonde is Mary Catherine Riley. She interviewed me about doing the cover for the Women's Forum *Bulletin*. I had thought she might be gay…but deep in the closet if she was. Guess I was wrong about that last part."

"Maybe not," I said speculatively. "She doesn't look all that relaxed. And she keeps checking everyone who comes in as though she's afraid she'll know them. Or they'll know her. I can remember doing that when I first came out. Whoops! She just spotted you."

The server returned to pour our coffee and Wren requested that she ask the two women across the way to join us. The attorney smiled her acceptance our way and they gathered up their purses and jackets, the smaller women somewhat reluctantly, I thought. Again I remembered my own uneasiness at coming out, and sympathized.

Introductions were made all around. Wren and Linda Dorsey did most of the talking.

At one point Linda said, "I'm glad you're here, Wren. I've been telling Mary Catherine that if you come to a place like this and see someone you know, that person is going to be a lesbian, too."

Mary Catherine smiled sheepishly. She said, "Theory and reality are a lot different to someone with my small-town Catholic upbringing." Bravely she risked touching Linda's hand. "But you know I've come to agree with you about those of us in the Forum being open and holding our ground."

Linda explained. "A small conclave is trying to shunt the open lesbians to the side—or even out of the Forum. Their claim that we push a gay agenda is totally false. My major interest is the preservation of old buildings and homes around town. Our president is big into pushing large businesses toward providing quality daycare for their employees. The fact that she's permanently on crutches doesn't mean she pushes an agenda for the disabled."

I had been running my fingers along the table edge as I listened. Now I stopped and interjected abruptly, "What drum does Nelda Cross beat?"

Wren looked at me quizzically but I ignored her. I fibbed, "I've been doing some research on Cross Communications and noticed she is a member of the Women's Forum."

Mary Catherine was the one to reply. "I think she's one of those people who just like to meddle around on the inside. She's part of the group going after the lesbians." Her manner toughened. "And she's always trying to influence the format of the *Bulletin*."

Linda inserted, "Mary Catherine's the editor. It's one of the few paid positions."

Wren explained for my benefit, "*Bulletin* is a misnomer. It's really a full magazine. You need to get your nose out of fiction and read some of the old copies Mary Catherine gave me."

I accepted the rebuke good-naturedly. "And give up on all my favorite female detectives?"

Wren held up both hands. "Okay!" She said to the others, "You wouldn't believe the number of women I have to share her with. She even brings them to bed." We shared a private, knowing glance.

The four of us sat a long time conversing over coffee. I was pleased to learn that Wren was being courted for Forum membership. Nor was I unhappy discovering that Wren, too, kept silent counsel until she was ready to reveal something. I watched Mary Catherine relax more and more. When Linda suggested dancing in the other room, she accepted almost eagerly.

Back in the bar, Wren and I were confronted by the Cat's owner Marilyn. who caught me looking worriedly behind the bar. She said, "Hal's all right, Lexy. He's in the back checking stock."

Her brother Hal was a survivor of prostate cancer...so far. I knew that he had personally paid the fees for our favorite server, Alice, and her little girl to walk Sunday in honor of Alice's mother who had recently been diagnosed with Parkinson's disease.

Marilyn, called the Admiral for her interest in boats and her vociferous commands, took a karate stance and chopped at me. "That half-pint kid taken you down yet, Lexy?"

I stared open-mouthed at Wren who immediately denied having passed on the story. Heads turned as Marilyn boomed, "She has! She sunk your butt! Tell me all about it!"

There was nothing for it but to tell, and loud enough for Melody and Hal who had returned to his place behind the bar, to hear. I wondered if Brie O'Mara would appreciate her daughter becoming the heroine of a lesbian bar.

Long about midnight we said our good-byes and headed home, a caravan of two beneath a sliver of moon and multiple stars, our way marked by garish man-made lights. At home in the bedroom I watched Wren climb into clean pajamas. She must have meant the no-sex injunction.

She caught my look but deflected it by asking, "Why the questions about this Nelda Cross?"

"Like I said. The research—"

She interrupted. "I know you're telling the truth, Lexy, but you always omit bits and pieces of your choosing. I play the good sport about it—but sometimes it's annoying."

I shoved rising guilt firmly back into its compartment, along with a retort about her not telling me about her proposed Forum membership. I understood the difference. Partly I didn't want her to know about the race because I didn't want to involve her—partly I didn't want her to know in case I lost.

I hid from her demanding stare by pulling her Christmas-gift sleeping tee over my head. It was light lavender with names of the women sleuths I admired written over it in variations of dark purple. I tried to look plaintive. "Are these the only women who are going to be close to me tonight?"

Wren tried to hold her stern expression but it began to slip. "Oh, get in bed. I need you close for warmth. But warmth is all you are getting."

I believed her. I considered it my penance for not telling her everything.

FOUR

I turned on my side and gazed at the still sleeping Wren. Her hair, a mix of blonde tones in the light of early morning, was fluffed about her face. The collar of her pajamas lay against one cheek, the point in the corner of her straight, firm mouth. Carefully I turned it back. Her lips parted and her copper lashes fluttered, but she didn't wake.

I slipped silently from bed and padded barefoot to my desk. Leaning back and putting my feet up, I propped Standish's folder against my thighs. It wasn't long before I understood clearly Barbara MacFadden's comment that he was a playboy in the literal sense of the word. Apparently his only purpose in life was to play. In two years of college, he began with organizing a dorm rugby team, the Stallions, that demolished all opponents and then assaulted campus structures. A Stallion shirt flew from every possible tower; private phone numbers were painted across the top of the administration building; all the furnishings of a professor's office were set in place on top of the history building.

Standish didn't graduate from college but he graduated to more adult games—diving in underwater caverns, survival outings in forests, deserts, or swamps, caving, skydiving, white-water rafting, mountain climbing. The folder contained newspaper clippings, columns from travel and adventure magazines, computer printouts. I didn't read them thoroughly, merely skimmed for the location and activity. He had ranged from the deep underwater springs of central Florida to the snow-covered mountains of Alaska. The datelines covered twenty years and no place appeared more than once except for Alaska. I found a follow up to the snowmobiling tragedy and filed it behind the first one.

I closed the folder wondering why one twin channeled all that energy into play and the other into work. If Andrew Standish had plans of his own for the orienteering event, they might be too formidable for three amateurs to disrupt. All we had going for us was his lack of awareness.

I lifted my head at the smell of coffee just as Wren touched my shoulder and leaned around me to put down a steaming mug. She tugged at the unruly spiky places in my uncombed hair. "When you start work without coffee, I know something has sunk a hook in you. Nelda Cross?"

I was glad I could hold up a clipping and point to the name of Andrew Standish.

But Wren wasn't appeased. "Are you sure there's no risk in that business tomorrow, Lexy? I don't like the idea of your boss using you. I can't believe it doesn't bother you."

"I'm just running a race, Wren." I didn't dare tell her it would be against Nelda Cross. "And if I'm being used, it's for the *Ledger*. I owe some dues there." I was thinking how much easier it had been for me to gain reporter status than it had been for Tamara Gantt. And I wanted to gain further ground there as well. The roots I was putting down with Wren made me want them on the job, too.

I sipped the coffee knowing it would be hot and strong. I put down the mug and removed my legs from the desk. Turning, I put my arms around Wren's thighs and pressed the side of my face against her stomach. I muttered, "You're even grumbling on the inside. What have I done to deserve such a grouch?"

She said, "Oh, hush." At the same time she lifted her pajama top up and over my head so that it was my cheek against her warm skin. Her voice was throaty and tense. "Don't breathe too deeply. I haven't bathed."

I hooked a finger in her bottoms and pulled. I ran my nose along the top of her gold triangle. "You smell good to me." She moaned and thrust toward me. I slipped the bottoms down her hips and gripped her firm cheeks.

Suddenly she seized my shoulders and forced me away. She said breathily, "You sure do know how to change the subject!"

"Wren!" I tried to pull her to me.

"No. If you're so set on racing, I'm going to see that you stay in training." She tugged up her pajamas. "I'm feeding you cereal this morning—and nothing else."

I glared at her retreating form but I was thinking, "Damn you, Andrea Standish!" I returned to my coffee and the Standish file. With all he had dared and accomplished, I couldn't see winning at orienteering being important to him. What if the importance was Nelda Cross or, through her, Chris Cross? But why? Who stood to gain? A cynicism I had never known as a teacher had crept into my work as a reporter. I wasn't sure I liked that.

In the kitchen at the small table we used far more often than the larger dining-room table, I grumbled over my cereal. "I don't like this stuff. I chew and chew and it doesn't go away. You could at least feed me oatmeal."

Wren responded sarcastically, "The maple syrup and brown sugar kind to which you would add butter?" At my enthusiastic nod she added seriously, "I want to keep you healthy, Lexy. All the brochures and information being prepared for Women's Health Week have gotten to me—made me realize all the things that can go wrong, all the conditions that the medical community hasn't properly evaluated from a female perspective. We are probably the only majority discriminated against so completely and casually."

Immediately contrite, I reached for her hand. "That's what this week coming up is all about. And why you and I are involved." I tickled her palm. "I plan to be around to aggravate you for a very long time." I made a show of lifting another spoon of cereal to my mouth.

She kept her mouth stiff but smiled with her eyes. Getting up to pour us another cup of coffee, she said, "What's your agenda for the day? I'm going to be at the Art League most of the day painting bottles." At my puzzled look, she explained. "We are giving away water and juice at our stands but we're decorating plastic bottles people can buy and carry with them."

"I'll buy one. I'll need a supply out in the wilds for a couple of hours."

Wren smiled. "I've already paid for yours, my friend. And painted it. Just be sure to pick it up before you go running over hill and dale."

"It's going to be more like through palmetto, around ponds and marsh, and under oak branches and Spanish moss. At least the bugs won't be bad this time of year, and the snakes should be curled up underground asleep." I finally got around to answering her question. "While you're painting, I've got a couple of follow-up interviews on the bank robbery last week. The family of the teenage girl who says she didn't know what her boyfriend and brother went in the bank to do, has agreed to talk to me. Then I want to canvass the convenience store and the filling station to see if anyone saw her in the car and saw how she was behaving. After I file that story, I've got several other projects in early stages. Can't be sure of the time I'll get home."

At the office I punched the computer key that would send my story to its next destination on the electronic road to appearing in tomorrow's *Ledger*. Meaning to scoop up my notes, I ended up scattering them on the floor. I rolled my chair all the way to the front wall of my cubicle and bent to retrieve them. As I was struggling to coax a small piece of paper from under a narrow table, I heard Andrea Standish speaking to someone in the corridor. Bent over as I was, I couldn't be seen.

I started to straighten and roll back to my desk but stopped as I heard her say sharply, "I don't want that said where anyone else can hear it. I'll not have the staff disturbed by possibilities I won't allow to happen."

The responding female voice was softer, but not weak. "I feel guilty telling you Andrew's intentions. But I can tell that he doesn't understand what this paper means to you. In just a few weeks I've discovered how much—because of my own background, I guess. He truly thinks that just being titular editor-in-chief would be enough for you. I've been battling my own father over issues of title and responsibility. So I know what counts."

Andrea's response was lost to me as they passed on by. Despite an ache in my lower back, I remained bent low, wanting to let them get out of sight. I assumed they would go past Worthington's office and up the stairs. At the sound of a low cough, I turned my head which was nearly touching my knees, and saw Barbara MacFadden in my doorway. Even though I stretched to secure the elusive scrap of paper, I knew I wasn't fooling her.

She proved it by saying dryly, "Is it protocol to eavesdrop on one's superior?"

Her mildly teasing tone emboldened me. I waved her to a straight chair beside my desk and asked bluntly, "Who was that with her?"

She answered promptly. "Fonda Allison. Andrew's fiancée. She came as a surprise in more ways than one."

At my expectant expression, she continued. "Though quite the ladies' man, Andrew has never linked himself with any one woman for a lengthy period of time. And never before proposed marriage."

"How long has she been on the scene?"

"She returned from Alaska with him about two months ago. He went there after his parents' funeral to test his skills on the ice slopes." Her tone was noncommittal but her expression disapproving.

33

I traced the edge of my desk with an index finger. "I read the article on the snowmobiling deaths. He was lucky."

The Iron Maiden's voice became precise and cold. "He's always lucky."

"You said the fiancée was a surprise in more ways than one?"

Her voice warmed. "She has substance. I was invited to a gathering to meet her and enjoyed the encounter. Her grandfather was retired Navy. He was stationed in Alaska and settled there after the war." I knew she meant World War Two. "He started a newspaper in Fairbanks and campaigned for statehood. Apparently it was as a reporter that Fonda met Andrew—covering the snowmobile deaths."

I hesitated several seconds before asking, "May I try out some other questions?"

"I'm still sitting here." The glimmer of a smile was gone before I was sure I had seen it.

"Are the details of the Standish's will or ownership of the paper public knowledge?" I was remembering my conversation with Wren on the way home Thursday night.

"I can't be certain of the accuracy of what I know. During the 1960s all print media were driven back into the trenches by television. Actually movie houses too. Rose Standish believed, and rightly so, that eventually some of the ground would be regained. But to hold on, they had to sell twenty percent of the *Ledger*."

"To Cross Communications?"

Barbara MacFadden shook her head. "They were not in existence then. It was to Media Acquisitions. They did, and still do, specialize in purchasing small portions of stock for their investors. That minimizes risk and involves less in operational expenses."

"And the remaining eighty percent?"

"As far as I know divided between the twins. Lyndall Standish continued to believe that someday his son would choose purpose and responsibility over play."

I considered that against the background of what I had heard a moment before as the two women walked by my area. Neither Andrea nor Andrew owned a majority. My intercom crackled and Joe Worthington's flat voice called me to his office.

Already outside my cubicle, the Iron Maiden turned back. "I wouldn't want to hear of any bruises or broken bones resulting from tomorrow's activities."

I said cockily, "Tomorrow I will be in my milieu. It's the others who had better watch out."

As I entered Worthington's office, he turned his computer so I could see that the story I had just filed was on the screen.

He said, "A little female bias seeping in here, don't you think?"

I immediately stiffened into my full height. "What do you mean? What bias?"

His chair creaked as he tilted back. "It's obvious you don't think the girl was in on the robbery. Can't have that in a news story."

I pushed the screen back toward him. "You show me where I've done anything more than quote the parents. They admit to their son's increasingly bad behavior and their objections to the boyfriend. But they say their daughter was living in a dreamworld where everyone she knew was a good guy. I didn't editorialize on any of that. Or on what the man in the glass enclosure at the gas station had to say. He watched her because he wasn't busy and she was pretty. Said she combed her hair and kept checking her face in a mirror. He insisted she didn't look like someone scared or worried about what was going on inside the bank. I've simply quoted him on that."

Worthington said, "I'm going to cut that line. I'm just granting you professional courtesy and letting you know."

Now I was angry. "Why?! It fits with what happened. Those idiot boys went out the wrong door. And when the alarms went off, the girl just looked around like 'What's going on?' What's going on with you, Joe?"

He worked a thumbnail between his front teeth before answering. "The D.A.'s charging her as an accessory. People are tired of teenagers all getting off—not being accountable. We need to be more of a team player with law enforcement."

I stared at him, my lips moving, but I couldn't form the words. Finally I said, "Where's the newsman who taught me about objectivity when I first came here? And how important it was for a newspaper never to be on anyone's team? Where's this coming from? Not the boss, I bet."

He had the grace to look uncomfortable. "There's more than one owner here. And I think you're forgetting your place."

"My place is not determined by some artificial hierarchy when we're talking right and wrong." I didn't care how pompous that sounded. "I don't believe for a minute you buy what you just said. Why are you playing the puppet for Andrew Standish? He's no newspaperman." I went a step further. "Or is it Chris Cross who's telling you what to do?"

Worthington dropped forward in his chair and smacked the desk-top. "The line goes—and anything else I decide is biased! I don't want another word about it—to me or higher up!"

Furious, I turned and stalked back to my cubicle. I hissed through my upper teeth at unseen adversaries. One of the reasons I'd left teaching was the encroachment of bureaucracy into the classroom, making it increasingly difficult to do the job right. Now I was encountering the same thing at the *Ledger*.

I sat with my elbows on my desk, chin in my cupped hands, a heel tapping rapidly on the floor. A different tapping sound came from behind me. I turned to see Andrea Standish and Fonda Allison, or so I assumed. I got up to take a couple of steps toward where each rested an arm on my cubicle wall.

Andrea said, "I had thought your eyes were blue yesterday morning. Now they're a thundercloud gray. You are angry."

"Just a policy disagreement. It'll pass."

"God knows I've had enough of those. I take it you lost."

"For the moment."

I interpreted the twist of her mouth as approval of my response, but her actual reply surprised me. She said, meaningfully, "It may toughen you for...other contests."

She glanced at the younger woman. "Fonda, this is Lexy Hyatt. Fonda Allison. She's also a reporter. From Alaska." No mention of her being Andrew's fiancée.

We exchanged polite comments and shoptalk while I noted her honey-brown hair, longish face, pointed chin and medium build. If she was running with Andrew tomorrow I wanted to be able to spot her, but instinct told me she wouldn't be. She looked fit enough but there was no aura of the athlete about her. There was, however, a determination in the set of her mouth and a directness in her gaze that made me glad she wasn't a competitor on the orienteering course or at the *Ledger*. All of a sudden I wondered if marriage to Andrew would include a position at the paper for her.

Andrea drifted away to speak with someone else. Fonda said, "Tell me; is this all the winter Florida gets? I haven't needed more than a lightweight jacket."

I replied, "We've had mild winters for a few years now. But some mornings can startle you with actual frost—not that that can compare to the cold and snow you must be used to. I'd like to experience it someday."

"I'd like to right now." She sounded sincere. "I'm so tired of all this green. I've even seen flowers blooming!"

I laughed. "You need a dose of Elinor Wylie."

She tilted her head to indicate she didn't understand.

I went on. "A Yankee poet. Came south once and went back north and wrote 'Puritan Sonnet.'" I quoted, "'There's something in this richness that I hate. I love the look, austere, immaculate, Of landscape drawn in pearly monotones.'"

Fonda's smile brightened the soft brown of her eyes. "A poet I need to read. Elinor—?"

"Wylie. W...y...l...i...e. Wrote during the early 1900s. Worked a lot with contrasting images and ideas. There's a poem contrasting black and white with distinctive imagery. And one entitled 'Nonsense Rhyme' that is anything but nonsense."

We talked awhile longer of poetry and newspaper work. I found myself liking her as much as I was coming to dislike her fiancé. I sighed inwardly. I had seen many mismatched couples who ended up complementing one another—even becoming stronger as a unit. Then there were those who ended up destroying each other. My stomach churned. How safe were Wren and I?

FIVE

I sat three cars back at a five-way corner waiting patiently for the light to change. Around me drivers gunned their motors and tried to inch forward as though they could force it to change by their aggressiveness. I turned a styrofoam cup slowly, the coffee half gone, and made a pattern of indentations with my teeth.

Andrea had effectively reminded me of my job tomorrow. My stomach was tightening in anticipation. However, the aroma of the coffee made me think of Fonda Allison. Conversation with her had been full-bodied. There was no raw Alaskan chilliness about her—instead, the scintillation of a hearthside fire. I chuckled at my fanciful imagery, no doubt caused by our discussion of poetry. Suddenly two sharp beeps drew me away from my thoughts as the light changed.

Wren wasn't home when I arrived but she had left me a phone message. I grinned all the way through it.

"This is your trainer, Butch Carlyle, speaking. I do believe I heard somewhere, sometime, someplace that athletes require lots of pasta the night before an event. So...find the plate in the freezer marked 'M/Cgr' and pop it into the microwave."

I did as I was told, knowing I would get a generous portion of her luscious macaroni and cheese and the green beans she insisted were good for me. I ate curled up in the corner of the couch watching a rerun of *Deep Space Nine*. Red-haired Colonel Kira was a favorite of mine.

Wren came in as I was washing up. She made a selection from the freezer and we sat at the table sharing our day. This was one of the parts of our relationship that had come to mean so much to me. I had always reviewed my day in my own mind—talked to myself about it—but sharing it with Wren was not binding as I had feared but freeing. I told her about the interviews and the conflict with Worthington over them.

38

She said, "That makes me feel a little guilty about how well my day went. We had a lot of fun decorating all those bottles. Everyone showed up for at least two or three hours except the High Priestesses of Oils." That was Wren's description of the very serious painters who looked down their noses at the graphic-designer and craft artists.

A while later, bathed and swathed in an X-size robe, I sat at my desk gazing at the picture of Miss Perry—her first name gone from my mind, if I had ever known it. It would be in my shirt pocket tomorrow. Dark with an elfin appearance, she had ruled my third grade class with happy eyes and an iron will. And we had loved her. Difficult to realize that she was frozen forever as she had been when I was only eight. Had she lived she would have been in her late fifties now.

Wren was in the doorway, a silhouette against the hall light. But I knew her features, every vital inch of her. I looked again at the picture, circling the face with my finger. "Grow old, Wren."

"What?"

"Promise me you'll grow old."

"Lexy?" She moved to my side and saw what was in my hand—and understood. Softly she said, "I will turn gray and develop wrinkles and stoop a little." She touched my shoulder. "I promise. Come to bed."

Trying to shake my mood, I said with mock irritation, "Why? You've put me on restriction."

She squeezed my neck. "Maybe I plan to talk dirty to you." Her voice became a low throb. "I want to hold you. I want you to feel how strong my heart beats."

I followed her—the Wren whose quiet strength of will had captured me the moment I met her. In the bedroom she removed my oversize robe from behind and with a gentle push sent me scrambling under the covers. My eyes closed, I listened to the sounds of her undressing, then shivered with anticipation as she dove in beside me and drew my naked form against hers. My nipples rose to point, my stomach dropped, my thighs tightened.

But Wren had meant what she said. She stroked my back and hips and murmured, "Relax. Let the day out. Tell me about Miss Perry."

And I did. And it felt good. The words flowed and the tension ebbed. And death lost its threat. I sighed and turned over, scooting back into the crescent of Wren's body.

She breathed against my neck and I went to sleep feeling her heartbeat on my back.

I turned over and stretched my legs. My body clock said it was somewhere around 5:30—but something else had been activated.

Wren stirred and mumbled, "What do you hear?"

"Nothing. That's just it. There's fog."

She lifted herself up on one elbow and glanced over me to the clock. "It isn't even light yet. How can you know?"

"I just do. My mother said she and Uncle Kurt always knew when it had snowed during the night before they ever looked out the window. I'm that way about fog. I can hear that special quiet. It's out there right now."

"Hear the quiet? Lexy!" She threw back the covers and her naked form was a pale blur in the darkness. The vertical blinds rattled as she parted them to look out. After a few seconds she conceded, "Okay, there's fog. The sentry lights next door are just a dull glow." She scrambled back to bed. "What kind of schedule are you on?"

"Registration for orienteering starts at eight o'clock. First people go off at nine. But I want to be there early. You?"

She replied. "I need to be there early, too. Why don't you ride with me. I've got a parking permit because I'll have a trunk full of bottles to deliver to our stand."

I readily agreed. Most participants were being asked to park at a nearby mall and catch busses to the starting area. I wheedled, "What say we get on our way and have breakfast at the diner?"

"You're afraid I'm going to give you cereal again." She brushed at the hair over my ear, then pinched my ear lobe and drew my face to hers. The kiss kindled passion and eclipsed my hunger. I tried to deepen it but Wren slipped from beneath me, saying tauntingly, "Hold that thought for another morning."

I made a face but she only laughed.

Forty-five minutes later we walked from the car to the diner entrance. I loved the neutralizing effect of the fog—the muted lights, the muffled sounds—even the feeling of breathing moisture with the air.

As we slipped into a booth, the waitress settled coffee in front of both of us and a small grapefruit juice for me. Wren shuddered as I downed the juice quickly. I tugged the local section from the paper I had brought in and Wren chose Arts and Leisure. I grumbled as I noted the deletions and changes in my story on the young girl's involvement with the bank robbery.

Wren said sagely, "Let it go for today. You've other things to tend to."

She was right, but the sour taste in my mouth wasn't from the grapefruit juice. A swiss-cheese omelet and toast helped. Her gift helped more. Over second cups of coffee she handed me a sack she had carried in from the car. I pulled out a water bottle decorated with unicorns—standing, prancing, galloping. In the center of one rounded side, a unicorn rose high on its hind legs. It was the color of my hair. I smoothed my thumb over it and looked across the table into the velvet of Wren's eyes, wide with sharing my pleasure. I nodded and she smiled—no other communication was necessary.

At the park I helped Wren carry boxes of bottles to the Art League booth. While she and another early arrival started arranging things, I wandered off and observed the scene. The late winter dawn was a variation in gray—daylight slowly spread from nowhere. This was no Carl Sandburg fog stealing in on little cat feet. We were in a thick cloud. I was certain it would be mid-morning before the sun burned through.

Most of the people scurrying about purposefully were organizers and service providers. Many wore hats, sweatshirts or headbands bearing the emblem for Women's Health Week—a sketch of the female form caught in a joyful leap. Orange vests appeared and receded into the fog as guides and medical aides prepared to move to their locations along the paths. I assumed the cluster of garish fluorescent green vests were the referees for the orienteering event.

Soon I heard the rumble and screech of the first busses. At first I couldn't see them, but laughing, chattering people began emerging from the fog and descending on the booths to make purchases. The emblem was given out free and would stick to clothing. I had dressed in dark gray jeans and a green plaid shirt. I decided to purchase a hat. If I was going to stick close to Nelda Cross, covering my auburn hair might be a wise decision.

"Will the fog be a problem?" Andrea Standish was at my side. Even in a black running suit with yellow piping she appeared regal, sophisticated. Water droplets beaded her hair as though part of a carefully arranged design.

I replied, "It will increase the challenge. Could be a help as much as a hindrance." I turned my left wrist upward and checked my compass. "But north, south, east, and west don't change."

Just as I was wondering at the wisdom of her being seen with me, she was absorbed into a large group of newspaper employees preparing to start out on the paths. When they dispersed, only Peggy Thomas remained with her. Normally Peggy manned the reception desk at the *Ledger*. Right now she was flipping papers on a clipboard and nodding at Andrea's instructions. Her pleasant face—round cheeks and chin and turned up nose—was set in concentration. Her brown curls, touched with grey, bobbed as though emphasizing her acceptance of Andrea's commands.

Peggy was a soft counterpoint to Barbara McFadden. Like a big sister Peggy guided new staff through the maze of written and unwritten expectations. To the public she presented a warmth and willingness to assist. But I had always sensed that she used this pleasantness to guard her privacy.

I then noticed a man of medium size and rugged good looks approach them. The fog had added kinks to his short sandy hair. Andrea was obviously surprised to see him but their handshake was warm and unhurried. He spoke with Peggy as well. Then Andrea pointed him toward the registration booth for orienteering and I observed him walk toward it. A prominent limp marred the movement of his right side.

The two women separated. Peggy joined me but kept her eyes on the sandy-haired man. She said, "I wonder if I ought to warn him that Andrew will be on the course."

I was immediately interested. "Why?"

Peggy adjusted her glasses. "His name's Warren Kessler. We all went to high school together. He was on a fast track—the real kind. Ran sprints and hurdles. Scheduled for a big college scholarship—till he played King of the Mountain with Andrew Standish." Her cheeks were flushed, I didn't know whether from the cold or anger.

"In what way?" I asked when she paused.

"Climbing a radio tower to plant the senior class colors. Warren got almost to the top and slipped, grabbed at beams and wires on the way down. That kept him from being killed but his right hip and leg took the worst of it. No more sprints and hurdles. No scholarship." She thumbed the sheets on her clipboard. "The boss lady is beckoning. Gotta go."

I thought about the six snowmobilers. Playing with Andrew Standish was a dangerous game. That thought caused me to shiver.

Or perhaps it was Tamara's fingernails raking down my back as she said, "Think our boss ordered the fog?"

I gave a short grunt. "She has power, but not that kind. At least not that I know of. There is a bit of the Celtic goddess about her, though."

I was answering Tamara but my eyes were on her companion. She was tall and long-limbed, slender but sinewy—and the blackest person I had ever seen. She was raven black and I had an irresistible urge to stroke her long neck. The bright points in her eyes, set deep above high cheekbones, read my reaction. She was made even taller by a new hairstyle popular among African-American women—the tornado. Her hair was divided into inch-wide strips like ribbon that swirled up and about and coiled loosely together at the top of her head. Two thin strands fell down from her temples and brushed her cheeks.

Tamara introduced us. "Lexy, this is my cousin Thea, or Al as she demanded we call her before she found out she liked being a girl." They exchanged private smiles. "Thea's running with me." She chuckled. "If you're worried about that hair getting snagged by a tree limb, that just might be a good thing. We might need someone's help—like the person going off after us." She cocked her head. "And that just happens to be Mr. Andrew Standish. We go off in twenty minutes. Saw your name a lot further down."

Tamara excused herself to go get some water. Her cousin remained with me and said, "I've heard interesting things about you at Leather Fever." Her voice was cavern deep but soft and coaxing.

I stiffened. Leather Fever was Marilyn Neff's other lesbian bar, located east of town. It attracted more of the fringe elements and had a blue-collar atmosphere. I enjoyed going there now and then but had never taken Wren.

I said only, "Haven't been there in a while."

She replied suggestively, "I know."

I changed the subject. "Thea? Al?"

She rolled her eyes and the flash of white was startling. "Althea. My mother named me Tiffany and handed me over to my grandmother the day after I was born. The way I heard it, many times, was that Grandma said she wasn't having no Black child in her house with a hoity-toity name like that. Grandma had worked in white women's houses during the 1950s. Some of them had the first television sets. When she saw a Black woman playing tennis with white women and holding her own, even beating them, she knew change was a-comin'. She told me she gave me the name Althea Gibson because I was the first Gantt child who could throw a rattle and hit something."

I knew she was partially imitating her grandmother's speech pattern, but there was something familiar about the voice itself.

"She's over eighty now but still watches tennis on television. It was great to see her stand up and cheer when Zena Garrison invited Miss

Althea to Wimbledon. But you ought to hear her fuss at the Williams sisters. Tells them it's all right to make all that money and flounce those beads, but they better remember who paid their dues so they could do that. I love that old woman but do we live in different times."

Something in her tone and her stare told me I was being put on notice—but I wasn't clear of what or why.

SIX

I scanned the registration board. Tamara was going off two slots in front of Andrew Standish, Paul Jared was three slots further down, and I was toward the bottom, three slots after Nelda Cross.

I thanked the man behind the counter for my map and whistle. Each competitor was provided with a whistle in case of injury or becoming hopelessly lost. I didn't plan on either eventuality, but I looped the cord around my neck and dropped the whistle itself down the front of my shirt. I patted the picture of Miss Perry in my shirt pocket.

Stepping away from the booth, I perused the map. On flat paper the topography appeared deceptively simple. But I knew that some stands of trees would be too dense to cut through on a straight line, some depressions would require skirting, and some contour lines would be high areas of soft sand. Thick underbrush wasn't indicated at all. And then there was the fog. The first marker looked to be somewhere right of the starting point in a clear area beyond a ditch or stream.

Looking up from the map, I glanced toward the entry point where Tamara and Thea were just being ushered onto the course. Nearby were Andrew Standish and Warren Kessler. I looked over my shoulder at the registration board and saw Kessler's name right above that of Paul Jared.

Often I felt called on to produce my share of fake smiles, so it was easy to recognize them on the faces of the two men. Their body language wasn't as easy to read. Both held themselves proudly erect but Standish's frame was hidden in army style fatigues and Kessler's in a loose blue sweatshirt and jeans. Kessler held a gnarled walking stick against his shoulder like a rifle in parade position. I hadn't noticed it before and wondered if he had kept it hidden at his side while speaking to Andrea.

45

Standish called to someone and Fonda Allison emerged from the fog. She wore a russet-brown running suit. In one hand she held miniature barbell weights that many carried and swung while power walking. Standish hugged her to his side, but I thought she took advantage of the introduction to ease from his grasp and shake hands with Kessler. She didn't strike me as a woman who enjoyed public displays of affection or would tolerate male possessiveness. Was she drawn to Andrew Standish, the man, or, with her newspaper background, to the co-owner of the *Ledger*?

Standish did most of the talking and Warren Kessler relaxed visibly when Standish turned to go join the line at the entry gate. I watched to see if Standish was teamed with anyone; not that I expected him to be.

I wasn't aware of Fonda Allison's approach until she spoke. "I feel like my complaining about the greenery and brightness Friday brought on the fog," she said.

"Then I have you to thank." I lowered my voice dramatically. "I'm looking forward to using it for cover as I try to slip around the competition."

The bright band holding her hair smoothly back from her face was decorated with the Women's Health Week logo. She tucked in short curls that had escaped. "I'm looking forward to walking that track in the fog. Gives me a chance to be more alone." Something in my expression made her hurry on. "I've been a little overwhelmed by all the people and activities since I arrived here. A lifetime in Alaska makes you expect a certain amount of silence…of isolation. Makes you need it."

I started to tell her that I shared those needs but felt reluctant to be so personal. It was as though I was being warned not to continue liking her, not to trust someone who would choose Andrew Standish for marriage. I sought refuge in talking about him.

"Your fiancé is about to go out on the orienteering course. I wouldn't expect him to be interested in something so tame after all his expeditions."

If she was surprised at the comment or my knowledge of Andrew's past, she didn't indicate it. "He's always interested in beating other people. Winning—the American disease."

"That sounds like a title for an op/ed piece."

Her enthusiastic smile made me forget that I didn't want to like her. "It was. Made my grandfather mad as hell—but he printed it anyway." About to say something else, she tilted sideways instead and peered around me.

I turned halfway and looked down into the solemn face of Kelleen O'Mara. She appeared even younger in neatly cuffed jeans with matching western jacket. Sandals had been exchanged for well-scuffed hiking boots.

Kelleen said simply, "I like your water bottle."

It was clipped to my belt in the small of my back where it wouldn't be likely to snag on something.

Fonda took a couple of steps around me to view it. She said, "I do, too. It's obviously been personalized for you."

Feeling inexplicably uncomfortable, I made introductions and explained about the Art League sale of decorated bottles, pointing out the booth barely visible through the fog. I mentioned Kelleen's martial arts accomplishments and described Fonda's newspaper roots in Alaska. Each asked questions of the other. Then I had to make more introductions as we were joined by Brie O'Mara, her hair made even wilder by the moisture in the air.

Kelleen told her about the Art League booth and Brie pulled money from a pocket. "Pick me out one that is bright and cheerful." She watched carefully after her daughter.

I said, "She seems an exceptional child, Mrs. O'Mara."

She answered warmly, "Ms. will do but I prefer Brie. And yes she is exceptional. And exceptionally independent. I've been quite pleased with her interest in you and your profession." She sighed. "I've worried a wee bit about her developing into a smart aleck little cock-a'-the-walk without proper consideration of others."

Fonda spoke before I could. "Oh, I didn't see any of that just now. She's too naturally polite. But there is a remarkable air of self-assuredness about her. Makes me think of...of someone I once knew." She touched my arm. "If you'll excuse me, Lexy, I'm going to buy a bottle, too." She moved away hurriedly.

Brie and I chatted about Kelleen, our jobs and the activities of the day. I learned that she was the events-coordinator for the Sun Star Convention Center west of town. But all the while I was juggling the feelings I had struggled with when I was teaching—how to handle the natural student interest, admiration and crushes that were far more complicated for me as a lesbian than for my straight counterparts. My indecision about whether or not to clear the air with Brie right now was made moot by Kelleen's return.

47

She handed her mother a bright and cheerful bottle—all aflutter with butterflies. Her own was decorated with a pair of dragons, fierce and elegant in dark green and red. She said to me, "Your friend knew what I would like."

I replied, "She's good that way. I think it comes from being an artist." Leave it to Wren to charm even the taciturn Kelleen.

Brie said, "Good luck on the run, Lexy. We're going to hit the track."

Kelleen extended a hand. "I hope you win, Ms. Hyatt."

I shook her hand. "You can call me Lexy, Kelleen."

Without a change in expression she said, "Some people call me Kell. My middle name is Cha." She turned smartly and marched off into the fog.

Brie's eyes widened and she pursed her lips in a combination of surprise and pleasure, then winked at me and hurried after her daughter. Considering Kelleen's features, I assumed the middle name was Asian in origin—and I knew it had been offered as a symbol of trust. I let out a deep breath slowly. I would have to meet that with some trust of my own.

I decided on another visit to Wren's booth before lining up. My mind still on Kelleen, I nearly collided with Nelda Cross. I muttered an apology as I dodged around her, but she appeared to take no notice of me as she headed for orienteering registration. I wasn't going to have any problems spotting her on the course. She was flashy in a hot pink running suit. Black boots matched the sheen of her hair. I watched her get in line and avoid eye contact with Andrew Standish, who was near the gate. Fonda Allison and Peggy Thomas were walking away from him and each other.

Wren took a break and joined me at the back corner of the booth. She said enthusiastically, "Our bottles are flying off the shelves! I was glad I had put my dragons out of sight. When Kelleen showed up, I knew it was the one for her. Wonder if that was in the back of my mind when I painted it?"

"Jodi would say it was." There was a swirl of coolness that always shrouded Wren when I mentioned or quoted a former lover. Jodi would probably say that I was testing Wren whenever I did so. I didn't want to believe that. I hurried on, "Who else have you seen?"

"Bunches. The Cat crowd...some neighbors...Art League and Forum people. Oh, and your boss. At least someone called her Miss Standish. She bought a bottle with pampas grass plumes—because it matched her hair, I think. She was wearing one of the headbands like a crown, which made her look like an exotic alien calmly observing the natives. See?"

She opened a sketchpad and I saw the accuracy of her description of Andrea Standish. With only a few bold strokes of charcoal, Wren had caught Andrea's ability to carry authority naturally—not exactly an expression of superiority, but one of appraisal.

I turned pages, enjoying the variety of faces. I stopped over a sketch of Fonda Allison. Wren's strokes suggested that she had been trying to turn her head, lower her eyes.

Wren said, "Don't know her—but she's carrying a weight of pain. Doesn't want others to see it. I probably should destroy that. Qualifies as invasion of privacy."

Before I could explain who Fonda was, Wren took the pad from my hands and flipped pages toward the back. She held it in front of me again and I smiled at the placid face of Kelleen. Her eyes were caught just beginning to glow and her lips parting slightly as though about to smile.

Wren said, "That's how she looked when I put the dragons in front of her. This artist likes seeing her work appreciated."

I said meaningfully, "Well, it's the artist herself that I appreciate." I saluted. "I'm off to play hide-and-seek in the fog."

Wren called after me, "Take care."

I didn't have to stand in line long before I was ushered onto the course and my starting time officially recorded. Although I had watched others plunge through underbrush on the right, I chose to skirt it at an even trot. I was pleased to discover that I had guessed correctly when I topped a low rise and saw that the underbrush became a tangle of thick bushes and young trees. As I trotted by it, the couple who had gone off in front of me struggled out of the tangle and fell in behind me.

In a short while I was able to leap a ditch and head for the first marker. The orange flag was driven firmly into the ground, a clipboard and hole-punch chained to it. I signed my name and punched a circle out of the number one on my map.

I checked the map for the location of the second marker. There would be twelve in all. Taking a swig of water, I noted the sun, still in the east, looking more like a dim moon through the shifting fog. Before me the vapor lay so thick that I could barely make out the large rectangle of woods the map indicated lay between me and the next marker. I chose again to gamble—this time that the course designers would allow for an easy run to the first two or three markers—and entered the trees at what I hoped was near the center of the course.

Cutting through in the fog required a slow pace. I heard some foul language and thrashing ahead of me as someone stumbled or became snagged. I had to tug my hat more securely in place more than once, as well as fight my way out of a net of Spanish moss. About halfway through, as best I could figure, I heard a friendly argument off to my left about what direction to move in. A female voice wanted to head southwest, the male argued for due west. I checked my own compass and shifted slightly north of west. Without a compass it would have been impossible to navigate through the woods.

When I cleared the trees I was frustrated by my inability to spot a flash of orange in either direction. I trotted off to the right until I decided I had chosen wrongly. I sped back to the left and was soon rewarded by the sight of two older women resting on a rock. Their frothy white hair was tangled with twigs. One waved toward where the orange flag was almost hidden behind a cluster of smaller rocks.

Quickly I signed and punched a star shape into the number two. The helpful woman said, "You hurry along, honey. We aren't racing anybody but ourselves." The other called after me, "But watch out for a she-devil in pink!"

As I stopped and looked back inquiringly, she said, "We got here first but she shoved us out of the way and grabbed the clipboard."

I started off again but called over my shoulder, "If I catch up with her, I'll give her a shove for you." Their chuckles floated after me.

I found markers three, four, and five with minimum difficulty, enjoying the task almost to the point of forgetting about Nelda Cross. I still could not fathom a reason for Standish to manipulate the run for her. Some kind of gain for one or both had to be the motive. Instinctively I knew Andrea wouldn't like me nosing beyond my assignment.

Unwisely I increased my speed. A low limb of an oak took my hat. I whirled around to scoop it up and lost my footing on a cluster of hidden pinecones. I sprawled flat on my stomach and was startled by two yellow eyes not a foot from my face. Behind the eyes was the plump body of a calico cat. She swished her tail and leaped gracefully up on a fallen tree trunk as though commenting on my lack of agility. I laughed and scrambled up.

Continuing through the trees I heard voices often, and now and then the shrill blasts of whistles. I saw only a young couple kissing against a tree. A referee was approaching to prompt them on their way. Right after marker number six, I passed a quartet that appeared to have banded together for conversation. But at number seven I encountered an agitated group of people. Among them were Paul Jared and Warren Kessler.

Paul explained without indicating any acquaintance with me. He said, "Seems the sign-in sheet has taken a walk. We've tried whistling up a referee."

An indignant woman barked, "I think someone took it to stop us!"

I thought to myself that it was very possible Andrew Standish had taken it just to slow things down. I suggested, "Why don't we fan out and check the ground. It might have been tossed nearby."

Anxious to do something, they all complied. Surprisingly soon, the woman who had spoken up cried out excitedly, "I've got it!" She brought it to me. "It was your idea. You click off first and get going."

I accepted the clipboard with the dangling hole-punch. Moments before I had noticed that Nelda Cross was not in the stymied group. Now I signed in right below her name. Had she managed to pass all these people or simply detoured to where Andrew Standish waited with the clipboard and hole-punch? Or, with the fog, he could have caught her between six and seven—letting her cut around toward eight while he tossed the equipment where we found it. I saluted the group and took off.

Paul Jared caught up with me. He trotted at my side but kept his voice low. "I passed the guy with the bad leg right after number one. Caught up with Standish close to three. Kept on his heels which he didn't like. He tried to lose me, then tried to get me to go around. I lost him after marker five. Hate to admit it but I got a little lost myself."

I liked his honesty. "You still probably spoiled some of his plans."

He flashed me a lopsided grin. "Hope so. Map looks like a clear run for a ways. I'm going to see if I can catch up to him if he's back on track." He dashed off into the fog, which was just beginning to lift.

With only five markers remaining, I increased my own pace now that it was possible to see ahead for a greater distance. If the fog hadn't started to thin, I would have had even more trouble finding the eighth marker. The orange flag wafted tauntingly in the middle of a deep rock-strewn depression. It was easy skidding down, though I wished I had thought to wear gloves, but climbing up and out was a struggle. Where rocks weren't the problem, loose sand was.

Kessler appeared as I finally scrambled out. I paused to drink from my bottle so that I could watch long enough to see him brace himself skillfully with the strong walking stick as he threaded his way downward. I slapped my hands free of sand and checked the map.

Arriving at markers nine and ten wasn't physically difficult but required competent map reading and compass use. The sun was overhead, only partially veiled by streaky remnants of rising vapors spreading like translucent scarves. In some places they seemed to weave among the tree limbs. At any other time I would have stopped what I was doing to watch the fog silently disperse and vanish, and color slowly return.

I came upon a wide area of undulating ground marred only by occasional clumps of prickly pear cactus. Half the distance toward a stretch of close-growing pines was Nelda Cross, jogging confidently. Taking advantage of my long legs, I raced across the field, leaping the wide patches of ground cover, glad that prickly pear was a spineless species of cactus.

I don't know if she heard or sensed me coming up behind her, but she looked over her shoulder and started sprinting for the trees. She went into the woods about fifty yards in front of me. I knew that by the clock I was surely ahead of her—but I wanted to pass her as well.

I glanced at my map to be sure of the angle I needed to follow once I entered the trees, then crammed it into a pocket. The openness of the field in the absence of fog was glaringly bright. I welcomed the dim interior below the high interlacing branches of the tall pines. The pink of Nelda Cross's running suit appeared and disappeared among the trees ahead. I sped after her, intent on gaining.

Suddenly I heard a popping sound and felt a sharp impact on my jaw. I stumbled—my hand flying to my face. I drew it away and stared at the red stain on my fingers.

SEVEN

Another popping sound sent me diving to the base of a large tree, landing hard on my knees. My mouth was dry and I could feel my heart thudding in my chest. I lost a sense of time as I huddled listening with every atom of my being. I wasn't at all sure I was shielded from my attacker's view. For a moment I thought I could actually hear my heart beating till I realized it was pounding feet coming up from behind.

Bracing himself with his staff, Warren Kessler knelt by me. He touched my chin with a gloved hand and turned my face more toward his. Angrily he said, "Paint! Some idiot blasted you with a paint ball! Lucky he didn't get your eye! What son-of-a ...." His face froze in hard lines. "I know exactly who!" He listened for a second, and I heard rustling sounds off to the right, then he lifted himself with the help of the gnarled cane. At my insistence that I was all right, he started thrashing his way toward a darker thicket of small trees and bushes.

I got to my feet and watched him disappear into the thicket. I touched my jaw again and found it smooth but wet. Checking my fingers, I realized that the red liquid was indeed paint. Kessler was right. I had been shot by a paint-pellet gun, the kind used by soldier wannabes in mock warfare games. Another of Andrew Standish's ploys?

Anger revitalized me. I sprang to my feet and tore through the trees, undeterred by bumps and snags as I zigzagged my way toward the brighter area that forecast the end of the woods. As I burst from the trees, I was so blinded by a brilliant noonday sun that I nearly missed the eleventh marker, planted in front of a pile of oranges obviously gathered from the squat tree shading them.

Again I signed below Nelda Cross's name after punching out a triangle. Breathing deeply, I smoothed my scrunched-up map and surveyed my surroundings. Before me lay a long wide lake of stagnant water beneath a lovely green patina of unbroken algae. Way across on

53

the other side Nelda Cross stood at the beginning of a broad path snaking its way between a series of thickets to the final marker. Her hand on one hip, she was drinking from a canteen but clearly aware of me. With an insolent toss of her head, she turned and began a fast jog up the path. No way could I skirt the lake and catch up with her.

Suddenly I realized where I was. The orienteering course had been laid out over two golf courses which had been only partially completed. I remembered hearing that the developer had guessed wrong on sub-division planning. The land had since gone back to the wild. That meant the lake was man-made and therefore should be shallow.

Hesitating only for the space of one deep breath, I stepped off the bank. The water reached only halfway to my knees. Ignoring the thick-ening stench and slime, I moved as fast as I could. I hoped Nelda Cross would round a bend of the path without looking back. The water deep-ened in the middle and I had to struggle across the soft bottom, but soon I had firmer ground under me and was able to lift my feet for long strides.

A couple of slips on the mud of the far side and I was out. I plucked algae strands from my jeans and shoes before hitting the path at a full run. I had no time for pacing—and the map had given me no indication of distance. It was catch her or not.

After longer than I wished, I completed an elongated 'S' in the path and spotted the garish pink. Contemptuous of my threat, she had kept an even pace. Her mistake—and I intended to make her pay for it. Using all the concentration I could muster (compliments of the Major and her martial arts instruction), I tried to touch down and push off silently, to flow with the path as though part of the air instead of in opposition to it. The distance between the two of us began to dimin-ish.

I almost stumbled when I saw her stop and pat at her clothing and hair. She was improving her appearance for the finish line! She looped her canteen strap from over her shoulder and neck, but saw me as she tilted her head back to drink. She lost a couple of seconds in being star-tled, then took off in a dead run.

I was at her heels when she swung the canteen back at me. For-tunately, she flung it by the strap and I took the blow on my thigh. Bet-ter thought or aim and she would have caught my feet. As I passed her, I grabbed the canteen and threw it into the bushes. Despite my being younger with longer legs, she was just as fit, more rested, and in dry shoes. She caught up to me and pulled a little ahead.

Rounding a wide curve I spotted a long patch of softer dirt ahead that had been churned by dozens of feet plowing through it. I shifted to the firmer dirt that bordered the path and passed her a second time. The long curve straightened and I saw the final marker waving from a table backed by clusters of people sitting and standing.

I skidded and slammed into a tree next to the table. The clipboard was thrust at me. I signed awkwardly as Nelda Cross slammed against me. Triumphantly I watched the official record the time next to my name. I turned away without looking at the panting, angry woman.

Accepting a bottle of Gatorade, I sat down in a lounge chair. Paul Jared came over and dropped cross-legged at my feet. He sniffed and wrinkled his nose.

I laughed with the little extra breath I had. "I cut through some pond scum." I saw him react to my face and explained about the paint.

His face darkened. "Tossing the clipboard was one thing. But that was dangerous." He glanced around. "I don't see anyone else with paint spatters."

I couldn't explain that I had been a target because I was nipping at Nelda Cross's heels. At least that was my belief. Instead I asked, "Did you catch up with Standish?"

"No. Never caught sight of him. But he hasn't come through here either. I've checked the sign-in sheet. And Tamara hasn't signed in."

I sat forward. "She hasn't! She went off way early."

At that very second I saw Tamara trotting the last stretch of the path. She gave us a wave, signed in, and plopped in the grass beside Paul. Huffing dispiritedly, she said, "I hope you two got your part done right. I got off track...Lexy! What happened to you?"

I explained again, thinking that I had better find a way to get the paint off to stop the reactions. Then I questioned Tamara. "What do you mean you got off track?"

"Thea and I were going slow—letting people pass us so we'd end up in front of Standish. But we came upon a woman who had sprained an ankle. Maybe broken it. We whistled for help but could hear whistles from other places at the same time. And the woman had hit her head when she fell. Thea didn't like the look of her pupils, so we headed back toward the starting point on as straight a line as we could figure. We finally crossed paths with a referee who called up a golf cart. They offered to run us back to where we went off course, but Thea said she'd rather hang loose..." Tamara cut her eyes at Paul Jared "...and girl watch."

Paul grinned. "Don't blame her. My son's always telling me I should do more of that."

Tamara went on. "I hung around a little. But then I decided to get back out on the course. Thought maybe I could be some help bringing up the rear. But I never saw anybody I knew. Hope the boss lady doesn't fire my sorry butt."

I muttered in a low tone, "You can ask her yourself, if you want." I nodded my head toward where Andrea Standish was getting out of a golf cart to check the sign-in sheet.

According to the map, we were somewhere near the railroad track maybe less than a mile from the entry point for the run. But I was sure she had come from the thickets scattered to the right of the path or from further around them to the north.

Movement on the path caught my attention. Warren Kessler, followed by several others in a scraggly line, was nearing the finish. With the staff-like cane and his obvious upper-body strength, he managed a gait that scarcely revealed his limp. There was no hiding the staff from Andrea this time, but I watched her carefully ignore it.

Noting the jagged tears in his sleeves, I realized mine were in the same condition. Along with my wet legs, paint-smeared face, and dirty hands, I must have looked the complete ragamuffin. Just as I was hoping Andrea would avoid contact with us, she caught my eye. Her only reaction to the condition of my face was a quick lift of her head and a slight parting of her lips. Noting the direction of her gaze, Kessler appeared to be explaining to her. Even at the medium distance between us I could see her eyes become slits. She spoke a moment more to Kessler and then headed straight for us, her *Ledger* trio in conspiracy.

Paul rose immediately and stepped aside for her. She said, "I believe your presence thwarted some of my...someone's plans, Mr. Jared. Thank you. And thank you, Ms. Gantt, for assisting the injured woman. I heard about it from the man whose cart I borrowed. I admire your commitment in coming out to complete the course."

Even in this casual setting she maintained boundaries of authority and decorum. Definitely not her mother's daughter in that respect. She glanced at my appearance without comment, saying coolly, "An excellent time, Ms. Hyatt."

A flash from deep within the mild blue eyes made me think she was going to say more, but we all lifted our heads and turned at a series of whistle blasts short and shrill.

56

A woman referee entered the path from the bushes and ran toward us, her large breasts bouncing under the green vest. A male referee rushed to meet her. The woman was both winded and disturbed. Paul grabbed a vacated lawn chair for her to sit in and Andrea commanded the others to stay back.

I couldn't hear the exchange but the woman spoke in brief bursts of words. At one point she gripped Andrea's shoulder and pulled her closer. Straightening, Andrea handed a cell phone to Paul. I was sure the three jabs of his finger were for 911. He nodded at something she said. Turning his back, he walked far enough away to be out of earshot of everyone.

Paul returned the phone and nodded again to whatever Andrea said. He called or motioned to the various referees standing around and some others. They followed him and he arranged them in a widely-spaced line blocking the path and the thicket area to the north.

I got up and worked my way through people to the marker table. I was reaching for the clipboard when Warren Kessler touched my arm gently with his cane.

He said, "Everyone's in but Standish."

"Did you see him out there?" I wiggled my paint-spattered fingers. "After I got hit."

His gaze was unblinking but he hesitated a fraction before saying, "No. He might not have been your sniper. I heard a bunch of kids' voices at one point."

At that moment Andrea's voice cut through the chatter going on around us. "Ms. Hyatt. With me." She was getting into the nearby golf cart.

I went around to the other side and swung in, my foot slipping on the broken shaft of a golf club. I threw it into the wire basket on the back. I kept a tight hold as she steered the vehicle and headed out over bumpy ground past the line of guards. After we rounded the north end of the lake I had waded across, she slowed and stopped. We were at the edge of the woods that I was sure had shielded...a mischievous kid?...an intentional sniper?...Andrew Standish? But I didn't know why we were here.

I heard sirens. Andrea took the cart across a relatively smooth field of tall grass toward a rusting fence. A wide section was open. I guessed that it had once contained long double gates. Runners of tough field grass sneaked under the fence as though intent on reaching the bare strips between two-story apartment buildings on the other side of the street. Lines from a Mark Van Doren poem surfaced: 'Then any bird saw, /Under the wire, /Grass nibbling inward/ Like green fire.'

A squad car, lights flashing, slowed and then, in response to Andrea's emphatic motion, entered through the opening in the fence. She left the cart to speak to the driver, pointing to the wooded area. A second squad car pulled in and there was more talking and pointing. The first car went toward the woods, the other around toward where we had left the orienteering crowd.

Andrea rejoined me and followed the first car, but stopped when I touched her wrist.

I said, "Can you tell me what's going on?"

She gripped the small steering wheel and stared ahead. "My brother finally crossed the wrong person. He's lying in those trees somewhere—dead."

I don't know if I was startled more by what she said or the dispassionate way she said it. "Could the referee be sure?"

"She's a paramedic. Said there was blood coming from his head. His eyes were open, and there was no pulse." She drove forward again pulling up to the squad car. She looked at me, clear-eyed and direct. "You're to cover this. Keep it as simple and lean as possible. Consult me if you have questions. My parents dead in a plane crash. My brother murdered. The vultures are going to start circling."

"It could have been an accident. I took a couple of tumbles out there. Tamara stopped to help an injured woman."

She removed her headband and fluffed her hair into place. Her tiny smile was chilling. "Andrew was more charmed than charming. Accidents bypassed him. They were what happened to other people." She turned her hands palms up and I saw extremely narrow scars crossing the width of each. "I only took his dare once—when I was seven. We slid down a wire from the peak of the garage roof. I didn't see him put on gloves—but I held on until I got to the bottom."

I looked at my right hand and the red on my fingers. Andrea said, "Did he do that?"

"I don't know."

One of the policemen returned from the woods and radioed a message. Then he began stringing yellow crime-scene tape. I followed Andrea as she approached him.

Carefully polite, he said, "If you'll wait here, ma'am, the detectives will be with us soon. You can accompany them to identify the body." He glanced our way often while continuing to stretch the tape, probably suspicious of Andrea's lack of agitation. And possibly of my appearance.

Soon a crime-scene van followed by two plain cars joined us on the edge of the woods. Exiting from a nondescript gray compact were detectives Glen Ziegler and Roberta Exline. I had first encountered them when they were assigned to investigate a death in Marilyn Neff's bar. Robbie had since become a friend. Their professional faces in place, they did not react to my presence before they followed the uniform.

Andrea did some pacing while I stayed in the golf cart—thinking. If Andrew Standish had shot me with paint and then been murdered, that certainly shrank the window of opportunity. But, given the orienteering event and the location, it didn't much limit the number of people with opportunity. I glanced toward the street—anyone could have come from there—or perhaps trailed after the last runners without being registered for the competition.

I wondered if Andrea knew of my involvement with two murders during the past year. Could that be why she wanted me covering this?

I left the cart quickly when Robbie came out of the woods and formally introduced herself. Her expression was somber; no gold flecks danced in her brown eyes as she cataloged my condition.

Robbie said, "Did this orienteering race incorporate war games?"

Andrea answered succinctly, "No. I wish Ms. Hyatt to accompany me. She will be covering the...the event for the *Ledger* and I guarantee cooperation with the authorities."

I saw skepticism flash across Robbie's face but she gave an accepting nod. She said, "Follow me and walk or stand only where told."

It was a short distance to Andrew Standish's body. He lay sprawled on his back. Blood dampened the dry leaves around his head. Near his right hand was what I assumed to be a paint-pellet gun. Though his open eyes were unseeing, his expression was something between a look of surprise and a sneer.

Unemotionally, Andrea joined Glen Ziegler to officially identify her twin brother. Police personnel were already moving out in a circle from the body, searching for clues and evidence. Two others hovered nearby waiting to get at the body itself. I stood next to Robbie.

Scarcely moving her lips, Robbie said very quietly, "Don't hold out on us, Lexy. Remember that I know full well how you work. How you protect your people."

"These aren't my people. They're the people I work for. I'm sim-

59

ply on the job here."

The arch of her eyebrows was pure cynicism.

Ziegler called, "Detective Exline, take Ms. Standish and Ms. Hyatt out and interview them. I'll supervise here awhile longer, then we'll both cover the other people."

Andrea's eyes flicked from him to me at his knowledge of my name. We returned to the golf cart, and Robbie questioned us and took notes. The compression of her full lips into a narrow line told me when she was not satisfied with the brevity of an answer. I told her truthfully that I had not seen Standish during the run—only near the starting gate early in the day. Andrea said the same. I chose to follow my boss's lead and made no mention of Fonda Allison and Warren Kessler being present with Standish when she was. But when I related being shot with the paint ball, I told her about a man coming upon me and then going to check the thicket after first making certain I wasn't actually injured. I made no mention, however, of his anger or possible knowledge of the identity of my attacker.

Andrea stiffened sitting next to me in the cart, but I knew that if Kessler related the story and I didn't, I'd be in deep trouble with both detectives. She relaxed when she realized I was not mentioning her consultation with Paul, Tamara and myself concerning her brother and the race. I wasn't trying to complicate the investigation—merely walking a fine line between loyalty and responsibility.

Ziegler came out and gave Andrea his card. He went through the drill about remaining accessible and reporting pertinent information. He asked if his car could get around to where the others waited. He denied Andrea's request to be present for those interviews. I knew that could be a matter of considering her a suspect or wanting to prevent her intimidating anyone. We were given permission to return to the front area.

About to get in his car, Ziegler looked over the top at me and said, "I assume I can trust you, Lexy, to make the standard comments about an on-going investigation et cetera."

Robbie added with an emphasis I understood, "And watch where you walk."

As they drove off, Andrea stated, "You know them—or they know you?"

"Yes," I confirmed. "I covered a murder they investigated about a year ago."

Nothing more was said on our ride back to the park entrance. As though nothing untoward had happened, Andrea went immediately to the orienteering board to check the standings. First place time went to a name I didn't know. I had secured second place. And it turned out that Nelda Cross was fifth, not third as I had thought, because she had started earlier and had actually taken longer to finish the course.

Three names were marked off—Thea Gantt, a woman who had to be the injured person assisted by Thea and Tamara...and Andrew Standish. I felt cold seeing the heavy line through his name. I turned from the board and saw Fonda Allison seated under the bare branches of a huge mimosa tree.

I touched Andrea's shoulder. She followed my gaze. She sighed as though telling Fonda what had happened was going to be more painful than absorbing it herself. Perhaps Ziegler was wise to view her as a suspect.

EIGHT

As Andrea angled her way through the many people milling about, I decided I didn't want to watch her tell Fonda Allison the news of Andrew Standish's death. I did want to hang around, though, because I was sure either Ziegler or Robbie would eventually do some checking here in the front area. And I wanted to clean up. Since there was a long line outside the women's restroom, I headed for the Art League booth, hoping to catch Wren alone. I was dreading telling her that once again I was smack in the middle of a murder. At this rate she was going to think of me as a liability, and no longer in jest, either.

Nearly there, I stared at the cozy tableau of Thea Gantt perched on a stack of crates while Wren sat much lower on a single crate sketching her. Thea watched me come up silently behind Wren and observe the sketch. Looking back at Thea, I realized how accurate Wren's strokes were in emphasizing the strength of the long lines. There was very little arch to her brows above narrow eyes. The long line of her nose widened gradually, turning down slightly above surprisingly thin lips. Her cheeks were flat and her jaw lines swept down to meet in a very small chin. The afternoon sun made a satiny sheen of her dark skin.

She moistened her lips and shrugged in a way that hardened the cords along her throat and deepened the hollow at the base of her neck. She said, more with curiosity than concern, "Looks like some- one's been in a fight."

Wren jerked her head up from her work and turned to see what Thea was referring to. She got up from the crate quickly, dropping the sketchpad on it. "Lexy! What happened to you? You've been—" and then with relief "—that's *paint!*"

I held up my hands to stop their questions. "It's complicated. I'll explain in a minute. Have you got anything I can clean up with? Can't get near a washroom."

Shaking her head in consternation, Wren took in my torn shirt, water-stained shoes and jeans and dirty hands.

"Sit down," she commanded and went to the booth.

Thea scooped the pad out of my way. Gazing at herself she said, "Hot damn! She makes me look good."

If she was trolling for a compliment, I wasn't going to bite. Part of me wanted her to leave so I could talk to Wren, and the other part of me was glad for the delay she represented. I wasn't going to announce Andrew's murder in front of her.

Wren returned with two bottles of water and a handkerchief. I saw the concern on her face as she tackled mine. She said, "I need to introduce you two."

I mumbled against her hand as she scraped paint flecks from around my nostrils, "We've met."

Thea stepped to where we both could see her. "Thought Tamara would be here by now."

I responded, "She'll be along soon. I was just talking to her."

Wren brushed at the short hair over my ear. "It's water-soluble paint. It'll wash out okay. Now, let's see those hands."

Thea slipped a crate closer for Wren to sit on, and got one for herself. We locked eyes as Wren poured water over my hands, then she blatantly looked Wren over from head to toe. She reached a hand to sweep a lock of Wren's hair from her eyes and received a thank-you smile. I tried not to react but couldn't stop from clenching my jaw.

Thea placed a hand on Wren's thigh. "Will you sign my picture and let me have it?"

Wren concentrated on scrubbing paint from my fingers one at a time, but said, "I'd be glad to."

Thea did not remove her hand until I glared at it and then at her. She arched a brow and I read the clear challenge.

Wren said, "Even though she's named for a tennis player, Lexy, Thea's a softball player like you."

"Still play?" I asked, glad of a neutral subject.

"A fall league. Sometimes summer. You?"

"I fill in for an outfielder now and then." I made a face. "Can't compete with those twenty-year-olds for first base any more."

"I know what you're saying, but I still try. I owned first base in high school. Even if Coach had something to say about that once or twice."

Wren stopped her work on my fingers. "Meaning?"

"Oh, she liked everybody at the ready all the time." She glanced at me. "She was a brighter redhead than you—but pretty even-tempered. I think that's why I liked to push at her."

Was I supposed to read something into that?

She returned her attention to Wren and her story. "I always knew when a gal would be hitting the ball my way. So when I knew they wouldn't be, I didn't see any sense in standing there like I was posing for team pictures. I'd just hang loose near the bag so I could tag 'em out if need be." She flashed Wren a cocky smile.

I saw a group of orienteers walking our way and pulled my hands, still wet, from Wren's grasp.

I said, "Be right back," and went to meet Tamara. Her brown face had a grayish cast. Either the questioning had been rugged or she had put too much into completing the run.

She stepped away from the group and joined me on a bench. She said under her breath, "I guess you know what happened?"

"Right. Been questioned and all that. You?"

"All of us. They spread us out and took us one at a time—but Betty Richards, that's the referee who found Standish, had already told us what she had seen." Tamara's face was calm but there was concern in her eyes. She asked cautiously, "Did you tell them anything about our little confab with Andrea on Friday morning?"

I replied, "Kind of let that slip my mind."

She relaxed. "Same with Paul and me. Figured telling that should be up to the boss. Guess you and I both had better keep our eyes and ears open—and watch each other's back. I don't feel so good about all this any more."

There was a bit of a stir at the starting point where a roving reporter and WCOL-TV cameraman who were covering the event had set up to do short interviews. Christopher Cross, his bulldog jowls rearranged into a smile, was seizing the opportunity to court the camera. He looked out of place in his dark suit and tie. His businesslike appearance was marred only by dusty shoes and some brambles on one pant leg. I wondered in what capacity he was claiming connection with the day's activities.

That was partially answered as Nelda Cross passed by at a fast walk heading for her husband's enthusiastic embrace. She smiled brilliantly for the camera. I wished I could hear the reporter's questions and their replies, but I was certain of what was being said some moments later when the television crew moved off to catch others.

Cross was hunched over listening intently to his wife. Then he straightened and took her by the arm. Rapidly they began walking

64

toward the parking area. She jolted him to a stop in front of the ori-enteering board. Even at a distance I could read the anger in her stance as she read the results.

She turned slowly looking everywhere—for me, I was sure. I leaned back enough to let Tamara's profile hide me. Confrontation, if that's what she wanted, could wait until I knew more.

I saw Paul Jared coming down the path, apparently in easy con-versation with Warren Kessler. I would try to catch him at work tomor-row and...and what? I tongued my cheek. Was I planning to cover Standish's death tamely as an in-house reporter—or investigate it? I knew the answer. I just wasn't ready to put it into words yet.

"What the matter, Lexy? You have such an odd expression."

"Do I? Are you going to collect Thea and head home?" I winced inwardly at the abruptness in my tone. "I need to break this news to Wren."

"Guess it's time to tell Thea, too." She sighed, turning. For the first time she noticed her cousin and Wren, dark and light heads bent close together as Wren shared her drawings. I had been noticing it. Tamara glanced at my right leg jiggling as I tapped my heel rapidly up and down in the dirt. She said carefully, "I'll collect her."

I stayed where I was. Wren came to join me. She said, "I think we should go before it gets cooler. You're probably squishing around in wet socks."

I wiggled my toes. "I think you're right. I feel some squishing. Been too much happening to notice it." I put my hand on her arm to stop her rising. "But I want to stay a little longer. I need to talk with...with Robbie or Glen Ziegler."

Wren frowned, on the alert. "So what's going on, Lexy? What were all those sirens for? Did someone get hurt?"

"Worse, I'm afraid." I took a deep breath. "You're not going to like this, and I'm really reluctant to tell you."

"Better spit it out then."

I described the referee arriving and reporting her discovery of Andrew Standish's body, and all of us being questioned. I admitted staying silent about Andrea's request that we keep an eye on her brother during the run. I could tell that Wren wanted to comment on that but held back. We were still careful about entering each other's territory uninvited.

But she did ask pointedly, "What's with the paint and getting wet?"

My skimpy version was that I had gotten irritated by the bad manners of a runner in front of me and went all out to beat her. I claimed to have no idea who shot me with a paint gun or why—which was true, on the surface.

I was relieved to see Robbie approaching us. She carried a white garbage sack. I said, "I'm glad you're here, my friend. I'd like to go over a couple of things if—"

Clearly in her professional mode, Robbie interrupted me. "It's Wren I need to see right now." She plunged into the sack and withdrew a sealed baggie containing several of the Women's Health Week headbands in various pastels. She tucked the bag under an arm and plunged into the large sack again. This time she withdrew a larger baggie containing a water bottle. She held it toward Wren. "Several people told me they bought decorated bottles from you this morning. Remember who you sold this one to?"

Wren bit her lip, looking from the bottle to Robbie to me. I checked it more closely and my hand flew to my back and an empty clip. "She didn't sell it to anybody. She gave it to me. I must have lost it in one of my tumbles. Where'd you find it?"

Robbie looked at me a long time before she answered. "Near the body."

"Are you telling me I'm a suspect, Detective Exline?"

"Lexy..." Wren cautioned.

"Sorry, Robbie. I'm tired, wet, bruised...concerned. I know collecting evidence and checking it out goes with your job. I really don't know where I lost it. Most likely when I got shot and ducked for cover, but ..." I shrugged.

She dropped the two baggies into the sack. "You know I don't suspect you—but the bottle changes things. Ziegler will probably want you taken off the story." She spoke faster to defuse my rising anger. "This is high profile. An owner of the *Ledger*. His sister and employees all over the murder scene. Everyone is going to have to walk very carefully through this one, including you."

To keep from saying something sarcastic, I swatted at the sack. "I'll want that back."

"It'll be awhile. I'll keep an eye on it. It'll have to be dusted for prints."

I didn't expect much from that. I thought of all the people I had seen wearing gloves. Others had them dangling from belts or peeking from pockets. "How was he killed, Robbie?"

She was still all detective. "The M.E. will determine that. And Ziegler and I will investigate. Ziegler and I," she added with force.

I hissed loudly.

Robbie's professional demeanor faded a little. "You hiss all you want. Stomp around and get mad. But stay clear. Wren, put a leash on her." She turned away from us.

"We're not into the leather scene!" I snapped after her.

Wren laughed softly at my retort, making it impossible for me to hold on to my anger. Still I said, "Go ahead. Side with her."

"You know she's right, Lexy. You're too close."

"And I wasn't close at the Cat! And the marina!"

Wren became stern. "You weren't involved. You're involved here. It doesn't matter that it's because of your boss and the bad luck of losing your bottle near the body. Ziegler and Robbie were able to look the other way those other times—even be of some help to you. This time they'll have to stand in your way." She stood up. "Home…shower…clean clothes…food."

"I can't be bought off that easily." I got up from the bench amazed by how stiff I had become. "But I can be detoured."

We walked the short distance to the Art League booth where Wren informed the two women there that she was calling it a day. Turning toward the parking lot, I bumped into her as she stopped abruptly. Glen Ziegler was seated on the bench under the mimosa tree with Fonda Allison. Andrea stood behind them impatiently striking her palm with a pair of what looked like expensive isotoner gloves. Robbie waited nearby.

Wren flipped pages of her sketchpad. "I drew her—the one Ziegler's talking to."

I said casually, "She's Andrew's fiancée…was. She's lucky."

"How so?"

"I met her at the *Ledger*. Kind of liked her. Didn't like what I was learning about him." I wasn't sure why I was working so hard to sound so bland. I was aware of Wren's contemplative gaze.

Ziegler joined Robbie. I saw her heft the garbage sack a little as she spoke so I knew she was telling him about my water bottle. He went back and spoke to Andrea. She apparently didn't like what he said. He followed his last statement with a curt nod and he and Robbie left.

Our next pause was in front of the orienteering announcement board. Shamelessly I basked in Wren's pride at my second-place finish.

But I wasn't as pleased when she asked, "Which one is the ill-mannered runner?"

At my admission it was Nelda Cross, Wren said sharply, "Too many intersecting lines here, Lexy. In art we'd call that setting up stress and tension—making a statement about conflict. One night you ask about Christopher Cross. The next about his wife, Nelda. Then the two of you clash. See what I mean about a picture developing?"

I stuck with her metaphor. "I'm not the painter, Wren. Just an observer of a work in progress."

"Not precisely accurate," she responded quickly. "You're so close to the canvas you've got paint in your hair." Her face relaxed into an expression of good humor. I could see her deciding to let me off the hook again by changing the subject. She said, "Kelleen and her mother came back through just before you showed up. I hope they saw this. It'll please Kelleen."

I grimaced. "Probably peeve her that I wasn't first."

"You don't like having things expected of you, do you?"

Wren's perception jarred me. I would take on something that I thought needed doing—but I didn't like it expected of me. I wanted to reach lines that I drew—not ones drawn for me by others. It had chafed me that Andrea wanted me to beat out Nelda Cross, but the insolent woman in pink had made me want it, too. I don't think I could have managed it otherwise.

The path to the car took us near Andrea and Fonda. Carefully I avoided looking their way, but Andrea's authoritative voice halted us.

Andrea did all the talking. "I will file a short column on my brother's death for tomorrow's edition. After that you will team with Tamara Gantt for in-depth coverage—under her byline."

I nearly smiled. Glen Ziegler and Robbie Exline had underestimated her. I cautioned myself not to do the same.

NINE

I propped myself against the hood of my car, contemplating the front of the *Ledger* building. An owner was dead—and by violent means—but everything looked the same. I scuffed a toe on the blacktop. What did I expect? A wreath on the door? The employees entering wearing black? Rose and Lyndall Standish had deserved that. Andrew Standish had done nothing to make his absence mourned here.

I had shut out all thoughts of him when I left the park with Wren late yesterday afternoon. First I had showered to get clean and then soaked for a very long time in a tub of scented water and suds. Then I had done stretches at Wren's insistence, finally admitting to her that I no longer felt stiff and sore. All that was left was a throb centered in my right thigh.

I smacked my car with both hands as I pushed away. Had Nelda Cross's canteen been in Robbie's sack of evidence yesterday? If so, it also had my fingerprints.

I arrived early, wanting to clear my desk, my computer, and my mind of all hanging projects and then rough out plans for pending ones. The orienteering run was behind me but the pace I needed to set for the coming workweek would be even more demanding.

I found Peggy Thomas already staffing the front desk. She motioned me over. "The boss lady wants you to lunch with her upstairs around one." She made it sound as though there were nothing out of the ordinary, but her next comment indicated otherwise. "Lexy, not many people are going to understand her...her approach to what happened yesterday. Don't be judgmental."

No one else was around or coming from the parking lot, so I decided to probe. "You said you went to high school with them. How were they then?"

Her pale brown eyes, enlarged by thick glasses, were serious.

"Depends on who you ask. People expect twins to be alike and to be close. They weren't. On the surface Andrew was all smiles and good cheer—Andrea was reserved, distant. You had to get really close, which few did, to find out that he was mean and conniving and that her manner was camouflage—mostly to protect herself from his constant attempts to muddy her waters."

"How did you find out the truth about them?"

Her smile was chilled with self-mockery. "Off the record, of course. Andrew asked me out when I was a sophomore. I was a plain Jane, Goody Two Shoes. Andrea heard him on the phone bragging about how he planned to get into a virgin's pants on a first date. She and I were lab partners in a biology class and I had told her about him asking me out."

Peggy removed her glasses and began cleaning them. "The short of it is she followed us and when I jumped out of the car, scared, embarrassed and crying, she picked me up and whisked me away." Peggy flashed me a wry smile. "Virginity intact." She settled her glasses back in place. "And she has never mentioned it to me since."

I changed direction. "Was Andrew trying to muddy her waters here with Cross Communications?"

"I think so, but all I know is office scuttlebutt. Heard a rumor Friday that Cross has or wants to get hold of the twenty percent of *Ledger* stock owned by Media Acquisitions."

With others coming into the building and the phone ringing, I had all I would get for the moment. I started down the outer corridor to my cubicle, but stopped in at Barbara MacFadden's to leave a note. Politely I requested any information on connections between the *Ledger* and Cross Communications that she felt free to share with me. I knew better than to demand information from the Iron Maiden.

Three hours sped by. I completed many minor projects and then concentrated on turning copious notes on the borderline legality of banking promotions, advertising, and disclosures into terse copy. I knew it would be examined carefully by staff lawyers and probably questioned by Worthington. But I had spent days sitting in waiting areas and listening to how old people, young people, and immigrants were confused, if not purposely misled. Often I had pretended to be an applicant and was stunned by how easy it was to miss the financial implications of requirements and procedures delivered rapid-fire in a specialized vocabulary or provided in pages of fine-print brochures. The banks were getting rich off fees and services that changed constantly and were nearly incomprehensible.

Then I made some calls, tying up loose ends before I filed my copy on the picketing of Bound to be Read, a local bookstore which was staying afloat by running daily and evening discussion groups and readings. They had been picketed during the two weeks featuring homosexual literature. The picketers had all claimed to be individuals with no specific connections or ties. I had discovered, however, that some of the signs and leaflets had been paid for by the office for the re-election of a rabidly conservative state legislator. I assumed that if the picketing proved successful, he would claim the connection when campaigning again.

I attempted to scoop the bulky, heavy Orlando phone book into an open desk drawer, but dropped it instead on my bruised thigh. Rather than swearing, I mumbled through gritted teeth, "Genesis, Exodus, Leviticus—"

I left off as Barbara MacFadden appeared in my doorway. Amusement brightening her dark blue eyes, she said, "I didn't know you were a religious woman, Miss Hyatt."

"I'm not. Something I learned from my grandfather when I spent summers with my grandparents in Indiana. He didn't believe it was right to curse." I waved her to a chair.

She spoke in a low voice for my ears only. "I attended a meeting with the legal staff and Miss Standish earlier. After the meeting she asked some very pointed questions about you. I answered them on the condition that I be permitted to be fully open with you."

I reached for a notebook but she hastened to say, "No notes for now." I folded my arms on the desk and leaned closer to where she sat at the side.

She continued, "The Standishes left separate wills which are still going through probate. Rose left her forty percent to Andrea; Lyndall left his to Andrew. It appears that was the only bone of contention between them. Lyndall wouldn't give up on his son maturing some day." A twist of her mouth said what she thought of that prospect in a man already forty years old. "Rose was in negotiation with Media Acquisitions when she died. Perhaps trying to see to it that her daughter would have a majority holding."

I spoke up. "If Andrea knew that, couldn't she have completed the purchase on her own?"

"She was in the process of trying to do just that, but they informed her last Wednesday that they had sold to Christopher Cross. She believed her brother was somehow involved."

I thought of the threat that represented to the *Ledger*—to Andrea herself. Cross and Andrew together would have majority control. Very muddy waters indeed. I asked, "What happens to Andrew's part now?"

"I'm not privy to that information."

Something zipped through my mind. Perhaps Fonda Allison wasn't so lucky after all. Had she been married to Andrew, she might now be co-owner of the paper with his sister. Instead she would most likely return to Alaska. Which, of course, was no concern of mine—or interest. I pushed back from my desk so forcefully that the Iron Maiden raised her brows.

She held a small piece of paper toward me just long enough for me to read the two names it contained. She explained before folding and pocketing the paper. "Two Cross people who have been here for about a month. Mr. Worthington was instrumental in their employment."

She left my cubicle and left me wondering if being 'Cross people' meant, as Tamara Gantt had indicated, being a right-wing crazy. Despite recent conflicts with Joe Worthington, I had never read him as being part of that movement.

I jumped guiltily as my intercom crackled with Worthington's voice requesting my presence in his office. Entering his glassed enclosure I expected something related to the Andrew Standish situation. Instead he asked me if I had completed the article on the picketing of the bookstore.

"Just now. Sent it through for tomorrow. Why?"

"Already a lot going in for tomorrow." He was shuffling papers—not looking at me. "May have to cut it too much to warrant a byline. Or cut it all together."

I stayed coldly calm. "What's going on, Joe? And it seems like I'm asking that a lot lately."

His calmness was almost a sadness. "I'm trying to look out for you, Lexy."

Suddenly he shoved his glasses higher on his nose. "That'll be all for now."

I heard the whoosh of the automatic door opening. A rabbit of a man, pinkish skin, unnaturally white hair for his age and a twitching nose, was entering.

Worthington said, "Come in, Mr. Neville."

William Neville? One of the names I had seen just moments ago.

72

I left without any comment, despite unanswered questions and increasing anger.

Back in my cubicle I stood, head bent over an open file drawer, where I could see Worthington's office. But the Neville had his back to me and blocked Joe from my view, so I could tell nothing about their conversation. What had he meant by trying to look out for me? Just a phrase to put me off or one with some substance? Concern for me as an investigative reporter or a lesbian?

I heard a throat-clearing sound. The Iron Maiden was back again but she, too, was watching Worthington's office.

She said, "The two names I showed you a short while ago—I checked their personnel files to see if there was anything pertinent to developing situations. I noted both listed religious affiliation as LCC. A very energetic sect, I've heard."

That rang a bell. I rushed to my desk and swept through the papers there on the picketing of Bound to be Read. I found the leaflet I was looking for and turned to show it to the Iron Maiden—but she had delivered her information and was gone.

I sat down and read the single, folded sheet. It was an especially harsh diatribe against homosexuality. It invited those wishing to do battle against the foes of soul-saving Christian doctrine to attend services of the Light of Christ Church—LCC. I checked the location in a cross-index of phone numbers and street addresses.

My stomach growled reminding me that I was expected to lunch with the boss. I hurried past Worthington's office but took the stairs slowly. I didn't know what to expect and I was wishing the Iron Maiden had told me what 'pointed' questions had been asked of her concerning me. I didn't want my position as reporter compromised. I didn't want my personal life to become an issue.

But I couldn't stifle my curiosity, either. Or my desire to ferret out what happened to Andrew Standish, why it had happened and by whose hand.

Though the door to the office suite was ajar, I knocked and waited. Andrea called for me to enter and then closed the door. She was at her desk on the phone but waved me toward a corner where two wing chairs sat, separated by a low table containing trays of finger sandwiches, stuffed celery sticks, and cheese straws.

Andrea completed the call, then joined me carrying a pitcher. She said, "I hope mint iced tea is acceptable. Fill your plate while I pour."

We munched food in a surprisingly easy silence. When at last she spoke, it was with a directness I was becoming used to and with less of the formality that always put me on guard.

"I've learned, Lexy, that you're not only developing into a good reporter who writes well, but also that you've proved your worth as an amateur detective. What exactly is your relationship with Detectives Ziegler and Exline and why do they object to your covering my brother's death for the paper?"

"Our paths crossed, as I think I mentioned earlier, when they were sent to investigate a murder in a bar that I frequent. Some personal lines of communication developed that had nothing to do with that specific situation—and that I would prefer not to expand on. The problem at the moment is that my water bottle was found near... near the body. On the basis of opportunity, I guess they have to include me among the early suspects." I knew I sounded stiff.

Andrea said dryly, "I rather imagine I'm their number one suspect. I was nearby, too. They haven't released the details of how he was killed yet so I don't know how they'll connect me. But God knows they'll be able to dredge up motive aplenty." She turned more toward me. "I don't want to be convicted because I happen to be a smooth fit for too obvious a theory. Andrew was devious—even malevolent. There are others who would want him dead." Her next words had the effect of figuratively shoving me against the back of my chair. "Will you look for them? Quietly, without danger to yourself?"

She hadn't said she wasn't guilty. Was she assuming I would think that or side-stepping the issue? I trailed a finger up and down the moisture on my glass and spoke without looking at her. "I'm willing to watch, listen and ask questions where possible. For personal as well as professional reasons." I was thinking of my bruised thigh courtesy of Nelda Cross's canteen and the splatter of a paint ball against my jaw. "But there's no guarantee of help in that." Now I looked at her. "Don't expect Glen Ziegler or Roberta Exline to be any more open with me than with you. And don't expect me to be a puppet whose strings you control."

I hadn't known I was going to say that. She actually smiled—and it made her appear more approachable.

"Miss MacFadden has correctly assessed you. She told me that under the mild exterior was mettle and fervor. In private I'm Andrea, Lexy. I think we'll make quite a team."

Our moment of camaraderie was interrupted by the voice of Peggy Thomas issuing from the intercom. "Ms. Standish, a Detective

Ziegler is here with me. He requests that you summon Tamara Gantt and permit him to interview her in your office."

Andrea said only, "Certainly. Contact Miss Gantt." Then to me, "I'd like you to stay."

Soon Ziegler was ushered in by Peggy, who left immediately. He compressed his lips when he saw me. I couldn't hear what he said to Andrea at her desk but she shook her head in disagreement.

When Tamara appeared in the doorway, Andrea offered her and Ziegler the two chairs in front of the desk. He remained standing by one and said, "I'd like to interview Miss Gantt alone."

Andrea countered, "I am correct, am I not, that Miss Gantt is under no obligation to answer your questions—alone or otherwise?"

Ziegler controlled his desire to sigh. "You are correct. Miss Gantt?"

Tamara answered smoothly, "I assume this is more about what happened yesterday. I don't think I can add to what I said then, but I can try."

He opened a notebook—orange like mine. Since we had once inadvertently exchanged ours, I was surprised that he continued to buy that color. Perhaps a shared stubborn streak. He took Tamara through her activities during the run. She described early sightings of Andrew Standish but none after she and Thea left the course to help the injured woman.

"But you went back out on the course?"

"Yes," she admitted. "I wanted to finish what I started even though I was pretty much behind everybody by then."

"Did you carry water with you?"

I couldn't see Tamara's face but she shifted in her seat, apparently as surprised by the question as I was. Where was Ziegler going?

She answered, "No. The woman I was paired with carried a canteen. I didn't think to get it from her."

"But you picked up a water bottle."

She was silent for a few seconds. "Actually I did pick up one—literally—off the ground. I saw it when I went behind a tree to—to answer nature's call. I was out of breath and my mouth was dry. I thought about drinking from it but there was very little in it and I also decided it wasn't a very sanitary thing to do. I left it there."

"What did it look like?"

Tamara answered without hesitating. "Unicorns all over it."

Ziegler didn't look at me, but I stared at him. Two things hit me. Tamara had been near the body since my bottle was supposedly found

75

near Standish—and my bottle should have been half full.

I said, "How did you know she picked up the bottle?"

Surprisingly, he answered me. "Her fingerprints were on it—along with yours."

Tamara twisted in her seat to look at me, then back at Ziegler. "Well, now you know how they got there."

I asked, "Were there any others?"

Again he surprised me by answering. "A couple of partials that didn't match anything on file." Wren's, I thought. "And some smudges that could have come from being kicked around. I know yours are on file because you were once a teacher. And you, Miss Gantt?"

"I worked one summer in a licensed daycare center. Being finger-printed was part of the background check."

Ziegler reviewed her story trying to pinpoint times and people she saw. He questioned me about where and when I could have lost the bottle. When he asked us both to describe our contacts with Andrew Standish at the *Ledger*, Andrea answered for us. She explained that he had never participated in running the paper—that few employees had ever seen or met him.

Ziegler began concentrating on Andrea's movements during the run. She explained that she had borrowed a golf cart from one of the referees and gone around checking during the fog, fearing that many people might become lost—and feeling responsible because of the *Ledger* sponsorship. After the fog cleared, she patrolled in a haphaz-ard way, never completely certain of her location. Did that sound as unlikely to the others as it did to me?

When the questioning was concluded, I followed Ziegler out of the office, dogging his heels down the steps and through the long corridor to the front. Then I managed to skip around him and hold the door open.

He tried to frown but his grin slipped through. "What am I going to do with you, Lexy? You're becoming a magnet for murder."

"Speaking of which," I inserted, "how was Standish murdered?"

"Classic blow to the head with a blunt instrument. That's already part of the official release."

"Weapon?"

He rubbed his knuckles over his chin. "M.E.'s office is working on that." He started down the steps, saying as he went, "Robbie and I mean it. Stay clear, Lexy. We've told your boss to give you other sto-ries to cover."

I smirked to his back knowing Andrea's response to that. Turning to reenter the building, I stepped back quickly as the door opened, brushing against me.

"Sorry." Tamara was rushing. "Domestic violence—hostage situation." The blunt phrasing and her hollow tone glossed over the horrors we both knew might be waiting. But she stopped and came back to me. "And I'm sorry about not taking your bottle with me. Would have if I had known it was yours."

"It's okay. I don't think I'm in real trouble over it. Ziegler is a good detective. He'll work hard to connect the dots right."

"Then maybe I shouldn't have held back on a couple of things."

"Like what?"

"Probably nothing—but I saw a flash of that electric green the referees were wearing further in the woods than I was when I stopped to pee. And then as I was getting back on the trail I heard a whirring sound. Those golf carts made that sound."

One of the staff photographers, his equipment rattling from his neck and shoulder, grabbed Tamara by the arm as he passed. She called back, "Later…"

TEN

I idled in a line of cars, waiting at a red light and concentrating on locking my activities of the last two hours away for awhile. I had been punished for my relief at not catching the domestic-violence call by being sent to cover 911 calls from an apartment building which housed foreign students attending Orlando Technological University. I was on my way back from the there.

I glanced down at the picture of a young woman. Born in Agra, India, home of the Taj Majal, she had a face that could have inspired its own memorial—strong classic lines framed by swirls of black hair, soft lips slightly parted, intense eyes. The picture had been given to me by a woman friend who lived in the apartment above. An EMT had given me a description of the brutally battered body shoved into the shower stall.

Following on the heels of the detective, I had garnered pertinent information, but only from female students. Glowering or coldly withdrawn, the men had refused to speak with me. In June, at nineteen, the young woman would have been honored as the youngest person ever to receive a doctorate degree from the university. Her field was international business and finance. The 911 calls were in response to loud shouting and thudding sounds coming from her apartment. The young woman's brother and cousin were seen leaving the building before the police arrived.

I heard from more than one person how strongly the two men had objected to the attention being given their relative and how unseemly it was for her to achieve beyond her station. I wasn't naive. I knew the status of women in many Asian and Middle Eastern cultures. I also knew that violence against women there was commonplace and accepted even to the point of execution and murder. But that didn't make it any easier to accept especially since apparently the murder had occurred on a local campus.

I had faxed in the story but it was not an issue I would shelve soon. For now, though, I was going off-duty.

I decided against going home before my Monday night class at the Martial Arts Academy. Wren was attending a seminar on the potential value of vitamins and hormones for the pre- and post-menopausal woman, sponsored by a group of gynecologists as part of Women's Health Week. She claimed that she was simply collecting information and would not be lining our kitchen windowsill with bottles of pills and capsules.

Though I dug in my heels like a contrary mule, I appreciated her efforts to improve my diet. Gradually she had weaned me away from fried, fatty, starchy foods to an acceptance of fresh fruits and vegetables in greater proportions. But I still balked at steamed asparagus spears, insisting that they had the texture and flavor of twigs.

Feeling like a kid getting away with something, I glanced in my mirror before doing a sharp right turn into a fast-food drive-through. Having just made certain there was no one riding my bumper, I was surprised to hear a squeal of brakes. The occupants of a white compact had apparently also decided on a fast-food fix and turned in after me. They took a second turn toward front parking.

I chose a cheeseburger and root beer, thinking how much I would really like two hot dogs and a frosted mug of root beer like my grandfather used to get for us at an A&W stand in Indiana. A few minutes later, munching and sipping, I decided on another detour. I took a street that I knew would cut through to Garden, the street that bordered the field running along the north side of the orienteering course.

There was parking only on the apartment side of the street, and no empty spaces, so I drove slowly, gazing over the field to the woods where Andrew Standish's body had been found. Knowing Glen Ziegler's thoroughness, I was sure he had dispatched someone to question apartment residents concerning people crossing that field on Sunday.

A horn beeped behind me and I waved a van past. I noticed another car hovering several lengths behind me. I sped up, then spotted a space I would have to back into carefully. I stopped and waved the car around before attempting a parallel parking procedure few Floridians were good at—including me. The driver hesitated, then, as I waited, zipped around me. It was very like the white car that had followed me into the fast-food restaurant.

I spoke aloud. "What do you mean 'followed'? You're getting paranoid. No one has reason to follow you." I shuddered, remembering a time I had been followed in the dark of night and during a thunderstorm. Without really tasting it, I finished my food, watching the field fade in the early winter evening.

I knew what I was doing. I was looking at the open space in the fence as the means by which an unknown person could have entered and lain in wait for Andrew. That way I wouldn't have to worry about the killer being Andrea. I sighed and reached under the seat on the passenger side, withdrawing an orange notebook. Might as well make my detour count for something.

I wrote down what I knew of Andrea's location at the approximate time of the murder. I did the same for Warren Kessler, myself, and Nelda Cross. Being meticulously objective, I added Tamara. I wished I could buttonhole Robbie to learn if the police had discovered anyone else involved with the orienteering competition who had some prior connection to Standish. I considered people who weren't on the course but had been in the area and added Fonda Allison, Peggy Thomas, and Christopher Cross.

I doodled at the bottom of the page. Hundreds had participated in the events yesterday and everywhere I turned I was learning that Andrew Standish incited lasting grudges. Who else—how many unknowns—qualified for my list?

A small group of kids was coming across the field. I got out of my car and walked to the opening in the fence to meet them. A skinny boy, maybe ten or so, was wearing one of the florescent green referee vests.

"Hey, guys," I greeted them. "Been exploring?" I knew that the crime-scene tape would be up still but doubted it would faze a bunch of inquisitive youngsters.

"Nah." This from a sturdy towhead. "Wanted to see where that guy was killed. Couldn't find no blood or nothin'."

"But you found that vest."

The skinny boy wearing it took a couple of defensive steps backwards. "Didn't belong to anybody. It was way up in a tree. Had to climb to get it."

An alert mother appeared on the sidewalk. She chastised the kids for being across the street, but seemed more concerned with my presence. She turned out to be the mother of the boy with the vest. I produced my *Ledger* identification and her wariness receded. But as I explained that the vest might be evidence and I wanted to give it to the police, the boy's wariness increased.

"Make you a deal," I coaxed. "You let me have the vest and I'll see to it your class at school gets a set of those nature maps *The Ledger* gives out. And tickets to some of the special wildlife parks around here." I could see him weakening and held out one of my cards. "And you can keep this. If you come across anything that might be big news, you give me a call."

He took the card and gave me the vest. I took his name, and the name of his school and his teacher's. I warned his mother that the police might get in touch with her.

She said, "They were through here yesterday, late. As far as I know, no one had anything to tell them."

I thanked her and repeated to her son my promise of maps and tickets. After three jerky movements forward and back, I escaped the small parking space. On my way to class I considered the green vest now residing in the trunk. Tamara had spoken of seeing a flash of that green. Had a referee killed Andrew Standish and then tossed the vest high and out of sight so as to blend in with the others? I planned to pry as much as I could from Robbie in payment for the vest.

I arrived at the Academy with barely enough time to change into my tunic before the stretching exercises. After the mental and physical demands of the past two days, I found comfort and renewal in the slow, precise movements. I was surprised at the ease with which I emptied my mind of everything except for the quiet authority of the Major's voice and the rhythmic responses of my body.

During a break, Kelleen approached me. She said, "Congratulations...Lexy. We saw that you had the second-place time." Without drawing a breath or blinking, she added, "Did you see the body?"

I was caught starting to say "thank you" and could only expel air in a breathy stutter. Finally I responded to her insistent gaze with "Yes. Yes I did."

"Why didn't you write the story?"

I told her the truth. "Since I was near the crime scene at the right—rather the wrong time, and he was part-owner of the paper I work for—that makes me technically a suspect. Reporters are supposed to be uninvolved and objective." There were a number of people who would love hearing me make that pretentious statement.

"Did you know him?"

"No. He was seldom at the *Ledger*. His twin sister runs things."

"Then when the police understand you are not involved, you could be objective."

"It isn't that simple."

Kelleen compressed her lips into a thin line. I was afraid I had sounded condescending, but then she relaxed, saying, "Oh. You're involved with people who might be real suspects." She turned away as the Major called us to line up again.

Though the course concentrated primarily on unarmed self-defense, tonight the Major took us through punching and kicking blows designed to halt or neutralize an opponent's force. I was uncomfortable and clumsy with the kicking routines, but enjoyed a sense of power using my hands and arms to punch, strike, and block. We all took turns challenging assistants wearing helmets and padded suits.

At the end of class I leaned against the wall, panting and exhila-rated.

The Major paused in front of me. "Have you ever considered a class in fencing, Lexy? I think it would solve your balance problems and that you would be good at it. Now, our Kelleen here..." She had materialized from nowhere as usual. "...She is her own weapon. She was born knowing how to walk inside the whirlwind." The older woman and the child bowed with the respect of equals.

By the time I reclaimed my street clothes from the dressing room, I was the last student out the door. I joined Kelleen who was looking very intently into the western sky.A sliver of a moon hung brilliantly against the dusty black sky. Two planets appeared to have dropped from it in free fall toward Earth. Jupiter and Saturn, I thought.

Without turning her head, Kelleen said, "It looks like an upside-down pendulum."

"Or the arm of a metronome about to start ticking to the rhythms of the universe."

Now she looked at me. "I don't know what a metronome is." Before I could open my mouth to explain, she said firmly, "I'll look it up when I get home."

Brie O'Mara drove up. She rolled down the window. "Well, if it isn't the long and the short of it."

Kelleen said, "Lexy had a good lesson tonight. And saw the body yesterday."

Startled, I shrugged helplessly at Brie, hoping she understood that I had not introduced the subject. Hurriedly, I said my goodnights and started for my car midway across the lot. But I paused before stepping off the curb. In a darker patch of the lot was a white compact. There was an all-night drugstore down the block with a few cars in front of it, but none anywhere near mine—except a van I thought belonged to the Major.

Reason said there were hundreds of white compacts in the city. Reason said there was no justification for the apprehension prickling the short hairs at the back of my neck. I shifted my clothes to my left arm and removed my keys from a pocket. I reached my car without seeing anyone, opened the door, and was bending to get in when a hand seized me roughly by the shoulder. My clothes and keys were knocked from my hands before I could react to the figure in a black ski mask.

Adrenaline surged and I struck with the heels of my hands just below the attacker's collarbones. I was surprised by the distance he fell back. A voice garbled by the mask said something indistinct. I could hear the Major's voice saying, "Wait for your opponent's move—then use it against him." He rushed straight at me. I braced against my car, lifted a leg. He took my foot in his abdomen and went down on a knee.

Foolishly, I moved forward and gripped the top of his ski mask. Before I could tug it over his head, he grabbed my wrist and whirled me around. I managed to keep my footing and was ready when he lunged again. This time I stepped sideways and jabbed with the hardness of my knuckles into the softness at the side of his neck while also tripping him. He fell flat and I heard the breath rushing from him.

This gave me time to scramble for my keys, just under the car. I was willing to sacrifice my scattered clothes. Straightening I was horrified to see the small, white-clad figure of Kelleen speeding toward us. Brie was wheeling her car to follow. Before I could yell at Kelleen to stop, she jumped into the air and sailed past me at shoulder height.

I barely had time to turn my head to catch sight of her foot hitting the chest of a second masked man. As he hurtled backwards, a tire iron clattered onto my trunk and fell to the paved surface. At the same time, car wheels screeched and Brie O'Mara screamed her daughter's name.

Grunting and limping, both men made for their car. Jumping in and starting up, they swerved toward an exit, nearly clipping the Major who was running toward us.

Clutching her daughter tightly to her, Brie said, "I looked in my side mirror before pulling away from the curb and saw you being attacked. I was trying to get my cell phone out of its case when Kelleen took off." She was struggling to stay calm.

Kelleen extricated herself from her mother's grasp. "I saw the other man come up from behind your car. There wasn't time to wait." She was calm.

I went down on a knee to pick up my clothes. "But Kelleen—"

She said, a trifle curtly, "I'm a brown belt, Lexy."

I pulled a strand of my blue belt through my hand. "Understood." I looked her in the eye. "I owe you big time, Kelleen Cha...Kell. I hold a marker for you. You can call it in anytime—no questions asked. Do you understand?"

Her smug face looked back at me. "Yes. I know all about markers. I read some stories by Damon Runyan. I pulled the book off the shelf at the library because I liked the sound of his name. He was a newspaperman, you know."

"I know." I was surprised that she knew of the early twentieth century writer noted for his celebration of offbeat gangsters and their colorful slang. For the second time that night I looked helplessly to Brie. This time she shrugged, calmer, perhaps resigned to the force that was her unusual daughter.

I refused Brie's offer to call the police, explaining that I had friends in the department I would contact. They left and I picked up the tire iron with my shirt so as not to disturb fingerprints—though I was sure I had seen gloves on both men. I put it in the trunk with the green vest.

The Major, who had stood by as an observer during my exchange with the others, said, "I saw a bumper sticker as they went by me—the letters LCC and the fish symbol that many Christian groups use."

I thanked her—for that and for more. "I may not be your prize pupil, but things I learned from you stood me in good stead tonight." We shook hands.

All the way home I puzzled over what had happened. I spun wheels within wheels. Joe Worthington had supposedly urged the hiring of two employees who were members of the Light of Christ Church. Why? I didn't know. I formulated a plan for checking out the church group. Joe I would tackle myself. Chris Cross and his wife apparently espoused ultra-conservative views. Connected with LCC? I didn't know.

And where did I fit in? I worked for the *Ledger*. Recently I was often at odds with Worthington. I had participated in the orienteering run. Beaten Nelda Cross. Her husband had bought into the paper. Was any of this connected with Andrew's murder? With Andrea enlisting me to snoop? I didn't know.

When I reached home there was a car I didn't recognize blocking my way to the garage, so I had to park in the street. Wren was in the doorway—someone else was on the small porch, caught in the spill of light from inside. She turned at my approach and I saw that it was Thea. The tornado hairdo had been flattened to emphasize her narrow, well-shaped skull. A wide swath of dark hair ran like a river around her long neck and over a shoulder and breast.

She said tauntingly, "Surely not your work clothes, Lexy. Or do you have a night job, too? Speaking of which, I do have a night job and need to get moving. Goodnight, Wren. Thanks for the drink—and for your most pleasant company."

The velvety seductiveness of her voice echoed unpleasantly in my mind as I watched her stride to her car. The echoing became an irritant as I tried to isolate and understand my feelings. There was something familiar about those deep-throated tones.

I was tired of questions I couldn't answer. I rasped gruffly at Wren, "I'll put my car in the garage—then maybe you'll serve me a drink, too."

I was too ashamed of my uncalled for surliness to see how she took that.

ELEVEN

I watched from the kitchen doorway as Wren poured hot water into a Chinese tea mug. She put the top in place and steam rose through the tiny holes.

"What's that?"

Wren's expression was speculative. "The drink you requested. Jasmine tea. It's what I served Thea. It needs to steep for three minutes—if that doesn't tax your patience too much."

I bit into my lip and lowered my head. She lifted my chin with the light touch of a single finger. "That was the first flicker of jealousy you've shown me. I rather enjoyed it. Now you know how I feel every time Jodi tugs at the back of your hair."

"You've never said anything!"

"Because I knew it didn't mean anything. Not even as a reminder of your past together. It didn't make me feel threatened, Lexy."

I heard the admonition in her words. "I know Thea's not a threat. But she unnerves me, disturbs my balance." I rushed on as Wren moved away to put cookies on a plate. "Something about her makes me want to put her on her butt the way Kelleen did me." Suddenly a delayed reaction to the events following class whipped through me. "Wren, I...I had a problem this evening."

In the living room, sipping hot tea and munching cookies, I told Wren what had happened. I concluded by saying, "I was terrified when I saw Kelleen coming across the lot. But she sailed past me like a battering ram and took out the guy I didn't even know was there."

"But why was he there? Both of them. What did the police say?" My exaggerated care in drinking the hot tea didn't fool her. "You didn't call them! Lexy!"

"I'm going to call Robbie in just a minute. I've got two or three things to go over with her." I did a risky zigzag. "I'm not being jealous now, but how did you and Thea get together?"

86

With only a mildly reproving look, Wren answered, "She was at the seminar."

I couldn't stop the suspicion that Thea had contrived to be there. I was not, however, foolish enough to voice my suspicion.

Wren continued. "She mentioned needing nourishment before going to work. Offering some seemed a polite thing to do. I enjoyed talking with her. I'm not the only one in this family who enjoys new people."

I held up my arms crossed at the wrists and said, "Okay...okay. What kind of night job does she have?"

"She never got around to saying." She gathered my empty dishes and said commandingly, "Call Robbie before it's too late."

I went to my desk where I had tossed my notebook earlier. I took myself through the entire day and jotted down what I thought important. I recorded Peggy Thomas's conflict with Andrew in high school, which led me to add Warren Kessler's injury while climbing the tower with Standish. I scribbled all I had picked up on Cross Communications and the little I knew about LCC. Under Tamara's name I listed her finding my water bottle, glimpsing the referee green, and hearing a golf cart. I concluded with all I could remember about the two men who had attacked me. Questions about Joe Worthington, Andrea, and Nelda Cross I underlined in my mind.

I turned out the desk lamp and called Robbie at home. She picked up on the second ring and to my businesslike "Detective Exline," she said, "I'm not going to discuss the case with you, Lexy."

"Not even in exchange for the evidence I scrounged up? You need to tell your crime techs to look up as well as down."

Silence—then, "What evidence and where did you find it?"

I responded, "How about I meet you in your office tomorrow morning?"

Silence again, but I thought I heard a resigned sigh. "Seven o'clock. Have it with you. And I don't want to hear the words quid pro quo."

I laughed. "You're the one bringing it up, Detective. Seven. Ill be there. Ah—Robbie, a couple more things. I covered the murder at OTU this afternoon."

"I don't have anything to feed you on that, on or under the table. But if first impressions prove right—that the brother and cousin did it—they may be hard to bring in. Too many compatriots willing to hide them—maybe get them out of the country. But at least we have a good extradition treaty with India."

"Looks like the women's motto for the new century needs to be 'We've got a long way to go.'"

"We will eventually. Even though I can't give you anything, did you pick up something I can pass on?"

"No. I did pick up something from an EMT, though, that seemed a little unusual. He said that when he was helping get the body out to the van there was a group of boys—men who kept muttering the word 'witch.' They shut up when he glanced toward them."

"Sure the word wasn't bitch?"

"I asked him that. He said no. Probably doesn't mean anything. Its just that from the picture I saw of her she looked like anything but a witch." Robbie was silent. Finally I said, "Robbie? You still there?"

"Yes. Trying to think of—Can you hold the line?"

"Sure." I heard her put down the receiver. It was a couple of minutes before she picked it up again.

"Found something, Lexy. Had to dig the magazine out of the recycling. It's an article on women being declared witches in India and attacked and killed."

"We're talking about right now!"

"Yes." Robbie was skimming the article and reciting portions to me. "It says that nearly two hundred women are killed throughout India each year like this. And over five hundred have been killed in the past ten years in a section called Bihar. Lots of times the killers are family members who claim that the women have caused them bad luck or earned something beyond their station. Doesn't sound like they're prosecuted for it either. You're right. We do have a long way to go."

She gave me the name and date of the magazine. She was going to pass on the issue she had to the detectives assigned to the murder. Now I had more to check out. I felt like I needed to tie reminder strings to every one of my fingers.

Robbie broke into my thoughts. "You said a couple of things. What else?"

Reluctantly, and as mildly as possible, I told her about the attack.

Robbie's exasperation was clear. "Why didn't you report it? When are you going to learn you're not a law unto yourself, Lexy!"

"I wasn't hurt. And I didn't want to involve the mother and daughter. Besides, I have ideas I want to—"

"No! You're not getting your way this time. It goes on the books. Expect a call."

I clamped down on a hiss. I didn't want to antagonize her further. The call concluded, I sat in the semi-darkness and let my responses to the events of the day and evening ebb and flow as I ran a finger over the face of a small radio. I touched the switches, circled the knobs, watched the red line as I turned the dial. Suddenly the feelings were all swept away as it struck me why Thea's voice was so teasingly familiar. She was the Mike Dyke!

The Mike Dyke was a sultry-voiced siren who broadcast sporadically over a pirate gay radio station generally picked up in the environs of GAG—the Gay-Asian Ghetto. The Ghetto was a collection of small homes and shops and restaurants encompassing several square blocks—an intriguing blend of Thai, Korean, Vietnamese, gay and lesbian cultures. I believed there was little harassment by the authorities or the citizenry because the Asian minorities came under the umbrella of politically correct treatment, even if the gay and lesbian community generally did not.

Between my relationships with Jodi and Wren, feeling alone and rootless, I had often cruised the GAG area seeking to pick up the Mike Dyke on the car radio. Her throaty, sexy, I'm-talking-just-to-you tones eased the pain as much as the haunting disenchantment of the love songs she played aggravated it.

So Thea was the Mike Dyke. I didn't think I would share that with Wren right now.

I sagged in my chair. I was tired. The day had been varied and both physically and emotionally exhausting. I was confused and angry over the threat of physical harm to me and, through me, to Kelleen. I straightened. And I wanted Wren.

She was in the shower. Her golden form, seen through the steamy, opaque glass of the shower door, performed a slow ballet of unknowingly erotic movements. I removed my tunic and kicked it out into the bedroom. I opened the shower door and stepped into the steam and fine spray.

Her hair in the back was wet and plastered to her head and neck. Beaded ringlets framed her face. The front of her body was coated in an uneven distribution of soapsuds. She kept her expression blank but she couldn't stop the eruption of her nipples into provocative darkish nubs.

I trailed my fingers through the suds. I was pleased to see her close her eyes and part her lips. A line of poetry bubbled in my mind. 'Splashing my passion/Across your smooth skin shores.' Without warning, I body-slammed her against the side of the shower stall, being careful to cushion her head with my hand. With ease I slid my body over her soaped one. Her mouth was warm and yielding. Her pelvis lifted against mine. The friction of my hair against hers was electrifying.

As I softened my mouth, Wren murmured against my lips. "Take me hard, Lexy. Make me know I'm yours. That you want me above all others."

I groaned and thrust her roughly under the stinging water to wash the soap from her. Then I backed away and sat on the hard white bench along the back wall. Wren turned and followed. She straddled my thighs and sat down. Slowly I spread my legs. Her eyes brightened with the pleasure. I leaned into her breasts, still smelling of perfumed soap, and her hands stroked my wet hair as I sucked her nipples larger, harder. She slid backwards to my knees. I began stroking her wet pubic hair, smoothing it up and to the sides. With just the tip of a finger I stroked her nether lips, so much fuller than those of her firm mouth. Her staccato breathing quickened my desire and I plunged my finger into the fluid passageway. She threw her head back and let out a tremulous sigh. I withdrew from her slowly.

Wren's head snapped forward. "No!" she cried.

"I want to give you more." I grouped three fingers tightly, knowing she would be wet and receptive enough to take them. This time I moaned with her as I thrust hard and so deep that the softness of her mound filled my palm.

She gripped my shoulders and began squirming and tightening on me as much as she could with her thighs spread so wide.

"You've got it all," I said huskily. I withdrew to my fingertips then thrust hard again. "See."

She kissed me, grinding my head against the tile. Then she eased the kiss just enough to gulp a breath before renewing it with greater force. It was almost an angry kiss. I pulled her head back with my free hand and bit into her neck, feeling the strong pulse. She lifted and pushed so vigorously that my feet slipped on the wet floor, spreading her wider.

"Look at me, Wren." I put an arm around her hips and stilled her movements. Then I was the power driving her toward climax. I watched the contortions of her face and a wildness like green fire in her eyes as she begged me to make it happen. When at last the explosion came, I was thrilled by her howl of triumph. I drew her higher on my thighs, tighter to me as she collapsed like a bow unstrung. Then the only sounds were our ragged breathing and the spray of the shower.

Noting my frown at her cramped quarters, Robbie said, "Glen and I are sharing with two other detectives. That means another desk, more file cabinets. The City finally approved an increase in personnel but no extra space to work in so..." She waved a hand over the crowded small room.

I placed the green referee's vest and a rolled up newspaper containing the tire iron on her desk, then perched on the corner rather than thread my way to a chair.

It was Robbie's turn to frown. "You should have wrapped this in something, Lexy."

"It was up in a tree for at least twenty-four hours. Then handled by a bunch of kids and ended up being worn by one of them. Didn't figure I could do any more harm."

"Probably not," she conceded.

Robbie took notes as I gave her the details, including the names of the boy and his mother. Her try for a stern expression didn't quite succeed as she said sarcastically, "You just happened to pick that spot to finish off your food."

I grinned. "Public street, Detective."

She became serious. "Only referees on the orienteering course wore green, right?"

"Right. All other vests were orange. Will you be able to find out which referee didn't return a vest?"

She shuffled through some papers, coming up with the one she wanted. "Doesn't look like it will be that easy. One referee didn't show. Sick kid. At least one vest would have been lying around somewhere. I'll have to find out where."

"Who will you check with?"

She opened her mouth to reply, then shut it firmly.

"Come on, Robbie," I wheedled. "You and I have too much history for you to think I'm going to play ostrich. You may have enough clout to twist Andrea's arm to keep me off the story officially—but you're not big enough to twist mine." I couldn't resist adding, "Despite all those work-out muscles you hide under that boxy suit."

Rather than respond, Robbie tapped my other offering. "And what's this? Carefully she unwrapped the tire iron. "Somehow I don't think they were after your tires. This could have done real damage, Lexy."

91

"It never touched me. And the other guy just managed to grab at me a couple of times. Your Christmas gift served me well."

Robbie put her elbows on the desk and ran her fingers up her forehead into her dark hair. Without looking up, she said in a resigned tone, "What else did you leave out last night? And what's your take on why?"

"Honest-scout truth, Robbie. I don't know any whys. But..." Her glare stopped the rest of my statement about how I intended to find out. Instead I told her about the bumper sticker the Major had spotted.

"Do you think that bumper sticker is a lead?" she asked.

"It's hard to see how. The connections are so flimsy. There may be a connection with the picketing of Bound to be Read. But my story on that is in this morning's edition. And there's something going on with Worthington and a couple of people who are members of LCC. But nothing in any of that explains violence toward me. Heck, Robbie. Those guys might have stolen that car and seen me as easy pickings to rob or carjack."

She gave me an 'oh, sure' look, but said, "I'll check that out. And have this dusted for prints. Will yours be on it?" I shook my head no.

"And I'll see if anything has come the department's way on that church group. Now, does that cover for this?" She pointed to the vest.

"Doesn't seem like quite enough, Detective."

"Look, Lexy, there's no way I'm going to give you evidence I may have to package up for a prosecutor." She scooted back to avoid a slant of morning sunlight slicing through the single window. "Besides, you know the rules. Check close at hand first."

I knew she meant the *Ledger* in general or Andrea specifically. But I said, "I've run into stories that connect Standish with people who weren't family or employees."

"We've been documenting some, too. Last summer he was hang-gliding off some cliffs in Hawaii. Dared everybody to lift off without the safety harnesses. Four joined him. One lost his grip right away and fell into the ocean. Was smashed to death on the rocks." Her voice was bitter. "No fault of Mr. Andrew Standish, of course. But we're not going to find our murderer in Hawaii, Lexy. He or she was on that orienteering course Sunday."

The phone rang and she began talking in monosyllables while taking notes. She pointed to the vest, mouthing a "thank you." I knew that was the end of our meeting.

A short while later I sprinted from my car to the bottom of the

Ledger steps to catch up with Andrea. I wasted no time on small talk. "Can you tell me who made arrangements for the referees on the orienteering course and things like that?"

"Peggy Thomas would know." She didn't mince words either. "Your detective friends hit both our legal department and my personal lawyer late yesterday afternoon. They had a judge's orders for examination of wills, books, a number of things."

I felt trapped between two loyalties. "Did they indicate any reaction to what they found?"

"Not that I know of, but I can imagine some. My parents left Andrew and me each forty percent of the *Ledger*. They stipulated that we could not sell any portion without first offering it to the other at a fair price determined by Legal and Accounting. I knew about that long before they died, but I didn't know until just recently of an added clause. If either of us married, that stipulation became null and void."

As another employee claimed her attention, I went up a few steps and sat on the flat stone ledge. I considered the import of that stipulation. Was that why the thrill-seeking playboy had suddenly chosen to marry? Was Fonda Allison merely a means to circumventing the terms of his parents' wills? Was she aware of that?

Andrea was standing in front of me. Almost as though reading my mind, she said, "I have Fonda in my home. Television reporters were outside the condo Andrew had rented late Sunday. She's all alone here, a long way from Alaska and family. I can't protect her from knowing that Andrew was using her, but I can protect her from the wolves."

Was Andrea's interest only in supplying protection? Or also in exercising control? Had Fonda moved from one predator's lair to another?

I asked, "Will she be returning to Alaska?"

"I assume so, but not until after the funeral. And I can't set the date until the police release...release Andrew's body."

The catch in her voice reminded me that they were not only brother and sister but also twins. His death so soon after those of her parents had to be severely wrenching her universe.

Again she read my mind. She spoke, looking past rather than at me. "A major disappointment of my childhood—of my life—was that we shared nothing beyond our physical likeness. It didn't help that most people assumed I was the one at fault. And now, even in death, he's managed to put me in a bad light."

She cut her eyes at me, gave a half-rueful smile, and went up the steps to the entrance. I sat chewing on my reactions. I wanted to trust her…to sympathize. But I feared manipulation.

"Trying to play hooky, Lexy?" Peggy Thomas sat beside me, stretching her legs out beneath her long stylish skirt and revealing her designer boots. "Wouldn't mind doing it myself if those phones ring today like yesterday… And trying to keep those television vultures out…" She pantomimed pulling her hair.

"I need some info, Peggy."

"Sure."

"Who are the people who actually managed the orienteering run? Set the course, produced the maps, handed out whistles, placed the referees? Stuff like that." I was hoping for specific answers to general questions. What I was doing Wren had recognized early on as playing my cards close to my chest.

Peggy responded promptly. "The man at the top, Stuart Merrill, goes around the state setting up events. Everybody else is local, operating from instructions he provides. I arranged a lot of the details. Got the Iron Maiden to produce the maps and keep them hidden until she gave them to Merrill Sunday morning. I knew there couldn't be anybody more reliable."

"You're right about that. So only you and she saw the maps in advance?"

"Oh, no. She worked with Merrill deciding on the placement of the markers and then produced the maps alone. I never saw one. One of our sports reporters got the supply of whistles and caution tape for marking off dangerous areas. I got the referees. They couldn't be connected with the *Ledger* so I went to Parks and Recreation for them." She made a face. "The boss lady made me give them a pep talk about responding quickly to whistles and keeping people honest in a nice way." She sighed. "This is terrible, I know, but I'm angry with Andrew for getting himself killed and messing up a good thing. He was always a damn easy man to be mad at."

As she hurried up the steps, I was left with her last words ringing in my ears. And a blurred image. I was certain I had glimpsed a map of the course as she had flipped through the sheets on her clipboard while standing with me early Sunday morning in the swirling fog.

TWELVE

Seated at my desk, checking my calendar about the next few days, I kept an eye and ear cocked toward the corridor. I wanted to catch Worthington outside his office. Finally he passed by on his way there.

"Joe," I called. "Give me a minute?"

He stopped but didn't enter my cubicle. When I motioned to a chair, he moved toward it reluctantly. "Save your breath, Lexy, if you're planning to fuss about the cuts I made in your bookstore write-up. You can put them back in when you do the follow-up."

I hadn't yet seen this morning's paper but decided not to admit that. "Right now I'm more interested in why. I thought part of what freedom of the press means is not being under anyone's thumb. How'd you get under the thumb of the Light of Christ Church?"

I expected denial, anger—at least irritation. What I got was a general slumping and a heavy sigh. "I've been wrestling with that for weeks." He dropped his voice to just above a whisper. "My wife and I have never been big churchgoers, but a few months ago a couple of her bridge buddies got her to go to LCC with them. Said it was new, small and personal, connected with real life. Carolyn took to it. Seemed like a good thing. Our kids and their families live too far away for us to see them often. I thought the church activities were a kind of substitute for her."

"Was pressure put on you to get involved?"

"Not that I noticed—at first. Carolyn joined some activities and then started letting different groups meet at the house. Somehow I got included before I could plan a diplomatic way to fade out of sight." He straightened and the old Worthington peered at me over his glasses. "You know how you nod your head to what someone says when you're not really in agreement with them, but it doesn't seem worth making your difference of opinion known? I got suckered in that way. By the time I realized I needed to correct false impressions, it was damn hard to do—especially with Carolyn so involved. And by that time I knew the members of LCC weren't going to hear my objections anyway. They've got real hard-core hatreds, Lexy. Blacks, Jews, immigrants, abortion... gay rights."

"I wouldn't think Carolyn would go along with that." I visualized the gentle, caring woman, I knew.

"They're clever people. When I stepped back and evaluated the situation, I saw that they had her involved in things she and I agreed with—fighting child abuse, aid to the elderly. And I had been helping plan some good projects for young teens. They had me backed against a wall long before I realized I needed to be resisting."

"Why did you help two of them get jobs here?"

He slumped back again. "By the time they hit on me for recommendations I had been nodding my head so long I didn't know how to suddenly shake it the other way. Ah, it's more complex than that. It was easier to convince myself that my relationship with Carolyn was more important than taking a stand against prejudice in the abstract. It was easy to pretend that the good she and I accomplished outweighed the bad done. You don't know it yet, Lexy, but it isn't as easy being the righteous rebel when you're well over fifty." He brushed his thinning hair. "Then Andrew Standish came back to town, and I got invited to power lunches with him and Christopher Cross. Andrew didn't reveal his connection to LCC. He always left it to Cross to do the talking, so it was Cross who told me about Andrew's interest in LCC, and it was made quite clear to me that things were going to change around here— and that if I hoped to keep my job I had better choose the right side."

"Andrew Standish isn't a factor here any more." I winced inwardly at my callous statement.

"Exactly what I thought when I read about his death in our own paper yesterday morning. But right off I got some not too subtle reminders that there were still things that could be done to 'educate' the public. I got the message loud and clear that Mr. Cross and the Light of Christ Church would appreciate my continued assistance." Bitter sarcasm coated his voice. "Less loud but just as clear was the message that turncoats would not be tolerated."

"What could they do to you without Andrew to back them up?" Hurriedly I answered that question myself. "Tattle on you to Andrea and hope she'd fire you."

"That's the way I read it. But Neville miscalculated and went too far yesterday. He's that toad who came in when you were leaving."

"I rather thought he was a rabbit," I said dryly.

Worthington put his head back and roared with laughter. "God, it's good to laugh! I haven't done much of that lately. He is a rabbit, isn't he? Pink and white and hopping all around like he's trying to be everywhere at once." He sobered. "He sneered at your back. Said it wasn't going to be long before all the perverts on the staff began finding out decent people didn't want to work with them. That was cold water in my face. Woke me up. Not just because you're a good reporter. Because you're the decent person—not him."

He stood up, embarrassed. "So I went home and talked with Carolyn last night. Should have done it sooner. Didn't give her enough credit. When I told her about the other side of the coin and how things were here...well, let's just say we aren't members of LCC any longer."

Why did I feel that he was still holding back?

At the door he turned. "I know I don't come off looking very good in any of this, Lexy. If Standish were still alive I probably wouldn't be telling you all this. Best thing that guy ever did was die."

I watched his head and shoulders as he went down the corridor. Andrew hadn't simply died, he'd been murdered. Someone was responsible for that. Had Andrew died because he had threatened the killer?

I was convinced now that I had been attacked by two members of LCC. But why? Why a physical attack? If there was already a plan to purge all us 'objectionables' from the staff...I remembered Tamara's story about Cross and his changes in staffing wherever he gained enough control. Was LCC his means to that end? Did he truly back them or just use them? Could he be funding them? But that still didn't explain the attack on me, unless Cross had somehow learned of my recruitment by Andrea for special assignments. I couldn't see how. Even Worthington didn't know...but he did know of my sudden visits to her private suite.

Frustrated, I turned to my regular work. I sent word to Research that anything on witches in India was to be routed to my desk. I took phone calls to banks, to contacts at OTU and to an Assistant DA. I was again rebuffed by the secretary for State Representative Yount, who funded some of the anti-gay literature passed out in front of Bound to be Read. I made a note to see if he was an open member of LCC. That gave me an idea. I went in search of the Iron Maiden.

She was not at her desk, so I went to the staff lounge for a coffee break. There I found her sitting across a table from a woman of medium age, medium size and medium coloring. The woman's bland appearance was relieved, incongruously, I thought, by a red scarf, red belt, and red shoes. There was nothing bland, however, in her haranguing tone.

"You are missing the point, Miss MacFadden! By selling so much advertising space to Jewish concerns, the *Ledger* risks being identified with—even fueling—their lust for money and power. It is aiding them in crowding out the businesses of worshippers of the true God."

I had my back to them, pouring coffee. I smiled at the Iron Maiden's deceptively mild tone as she said, "I thought Jews and Christians worship the same God."

"Oh, no! That is Jewish propaganda. It is how they try to avoid responsibility for killing Christ. And hide their vile efforts to kill his message today."

"Which message would that be, Ms. Vitak? Love thy neighbor? Live by the Golden Rule?"

I pressed the smile from my lips and turned around. I recognized her name as the other half of the LCC pair planted by Christopher Cross.

Still employing a mild tone, the Iron Maiden asked, "Who are these Jewish concerns you think should be denied the legal right to purchase advertising space?"

She leaped so eagerly into the answer I didn't think the woman even heard the moderate emphasis on the word legal. She rattled off a stream of names, concluding with Greenburg Florists.

I said, "If that's Thelonia Greenburg, I know her."

She jerked her head around and glared at me for my interruption. Following the Iron Maiden's lead, I said equably, "I don't know her background, but she is a practicing Wiccan. I covered her petition for booth space when Orange State University sponsored a Religions of the World mini-convention promoting education and understanding. She made a very intelligent, eloquent appeal and won the right to participate."

"That's an abomination!"

Now a coldness invaded the Iron Maiden's voice. "I found Ms. Hyatt's article very interesting and informative."

The woman's eyes cut back and forth between us, finally locking on me. "Lexy Hyatt? Exactly what I would expect from someone of...of your...your perversion!" She harrumphed and rushed from the room, slamming the door.

I took her vacated chair. "Surely she won't be kept on staff spouting beliefs like that."

The Iron Maiden replied, "I heard a rumor this morning that there would have to be cutbacks in advertising. I would expect it to be a matter of last hired, first fired. A similar situation in the promotion department, I believe."

"Hippity hop out the door, little rabbit." I laughed at the lift of her brows. "Never mind. Private joke. Ah...I was looking for you. I have a request that isn't, talking about things Jewish, truly kosher."

"Does that mean it is unrelated to your position as reporter?"

"Yes and no." I folded my arms on the table and leaned forward. "For a story I'm working on, I would like to know if and how Legislator Yount is connected to LCC. I'm persona non grata around his headquarters. For personal reasons—but also possible connections to recent happenings here—I'd like reliable information on LCC acquired from the inside, if possible..." I let my voice trail into silence.

Insightful Barbara MacFadden knew what I wanted without further explanation. After only a few seconds of thought she said, "Some of my cohorts at the Billet would delight in such an assignment. Mr. Yount I will see to. Something else?"

"You were in charge of the maps for the orienteering run. Did you give one to Peggy Thomas?"

"No. But once I deposited them at the registration booth and they were dispersed to participants, there was no longer a need for security. Before that I refused several requests for copies."

"From whom?"

"Ms. Standish." Then with a degree more emphasis, "Mr. Standish. And Mr. Worthington when he and I walked in from the parking lot together."

"Joe Worthington was there! I never saw him."

"He was there quite early dropping off his wife Carolyn and a box of *Ledger* caps. He voiced an interest in the layout of the course. Said he would have liked to participate had he been younger and more fit."

"Do you know if he stayed around?"

"No. However, his wife said in parting that since he had an appointment with Mr. Cross, she would get a ride home with one of her friends."

I digested that with the last of my coffee. Had that meeting been on or off the park grounds? Before or after Nelda Cross told her husband what had happened out on the course? Had it even taken place?

Several others entered the lounge and the Iron Maiden took her leave, but not before washing her cup thoroughly. I noticed that she took it with her rather than leave it with the communal clutter of cups and mugs brightening several shelves. I rinsed out my own and set it deep in the highest shelf, trusting that made it safe from other hands and lips.

I pulled open the door to leave and inadvertently yanked the knob from Fonda Allison's clutch. I put out a hand to brace her as she teetered forward. I was aware of all the chatter behind me stopping abruptly and, by Fonda's glance past me, judged that they were staring as well. I stepped out into the hall and let the door close.

She said meekly, "Guess I don't want any coffee after all. Been stopping conversations wherever I go." She shrugged wistfully, looking much younger than I had originally assumed her to be. "Almost wife and all that ..."

Impulsively I suggested, "If you don't mind a stop or two first, I can offer lunch in pleasant surroundings." I was pleased when she quickly accepted.

Moments later we were in my car. I took care not to ask any probing questions right away, but she talked freely by her own choice.

She praised Andrea for her support. "But her place didn't provide refuge this morning. The phone rang constantly and I could hear the messages. Several were reporters wanting information about me. One was for me, a woman detective wanting a call back. I know I should have, but I ran down here instead. I don't really know where else to go!" Her smile was winsome.

"And you'll be returning to Alaska as soon as possible." I made it more a statement than a question.

"Yes. It's home in spite...in spite of some inadequacies. Here everything is large and bright and antiseptic—can't even smell the ink—compared to our dinky old news office at home."

Had those inadequacies thrust her precipitously into Andrew Standish's arms? Her next comment justified the thought.

She said, "I've been facing the hard truth that I succumbed too quickly to Andrew's charm and promises of a whole world to cover. But we came here first and he revealed a side I didn't find particularly attractive." She shifted awkwardly under the constraint of the seat belt. "Sorry, Lexy, I didn't intend to get so personal."

We were stopped at a light. I reached over and loosened her seatbelt. "It's all right. I'm a good listener."

She gave me a long look, her eyes the soft champagne of a Burmese cat. I looked away in time to see the light change.

"Actually," she said slowly, "I wouldn't mind practicing on you. I know that detective will have to ask very specific questions. I want to tell her the truth but I don't want it sounding wrong or being taken the wrong way. Especially where Andrea is concerned."

I stayed quiet and let her set her own pace.

She continued. "About ten days ago Andrew had more than his usual amount to drink. He made a toast, saying, 'Here's to our marriage and to my evil twin's divorce from the paper.' That last part made no sense until he explained that his father's will contained a clause exempting him from offering his part of the *Ledger* to Andrea once he married. I realized immediately that left him free to sell it somewhere else—to offer it to the highest bidder. He tried to smooth things over by telling me that he'd be selling out to give me the world." She huffed an angry sound. "I don't know which makes me madder—his thinking I would believe that or that I'd be pleased by it." Almost tonelessly she added, "I told Andrea."

I thought back to my early morning conversation with Andrea. I was sure she had implied the marriage clause was part of both Standish wills. Fonda appeared to think it had only been part of Lyndall's. Did it matter? I tried to imagine how I would feel. Betrayed, I thought. Betrayed by my father and horrifically angry with my brother.

I pulled up in front of Bound to be Read. A car passing behind me honked and a black arm waved. Thea? I wasn't sure. I told Fonda I wouldn't be long but she expressed an interest in browsing while I attended to business. The manager was at one of the computer terminals in the long front counter. I took notes as he told me the latest.

"You should have been here Thursday night, Lexy. That was the last discussion concentrating on homosexual literature. It was lesbian mystery night. Right up your alley. They got to discussing how so many of the popular straight female detectives are poured out of a dyke mold. Even though the authors give them boyfriends."

"Which they've been killing off lately."

"That got talked about, too. But there wasn't any picketing that night. Instead they've been showing up inside since Friday."

"Harassing customers?"

He frowned. "Not so you could put them out. Two or three patrol the aisle featuring Women's Studies, that catch-all section on spirituality, goddesses, and healing, and lesbian books by and about. They

101

don't say anything. Just get close enough to see what books are getting from the shelves and look disapproving. Sometimes they follow the customer up here to the front. A couple of others planted themselves in the back corner."

I knew what that meant. That was where the gay and lesbian magazines were displayed almost out of reach. Really short people had to request assistance from someone taller or find a stepladder. That intimidated some not to purchase the magazines. I'd bet the 'observers' in the women's aisle had the same effect. Something else to be angry about.

I shifted my stance and realized that Fonda was only a few feet away, perusing the colorful display of calendars now on sale. I didn't know how long she had been there or how much of our conversation she might have heard. I wasn't concerned about whether or not she drew conclusions from my conversation with the manager that I was a lesbian. I didn't want her to be reserved or uncomfortable with me. I didn't want anything interfering with this opportunity to draw information from her.

I took Fonda to one of my favorite places for lunch—Feathers. I loved the clean, bright freshness of delicate feathers floating in the thick glass framing the entrance and the light golds and greens of the decor. Though we kept our conversation light and impersonal during the meal of fruit, nuts, and slivers of grilled chicken cupped in a bed of romaine lettuce, I sensed a strain. Her worry about being questioned? Discovery that I was gay? Concern for Andrea? Guilty feelings at standing on the brink of withdrawing from the marriage at the moment Andrew was being killed?

More than once I thought of Wren's sketch of Fonda—the painful reality of it. More real, I thought, than the many faces she presented to me.

Back at the *Ledger* she directed me to where her car was parked, saying, "I've decided to go back to Andrea's and call that detective. The lunch," she smiled warmly, "and the company have made me feel very much my true self—a person who steps forward to meet things. I'm not normally a person who skirts issues." Her smile faded below a very direct gaze. I felt as though something more was being said.

"It's probably Detective Exline you'll be meeting. Be open with her, Fonda. She's professional and fair. And I can warn you from personal experience that she will know if you're leaving something out."

"I'll heed that warning. Thank you." She hesitated over leaving the car. "I'm mostly worried about how it'll look—my not grieving hysterically."

"You don't seem any more the hysterical type than Andrea. I..."

She interrupted, "Who's probably catching flack for it." I couldn't really dispute that so I didn't respond. Fonda continued, almost as though talking to herself, "When I was walking along the track Sunday morning wrapped in the fog, it was almost like being back in Alaska. Right then I knew I couldn't turn another page with Andrew. He was a book I was going to close and then go home. I planned to tell Andrea first. Get her advice." She sighed and smiled sardonically. "Best laid plans and all that..." She left my car resolutely.

I continued to sit in the car. Questions skittered through my mind. How to write about the repressive tactics in the bookstore and stay objective? Was fear of witchcraft really a factor in the young doctoral student's death? Were the police concentrating on Andrea? Why did Fonda seem to present contrasting versions of herself? Why had Worthington been interested in the layout of the orienteering course, and why hadn't he mentioned being on the park grounds Sunday? Had the black arm waving been Thea, who was suddenly a recurring irritation in my life?

THIRTEEN

I decided on a brisk walk before parking my body at my desk for the rest of the afternoon. I circled the large newspaper building once and then halfway again. I stopped where the wide incline dropped downward to the basement entrance. Descending, I had to lean backwards to keep my balance.

An officious young man demanded identification before granting me entrance to the floor. The lighting was different down here—more concentrated in various areas, shadows in-between. The surging barrage of sound echoed off many hard surfaces. I climbed a short rise of metal steps and tried to spot Paul Jared—which proved difficult because most employees were wearing caps and tan coveralls.

Paul spotted me and called down from a higher level, "Lexy."

Quickly I made my way up to him. "Do you have a few minutes, Paul?"

He nodded and we backed up to a bench along the wall. He scrutinized me from top to toe. "You sure did clean up good."

"I was a mess, wasn't I? If you don't mind, I wanted to know if you heard anything of value when you all were being interviewed by the police Sunday. I suppose I sound like I'm being nosy—but I feel involved still."

"So do I, since we were out there because of Standish. Before the police separated us, I got a little from the referee who found him. I think she talked kind of openly to me because I had gotten her the chair. She said it looked like he had been hit on the side of the head near the ear. And after she checked him and saw he was dead, she stumbled over a gun. There was bright red blood on it."

"The paint gun!"

"That's what I thought, too."

"Anything else?"

Paul was obviously hesitating. "I don't like saying anything because

104

I liked the guy. But the paint on you doesn't make you guilty. Could be the same for him."

"What guy?"

"Kessler. The guy with the bum leg. He and I got to talking after the police finished with both of us. Just flapping our jaws, getting back to normal." Paul removed his cap and wiped his brow. "All the murders on television and in the pages of our own paper here don't prepare you for it happening to someone you know.."

"I know that too well. Kessler had paint on him?"

"Either blood or paint. While we were talking, he stripped off his gloves. They looked wet. They were the short, tight kind—open on the backs of the hands. I saw a couple of spots of paint, I'm pretty sure, in the hairs on the back of one of his hands." He toyed with his cap. "There's no need to tell anyone is there, Lexy?"

At my questioning look he hurried to explain, "I got to talking about my boy going out for the freshman track team and how I wished I could be more help to him in his training—especially with the hurdles. But I was a basketball player. Turns out Kessler was a big track man in high school. He's going to meet us Saturday morning and watch my boy. See if he can give him some pointers."

I recognized his expression. I had experienced the feelings that prompted it myself—not wanting someone I had come to like to be guilty of murder. But my instincts were jabbing hard fingers into my gut. "There's something more, isn't there, Paul?"

He ground his teeth. "Yes. But the fact that he told me—he brought it up—that should clear him. He told me he was all set up for a college scholarship. Said he messed it up himself being a dumb adolescent shithead and taking Andrew Standish's dare to climb a radio tower. Well, Standish grabbed Kessler's ankle to stop his climb so he could scramble around him and get to the top first. Kessler was just reaching for a new grip and it cost him his balance."

"Did he tell anyone?" I was sure I already knew the answer.

Paul shook his head. "When Kessler came to in the hospital, he heard right away what Standish was saying. That he had tried to grab and hold him but lost his grip when Kessler's shoe came off." At my grimace he said, "I know. Kessler said that it took so much just to learn to walk again he didn't have any energy left over for holding a grudge."

I had liked Warren Kessler, too. But I had seen his stiff bearing with Andrew Sunday morning at the entrance to the orienteering course. And I had heard the anger and contempt in his voice when he speculated that Standish had shot me with a paint gun.

I returned to my desk by wending my way upwards and through the building. I read and responded to messages, then called all the bookstores who had gay and lesbian sections to see if they were also experiencing "patrols" in those areas. I finally got hold of the Assistant D.A. who was assigned to prosecute the girl who had been in the car along with the two would-be teenage bank robbers. I got some wishy-washy quotes about why the girl had been included. I wondered if I would get any flack from Worthington on continuing to cover that situation now that he was out of LCC and Cross didn't have the backing of Andrew Standish. I began looking over some confusing information supposedly explaining on-line banking. More and more I was discovering that the highly touted information highway was full of potholes for the uninitiated.

Late in the afternoon Robbie called. "No prints on the tire iron, Lexy. And nothing to identify it according to the car it might have been in. It was one of the old kind that went with big cars that carried real spares."

"What about the vest?"

"No prints there, either. No surfaces to retain them. And, like you said, it had been hanging out all night, and handled by a bunch of kids. Including the big one I'm talking to right now."

"Easy there, detective. Let's not get personal."

She came back at me seriously. "Exactly what I've been trying to break you of."

"Come on, Robbie. I brought the vest in to you. You can at least let me know if it means a referee is in the pool of suspects."

There was silence, then she said, "Doesn't look like it. Everyone who showed up picked up and returned a vest. The organizer, Stuart Merrill, distributed them himself. The referees gathered at the exit point of the run and were driven out to their assigned areas in golf carts. The unclaimed vest was left in a cart in case someone was found to cover for the ref staying home with the sick child." Before I could ask, she said, "No one was."

I thought for a second. "What about maps? Were the referees given any? Might not have needed them if they were assigned specific areas. But if any were left in the cart with the vest…"

Robbie interrupted, "And if someone took the vest as camou-

106

flage—people see the vest but not the person—he or she might have needed a map. Good idea, Lexy. I'll check it out."

"Now that I'm in your good graces again, I don't suppose you'd tell me about any interesting interviews you might have had this afternoon?"

There was good-natured resignation in Robbie's groan. "Okay. She did call. She did come in. She cooperated in a thorough interview. She even passed on your remark that I would be professional and fair."

That confirmed that we were talking about Fonda Allison. Robbie said, "Ziegler has a contact in law enforcement in the Fairbanks area. Got a report from him this morning. He put her high on everybody's list to like and admire. But it seems she was having either generational or gender-bias problems with her father. He's general manager of a newspaper concentrating on the financial world. He was trying to block his daughter from a editorial position."

The 'inadequacies' Fonda had spoken of, no doubt. "Did the contact have anything on Standish? I'm assuming you know he met Fonda in Alaska."

"Nothing of any particular value. Standish either was or made a big show of being sorry and contrite about a snowmobiling tragedy a few months back. He even attended the funerals of the two locals who died on the slopes, and made donations in their names to conservation groups."

The cynic in me believed Andrew enjoyed the limelight. But that and his apparent newspaper background coupled with Fonda's problems with her father could account for the marriage decision she had soon come to regret. When I had decided to switch from teaching to journalism, I tossed and turned night after night for fear I had chosen wrongly. Fortunately I had slowly come to trust my decision. If I hadn't, like Fonda I would have gone back to that crossroads and chosen differently.

Lost in my own thoughts, I had missed some of what Robbie was saying. I caught a reference to LCC. "Whoa, Robbie. Back up. I missed that last part."

"I was telling you about the little the department has on LCC. What it boils down to is a handful of complaints from spouses or parents over what they see as brainwashing and hate indoctrination. And some businesses have objected to literature being handed out to their customers. Not something you can move against. First Amendment rights and all that. Also a couple of complaints by middle-aged children that their parents are leaving large sums of money to the Light of Christ Church in their wills."

"Have they been around here long?"

"No. Less than two years. But there are much longer established groups in St. Petersburg and Jacksonville. If anything comes your way, I want to hear it."

"Right, chief."

"Don't I wish." With that Robbie broke the connection.

As I hung up the phone, Worthington's voice boomed over my intercom. "Lexy! Apartments on fire. Now!"

I scooped papers into a drawer, stood up, and waved acknowledgement to the news editor watching from his office.

I arrived home about five-thirty, slammed the car door, and rushed into the kitchen. Wren, rinsing out a cup, said, "I'm glad you're home. I want—"

"I have to shower."

I tossed my clothes on the bedroom floor. As soon as the water was lukewarm, I stepped into the shower and turned slowly until it was as hot as I could stand. I lathered my hair, then soaped myself thoroughly, even between my toes. I stood for a long time letting the hot water cascade over me before drying off in a fog of steam.

In the bedroom my clothes no longer littered the floor and Wren sat waiting for me. I dropped down beside her. She took the towel and began rubbing my head vigorously. Then she looked into my eyes searchingly. "Want to tell me about it?"

"No, not in any detail. An apartment building was on fire, but they got everyone out except for the guy on first floor where the fire started. A fire trap if I ever saw one. People were screaming and jumping from windows onto those big mattresses. I got covered with dust and ash even though I was at a good distance. It was the smell…"

"I was going to ask you to play chauffeur and drive me down to the Women's Forum building so I can deliver my cover design for the *Bulletin* to Mary Catherine. But you stay here while—"

"No. I want to play chauffeur. I need to do something."

Wren stroked my cheek with the back of her fingers. "Get dressed. I'll be in the car."

We headed west where the low sun, behind non-threatening clouds, beamed through scattered openings. Wren asked about the meeting with Robbie and I filled her in. I told her about Worthington's revelations concerning his involvement with LCC and his decision to break it off. I included a little of Fonda Allison's situation and Robbie's information about her.

Wren commented, "No wonder I saw pain in her face. She was probably berating herself for making wrong choices at every turn. I'm glad your boss is being helpful."

"I think Andrea has experienced her own share of pain over her twin." Silently I added, Along with Warren Kessler, Peggy Thomas, Worthington...and who else? I switched topics to my banking research, agreeing that we needed to review our own options in light of what I was learning.

I was able to park close to the entrance of the Forum building. I admired the designs in the brick and the scrollwork along the top. I hoped this building, too, would continue to be safe from the threat of the wrecking ball and bulldozers.

Wren held her magazine cover toward me. Ten faces demanded my attention. There were interesting variations in age and facial structure, but I recognized two—Thea and Kelleen. My nostrils flared at the sketch of Thea, but I smiled over the one of Kelleen.

I was sure Wren caught both reactions, but she said only, "I'll be sending two copies to Brie O'Mara."

I responded, "And maybe include a membership application if that's how the Forum does things. She's the Events Coordinator at Sun Star Convention Center."

"Good idea!"

I tagged along with Wren into the building. She waved me to a chair outside Mary Catherine's office and pointed commandingly to a stack of *Bulletins*. Obediently, I started looking through them. I heard the editor's murmurs of pleasure and then they began discussing color and placement of printed information. Their voices faded away as I concentrated on an article that advocated saving the few brick city streets still in existence.

Minutes later something made me look up—and into the glaring eyes of Nelda Cross. Deliberately, I returned my attention to the magazine in my hands. She snorted her displeasure and entered the office. I listened purposefully this time.

She overrode Mary Catherine's polite introduction, saying in a strident voice, "There are too many faces there. And those two need to go." I had no doubt that she was pointing to the sketches of Thea and Kelleen. "They don't represent the Forum."

Mary Catherine said, more forcefully than I expected, "They're faces of women participating in Sunday's events for Women's Health Week. But since the *Bulletin* is none of your concern, what can I do for you?"

The momentary silence told me Nelda Cross had been put back a step—and no doubt didn't like it.

She said, "I have an announcement I want placed in the members' newsletter. My husband is granting us a block of time on WCOL-TV next week after the evening news for a presentation of the Forum's goals, values and contributions. I'll be running it, since I have experience in front of the camera."

Mary Catherine replied, "Since I'm on the board, I know this hasn't been presented for approval."

Nelda Cross was flippant. "Oh, of course they'll approve. What better publicity could we receive? I'm surprised you don't understand that." Her voice coarsened. "I want to know what that...that woman is doing out there. She attacked me on the orienteering course and cost me the race. I had planned to lodge a complaint with the sponsor, but when I found that she worked for the *Ledger,* I realized it would do no good."

I touched my bruised thigh and walked to the open doorway. Wren's icy tone cut through the tense atmosphere. "You're talking about my partner, Ms. Cross, in a way I don't appreciate. I know she didn't attack you." Wren's face was still and coldly austere. Mary Catherine's eyes were wide above flushed cheeks.

Nelda Cross whirled to run full force into me.

I stepped aside, managing what I hoped was a disdainful smile. "Forgive me for being in your way—again. No contamination, I hope."

Now Wren's eyes were wide and Mary Catherine swallowed back a laugh. Nelda Cross stormed down the hallway.

I stepped into the small room. "I didn't mean to cause a ruckus."

Mary Catherine stood. "You didn't. I suppose she's run off to tattle to the president. I don't think she'll get very far this time. Linda and a couple of others met with the officers yesterday evening to complain about her attitude and behavior. Yesterday morning she was offensively rude to Maydenne Ramos."

Wren exclaimed enthusiastically, "She's the artist who does murals. Incredible colors!"

Mary Catherine glowed. "Yes. You'll have to come peek at what she is doing on one of the walls in our large meeting lounge. She doesn't mind people watching. It's neat seeing the forms and design emerging a little at a time."

"What's Cross's problem with her?" I asked.

Mary Catherine frowned. "The fact that Maydenne's Hispanic, I think. Nelda acted like Maydenne was a cleaning lady making a mess—at least that's the way Linda described it. Linda said she wanted to grab a brush and paint a white streak through that black hair to show what a skunk Nelda was."

We all laughed.

Then Mary Catherine said, "I was sorry to hear about the attack on you, Lexy. I hope you weren't hurt."

I stared at Wren, who shook her head and looked as puzzled as I felt. I asked Mary Catherine, "Where did you hear that?" I tried not to sound as unsettled as I felt.

"On the radio, coming to work this morning. There's a station that plays religious music early every morning. I tune out the man and woman who talk. They sound so sanctimonious—but I like the music to start the day. I heard your name so I listened. It was short. Just something about your being attacked in a parking lot in what might have been a robbery attempt ..." She looked uneasy. "...or connected with your being a gay employee of the *Ledger*."

Wren made an angry explosive sound. I tried to react in a manner light enough to put Mary Catherine at ease. I said, "They could have at least said lesbian."

In the car I fumed silently. Finally Wren said, "What's your take on that?"

"I'll bet Cross Communications owns the radio station. The sanctimonious pair are probably LCC people. And if I'm allowed to be paranoid, the whole thing may have been set up by Cross. He could be continuing plans to compromise people like me at the paper even though the deal with Standish has fallen through. But if so he's made a mistake."

"How's that?"

"They most likely assumed I reported the attack and it would be on the morning police log for anyone to see. It's probably there now thanks to Robbie, but it wouldn't have been there this morning in time for that broadcast. That gives me an edge."

Wren frowned. "To do what?"

I reached over and turned the collar of her windbreaker rakishly up into her hair. "Nothing. In fact, what I want right now is a drink to get the nasty taste out of my mouth."

"With food," Wren said. "I had very little lunch with only myself as company."

I let her take my mild grunt as compliance. This didn't seem the time to mention my satisfying lunch with Fonda Allison.

Wren said coaxingly, "Let's do something different to really change the tenor of your day. Take me to Leather Fever."

FOURTEEN

We arrived at Leather Fever in the gray between sunset and the dark of night. Four motorcycles nudged the front of the squat building and a few trucks were scattered in the gravel of the parking lot. They were the only indication the bar was open since the floodlights hadn't been triggered yet and no neon signs pulsed their flashy identification.

I watched Wren's admiration of the large wooden door, its rich brown, umber and copper colors. As I held the door for her, I inhaled the smells of wood, wood oil, leather, and beer. We drank in the sights—the long polished bar, the traffic lights flanking the jukebox, the railroad lanterns on the tables as we went to the bar.

"Interesting colors," Wren said. She was looking at two young women in fringed jackets and leggings. Each sported a brilliant coxcomb above nearly shaved sides—one in blues and greens, the other reds and yellows.

"I've never figured out which one bottoms and which one tops," C.K. Chen, manager of the Leather Fever, said from behind the bar.

"Have you been demoted to bartender, C.K.?" I asked.

She answered me, but her almond eyes were measuring Wren boldly. "Only for special customers. Sheila's in the back stirring the pot. Bourbon?"

"Not tonight. This is a beer and barbecue night." I turned to Wren. "Barbecue and hotdogs are the only offerings. The barbecue is the chunky, pot-stewed kind. And just one serving won't do."

"Then I'll have two. And beer. Something dark." She gave C.K. a small smile. "I'm Wren."

"Pleased to meet you, Wren. I had been worried that we had a celibate here." She tilted her head back and colored lights bounced off the planes of buff-brown skin. "I won't be worrying about that any more."

I stared, Wren chuckled, and C.K., swishing her short, narrow mane of glossy black hair, turned to get our beers. She placed two cold longnecks in front of us saying, "Sheila will bring your sandwiches in a few minutes."

I picked up both bottles and led the way to a side table.

"Celibate, huh," Wren said lightly. "That's nice to know."

I took a long sip of beer, savoring the sharp bite of it. "I told you this was a place I liked to escape to now and then. I never said I was celibate—that's her assumption."

Immediately Wren became serious. "I don't mean to interfere...."

I seized her wrist. "No. It was never an escape from you. It was before you. It was escape from...from...."

Wren understood better than I did. "Other people's expectations again, isn't it? Or perhaps more a matter of disputing their expectations."

I smoothed moisture from the side of the bottle before answering. "Perhaps." I changed the subject. "What do you think of C.K.?"

We both looked to where the manager stood, leaning over a table of older women. Dusky gold leggings sculpted her thighs and disappeared into dark brown riding boots. She wore a shirt of antique white brocade beneath a leather vest, the long sleeves tied with dark leather thongs just above the elbows.

Wren answered, "I always thought that Jodi was pure feline. But this woman is all night animal. I'll bet she snarls when she takes her prey to bed and plays with her claws extended."

"You're not expressing interest, I trust. Oh...." One of the older women had scooted her chair back and a little sideways. Soft white hair floated above a face of sharp lines, the wrinkles lessened in the dim light. "That's Possum Perkins!"

"Who is?"

"She used to coach part-time for a semi-pro women's fast-pitch team here in Orlando. She'd hold clinics every summer for us high school players. And she saw to it we got tickets to the Women's College World Series when it was here. I went to every game I could." I grinned. "Experienced some of my first strong crushes, too. Looking back, I realize Possum kept a close eye on things. We got to meet with the players and ask questions and all that—but there wasn't any real fraternizing."

"Where did she get that nickname?"

"Possum? She told us she had a coach once who told her to point her long possum snout at the pitcher and dare her to throw strikes. Got called Possum after that. Look at her, Wren. She has to be every

114

bit of eighty, but I bet she can still throw a ball that would sting you through your mitt."

"Was she a baseball player, too?"

"Oh, yes. They did an article on her when that movie *A League of Their Own* came out. She had played for the Atlanta Blue Sox and the Lorelei Ladies when she was just out of high school. Then made one of the first pro teams in the 1940s, but played only about half a season. She was quoted saying something like 'I was just a Georgia farm girl. Didn't take to the travel or the close living. And there were too many rules taking the fun out of things. They even made us wear skirts!' So she returned her pay and got her amateur status back—even made All-American in her thirties."

I paused to drink before continuing, "I think that's why I admired her so much. She kept the fun in it during those clinics. Never let us get cocky about our skills. I heard somewhere that she could have been a pro golfer, too. Right up there with Babe Didrikson and the original LPGA Hall of Famers. But she preferred team sports. Do you mind if I go say hello to her?"

"Of course not." Wren surveyed the room. "There's plenty to keep my eyes and mind occupied. I think I saw Xena a minute ago."

It was obvious that Possum was in the middle of a story, so I pulled out a chair from a nearby table and sat down to listen unobtrusively. Possum was saying, "They called their pitcher Scorch. And for damn good reason. Never been singed so much in my life! Don't know how her catchers stood up to those pitches. None of us could lay a bat on a ball. When I went up to the plate for the third time, someone in the crowd yelled, 'Get a board!' Well, I went back to the dugout and got an old piece of planking from the dugout bench I had seen propped in the corner."

"You didn't!" exclaimed a rosy-cheeked woman.

"Sure did. The umpire was having a conniption fit, the crowd was applauding, Scorch was winding up. When I saw her arm start forward, I stuck that board right out over the plate. The ball hit it so hard it numbed my hands—and dropped down dead in front of the plate. I ran to first base and stood there laughing while the catcher and the umpire yelled at each other and the crowd went wild. The ump called me out and thumbed me back to the bench. When I crossed in front of Scorch, she said, 'You got a hit. Drinks are on me tonight.'"

While the other women laughed, Possum turned her head and looked over at me. "One of my high school kiddies, right? First base."

I leaned across the space, offering her my hand. "Yes, ma'am. Lexy Hyatt. I miss those days."

"So do I."

She introduced me around and we talked for a few minutes about past and present. When I excused myself to return to Wren, I nearly stumbled over my chair. I had eyes only for the hands turning down Wren's collar and patting it into place—hands that belonged to Thea Gantt. Sheila was placing our sandwiches and two more beers on the table. Thea whispered something in Wren's ear, then moved to the bar with a cocksure strut.

Wren smiled warmly. "You're just in time. These smell delicious." I glanced at the food as I sat down, but couldn't stop my eyes from straying toward the bar. Thea, in pearl gray denim, a silver choke collar, and brushes of glitter over her eyelids, returned my stare arrogantly.

Without looking up from cutting her sandwich in two, Wren said firmly, "Lexy...I'll have none of that tonight." Then she lifted her copper lashes and the lantern light caused her solemn eyes to glow.

I was jolted again by how she could invade my senses, strip me of all control. I touched my knee to hers, taking comfort from the answering pressure.

Being a Tuesday night, Leather Fever was relatively quiet, though many came and went. C.K. had to settle a dispute at the pool table and oust a diesel dyke who kept lifting a delicately boned gymnast in a faux leopard-skin bodysuit over her head and twirling her. Wren enjoyed it all—the variety of leather and hardware, the imaginative designs on clothing and skin, the racy language, the general atmosphere of rebellion.

Now and then a regular I knew slightly would pause at our table. I appreciated their reactions to Wren, and I marveled at her ease and versatility in responding. I became so relaxed and content that when Thea turned a chair around and straddled it, I actually smiled at her.

She said, "Saw you talking to Possum. Something isn't she? That old woman ain't never going to be an old woman."

"I can agree with you on that."

Thea glanced at Wren, who was concentrating on some close-quarters dancing going on nearby. She said, her voice slow and thick as dark molasses, "There's more we agree on."

I wasn't going to let her spoil my good mood. I asked, "Did you ever work with Possum?"

116

"'Bout twenty years ago, when I was a gap-toothed, kinky-haired, sassy little kid. She came into the Trees and organized a bunch of different age groups for Youth League Softball. I didn't know then what a big deal that was. Didn't know how she had to fight City Parks and Recreation to get us included. Didn't know yet what my color meant." The velvet of her eyes had become onyx.

I responded, "When I began to know, it was with very incomplete understanding—until I read a poem by Langston Hughes. It was about how puzzled a little girl was when seeing her first merry-go-round." I recited, "But there ain't no back/ To a merry-go-round!/Where's the horse/For a kid that's black?"

Surprisingly the hard onyx became velvet again. "You're all right, Lexy Hyatt."

Wren twined her fingers in mine. "Of course she is. But I didn't hear what you were talking about to lead to that conclusion. I was listening to the music."

Thea leaned forward over the back of the chair. "Girl! You weren't listening to anything. You were taking in all those butches who are packing."

I had never seen Wren blush before. The comradely laughter I shared with Thea didn't help.

Still laughing, Thea high-fived the air and went toward the exit. As soon as someone punched in choices for less frenetic music, I led Wren to the dance area. After two numbers we made our own way out.

Outside Wren shivered. "Feels like it's decided to be winter."

Briskly we walked to the car. Once seated, I stopped her from reaching for the seat belt, pulling her roughly to me. I whispered huskily into her hair, "Let me raise your temperature."

Our kiss was long and searching. We explored each other's mouth.

Between gasps Wren said, "It's been a long time since we necked in a car."

"There's more we could do," I teased.

"Oh, no. I can't believe we're making out in public."

I said reprovingly, "In our own car behind thoroughly steamed windows does not qualify as in public." I added playfully, "Does come close though. Would you believe it? My Wren a wanton woman!"

She smacked my shoulder. "Wash your mouth out with soap!" She rubbed her forehead against my shoulder. "It was a good evening, Lexy."

We rode home in a comfortable silence, but the ringing of the phone filled the house when we got there. I remembered that I had deactivated my pager and pushed it under the car seat when we arrived at Leather Fever. I grabbed the wall phone in the kitchen.

Tamara, her voice a thin monotone of strain…or anger, asked if I could come down to the side parking lot at the paper. "There's something I want you to see, Lexy."

"Be right there."

"A story? This late?" Wren was apprehensive.

I nodded. "But I don't think it will take long. I'll probably be warming my cold feet on you before you get soundly asleep."

"You'll be careful?" Her words floated somewhere between a request and demand.

"Most definitely." I brushed her cheek with my lips but I knew I hadn't stilled her fears. The attack on me last night was on her mind. I was grateful she wasn't trying to shackle me with it. I felt a little guilty at my impatience to get on my way and find out what was going on with Tamara.

I saw the blue and red flashes before I reached the parking lot. I pulled up next to a large sedan. Leaning against it was a broad-shouldered Black man who turned his head toward me. I was sure the glare was already set on his face rather than triggered by me.

As I approached where Tamara stood speaking with a patrolman, I caught a foul odor emanating from her car. I didn't need the message scrawled on the door below the broken-out window to identify the smell as cow manure. The message proclaimed "Nigger Shithouse" and the back seat had been shoveled full.

The officer was saying, "I'm sorry for this trouble, Miss Gantt. We'll be doing what we can."

I knew from my days covering the police blotter just how many vandalism reports were filed and how few were solved. But I believed there was more going on here than a vandalism.

Tamara explained immediately. "Davonne picked me up for a night on the town, since I'm going to be busy the rest of the week with the Hurston Festival. This is what we came back to. He's pretty angry—and a little angry at me for making him stay out of it. What do you think, Lexy? Dumping on me simply because I'm African-American or because I'm an uppity nigger daring to work for the *Ledger*?"

"Tomorrow morning might tell you."

"How so?"

Before I could answer, her date called, "Wouldn't you ladies like to move upwind from that car?"

Tamara said under her breath, "What he really wants is to hear what we're saying."

I initiated a move to join him. Tamara made introductions. I said, "Tamara mentioned once that you worked for a station bought out by Christopher Cross."

"Did. Left before I got shoveled out." The phrase made him glare again at Tamara's car. "Why?"

I went on, "Do you know if it's the one that now plays religious music every morning?"

"I've heard that it does. It's WCXC now." More strongly, "Why?"

I turned to Tamara. "Listen to them in the morning. See if there's a reference to this—and what kind of slant." I told them about my attack the previous night and that someone had heard about it on the radio this morning. I ignored Davonne's uncomfortable shift when I spoke of being a lesbian. I finished with, "Anything I can do here to help?"

"No," Davonne said curtly. At Tamara's frown he added belatedly, "Thank you. I've called a place to come tow in her car and do what they can. We have to deal with this kind of thing all the time."

"Davonne," Tamara said sharply, "put a sock in it. Lexy's a friend. She has to put up with her own brand of..." she glanced at her car, "...shit. Thank you for coming out, Lexy. I wasn't buying this as a random act of violence. Wanted your take on it."

"I plan to tell the boss lady tomorrow about the attack on me. Okay if I include yours?"

She agreed, and shook her head in resigned amusement as Davonne yanked open his car door for her.

I didn't think that dating relationship was in for the long haul. Without acknowledging my purpose, I took a shortcut through GAG, the Gay Asian Ghetto, on my way home. Despite the first winter chill of the season, I drove with the window down, partially to clear my nostrils of the foul smell and partially to clear my mind of disgust. I remembered a teacher who once stressed the necessity for tolerance if humans were to survive and make progress. From that attitude, she claimed, we could then rise into respect and cooperation. Without it, we would decline into prejudice and discrimination. LCC, whom I believed was responsible for the condition of Tamara's car, seemed bent on that decline. I would never be able to fathom why.

119

I turned on the radio, barely listening to the ebb and flow of voices and music as I slowly scanned the dial. Then my hand froze as I caught the deep-throated, alluring voice of the Mike Dyke.

Thea intoned provocatively, "How did that grab all you lonesome gals out there? Nothing like Janice Ian's 'Ride Me Like a Wave' to heat the sweet juices...activate the hungers...release the needful cravings."

I drew cold breaths deeper and deeper as I heard her say, "Had a little taste of all that myself tonight. A bit of honey teasing my taste buds. A soft glow that drew this dark moth. I'll sleep tonight in golden dreams. I'll—"

Brutally I punched the radio to silence. I smacked the dash above it hard and stingingly, shattering the brief feeling of camaraderie that had existed earlier.

FIFTEEN

When I finally slipped into bed I was certain that Wren was feigning sleep so as not to seem too concerned. Still edgy from what I had heard Thea as the Mike Dyke say, I was happy to accept the ruse. Still, I snuggled against her back and thighs and whispered into her hair, "Goodnight, my wanton woman." I sensed that she smiled.

In the morning I got up without waking Wren. I sat at my desk, sipping strong instant coffee and tuned the radio to quiet music, keeping the volume low. I took out the folder on Andrew Standish from a bottom drawer and reread the contents. His death changed how I saw him; he was no longer the athletic thrill-seeker surviving while others were injured or killed.

I found the hang-gliding episode that Robbie had mentioned. Benny Moja had been killed, and two others were permanently disabled when they dropped into the ocean and were smashed against the rocks. The gusting, powerful winds had caused Standish to lose his grip with one hand, yet he managed to maneuver the fragile contraption out far enough to avoid waves slamming the rocks.

In another article he was praised for his clear thinking and effort in righting a large raft, thus saving several people. They had been rafting down a North Carolina river made wilder by the runoff from recent torrential rains. The group had put in below the designated starting point where rafts were being held up. At the instigation of Andrew Standish, most likely. Did he care that Keith Toliver drowned? Or that Tracey Wood, age twenty-three, was blinded when struck in the head by a loose paddle?

I read a second article on the snowmobiling deaths that I had passed over before. This one contained quotes and observations by the ranger who investigated. Though couched in very careful language, he recounted the impressions of two survivors about how Standish had cut off the snowmobile nearest him and caused it to skid and lose momentum. My thought was that even under the threat of death, Standish wasn't about to let anyone get above him in high-marking the slope.

The names of the dead daredevils were listed: Lawrence Akers, forty-five, Napoleon, Indiana; Brit Powell, thirty-two, Fairbanks, Alaska; Chad Newsome, thirty-three, Green Cove Springs, Florida; Martin Quenzler, twenty-five, Utica, New York; Henri LeBlanc, forty-one, Fairbanks, Alaska; Vernon Haralson, nineteen, Appleton, Wisconsin. Out of all those men, why was it Andrew who survived?

The coffee soured in my stomach. I'd had enough of death. I seized the papers and patted them evenly together to return them to the folder. A small clipping escaped and fluttered to the floor. I trapped it with a toe and drew it close enough to pick up. I had missed it the first time around. Before I could read it, one of the voices on the radio mentioned the *Ledger*. I bent forward to hear.

A male voice was saying, "Last night another employee of the *Ledger* invited criticism. Using the newspaper property as her private parking lot, Tamara Gantt, a African-American woman, danced and drank the night away at the Peacock Club. While she partied, her car was vandalized. Will she be expecting the *Ledger's* insurance to cover the damages?"

A female voice chimed in, "The club has been the scene of many arrests for public drunkenness, possession of narcotics, brawls, and several knifings. It would seem that the management of the *Ledger* has been negligent in its background checks of employees."

I felt like punching the radio. Those charges applied when the place was known simply as the Club. It had been taken over by a husband and wife team who had turned it into a safe, attractive lounge and renamed it the Peacock Club. I was most angry at the dextrous intimation that Tamara had featured in some of those arrests.

Wren's hands on my shoulders startled me. She placed her chin on the top of my head. "I go to bed alone and I wake up alone. Is the honeymoon over?"

I turned off the radio, reached back and gripped her thighs. "Let's see. Last week we had sex Sunday, Monday, and Thursday. This week it's been only Monday. Of course, today's only Wednesday."

She butted my head with her chin. "Do you keep a calendar?"

"I'm was a school teacher, remember? I know how to keep all sorts of calendars going in my head."

She reached around and picked up my cup. "Cold and bitter. I'm going to brew us something good. Although I ought to drink this to put myself in a tough mood."

I turned around. "Why?"

"I plan to contact Cross's radio station and withdraw my logo design."

"You don't have to do that, Wren." But I was pleased.

"Yes, I do. I value what I create. It's a reflection of me." More firmly. "I have principles and I don't sell out. Now, come shred the cheese while I brew coffee and beat eggs."

Fueled by good coffee and a cheese omelet and motivated by a forty degree morning, I took the broad steps of the Ledger two at a time. Just inside the entrance Peggy Thomas was sorting pictures across the top of her counter.

She pointed to a small stack. "Check those, Lexy. See what you think. So far they're what I've selected for our display board."

The first picture was of a group of women in *Ledger* caps doing stretching exercises in the fog. Next was a young couple scrutinizing their topographic map at the entrance to the orienteering run. The man was pointing out something on the map and the woman was holding a whistle to her mouth. Another photo was of three generations—grandmother, daughter, and granddaughter starting out on the track. Their shirts bore the same picture which looked like it came from a high school yearbook. I wondered who the young woman was to them? I smiled at a picture of a young father down on one knee putting a Women's Health Week headband around the tiny waist of a little girl. I hoped that the mother stood somewhere near and that they weren't walking in her memory.

As Peggy answered the phone and took notes, I shuffled through some of the other stacks. I stopped at a wide-angle shot of people getting off one the busses near some parked cars. Near one car, Sarah Vitak, who had recently harangued both the Iron Maiden and me in the lounge, appeared to be handing a sheet of paper to Joe Worthington.

I picked a different picture from the pile and held it toward Peggy as she returned to the counter. "You and Andrea look like you're having a tug-of-war over the clipboard."

She took the picture from my hands. "We were. She gave it to me when I arrived. It had lists of people and their responsibilities. I added other things I needed. Later she wanted it back."

"Who won?"

"I did. I'm the one who really needed it. Now and then that obsessive-compulsive control element of hers flares up. Not many people can squelch it. I can if it is truly necessary. Barbara MacFadden can. Heard her do it when Andrea was asking for some vital statistics on your...personal life."

She returned some greetings from arriving employees and drew the pictures toward her, effectively halting my rummaging through them.

Slowly I made my way to my cubicle, exchanging my own good-morning greetings, but my mind was elsewhere. What was Andrea's interest in my private life? Was the tug-of-war over the clipboard because of the map I was certain it had held? What was on the sheet of paper given to Joe? Why not just ask him? I sped up and passed my own office, heading for his.

His head tilted back, Worthington was reading the display on his computer screen. Then, massaging his neck, he said, "Don't ever get bifocals, Lexy. They'll drive you crazy a thousand ways." He lowered his voice. "Had an interesting call from the president of the Chamber of Commerce late evening yesterday."

"Oh?"

"Seems a couple of bank managers noted your recent interest. Brought it up at a Chamber luncheon to compare notes. The gist of the oh-so-polite call was to touch base with us on our—" He shifted into a pompous tone "—'shared interest in maintaining the public's faith in its institutions.'"

I stiffened in irritation but then saw the twinkle in his eyes. "And your reply was?"

"I told him that if your interest was as a private citizen, it was none of my business. If you were a reporter developing a story, I would be glad to hear his comments—after the story was published."

"It's good to have the real you back, Joe."

"Good to be back. There's one more thing, though. He mentioned Cross as though he expected that to carry some weight. Cross and Andrew must have believed they had the *Ledger* all sewn up, and spread the word around." He read something in my expression. "I know. They had me all sewn up. I guess I was counting on the boss lady standing up to them. She's her mother's daughter. She'd have found a way to beat them."

Not in a thicket on the orienteering course, I hoped. I took advantage of his bringing up Cross to move in the direction I wanted without being too blunt and obvious. I said, "Cross stuck his finger in the

Ledger pie on Sunday. He had the nerve to give a television interview with his wife. Did you run into him? Someone said they saw you there with Carolyn."

Worthington looked displeased, but answered, "No, I didn't. Not face to face, anyway. I got word from him about something he wanted me to do. He wanted me to download a bunch of stuff on personnel. He was savvy enough to know that Sunday would have been an easy day to do it without anyone noticing. I was told that he had authorization from Andrew Standish to receive the information. I looked around for Andrew but never saw him. I was a little hot under the collar—both at Andrew for thinking it was okay to give Cross info like that and at Cross for treating me like a flunky."

"Was I on the list?"

As an answer he unlocked a drawer, drew out a piece of paper and gave it to me. I recognized the names of three gay staff members and several others who were African-American. There were also some names listed that could've been Asian and some Jewish. My own name was third on the list. It was a hit list! Cross—LCC—they intended to assassinate our characters and render us impotent, if not drive us from the paper.

"May I keep this?" I asked.

Worthington nodded. "I wanted to cram it down Andrew Standish's throat! What I did do was come back here. I did a little work but mostly I got madder and madder."

"When did Cross expect the printouts?"

"Right away. Sunday afternoon." He pointed to the paper in my hand. "Note's on the back."

I turned it over. In small, straight-line writing it said, "Will be parked along Garden Street mid-afternoon."

Worthington said, "I drove along there, not knowing if I was looking for Cross or Sarah Vitak, who had given me the paper. I intended to tell whomever was there that I found a lock on the personnel files. Couldn't pull them up." Obviously unhappy with himself he added, "Mad as I was, I was still covering my ass with them."

"Who was there?"

"I saw Cross's fancy black Lincoln. Then I saw Cross himself—in a big, empty field across the street. Couldn't tell whether he was coming or going. He was just standing there. I realized that I had been counting on it being Sarah there—knew it would be easier to lie to her. I didn't think that Cross had seen me, so I sped up and got out of there. I was surprised when I never heard from him Sunday evening. Found out why Monday morning."

"You told the police, didn't you?" It bothered me that he kept revealing things in droplets—and only when confronted.

He shook his head. "No. Seeing Cross there also put me there. And I had said some damn strong things about Andrew in Sarah Vitak's hearing. It's all right to dump a little judgment on me, Lexy. More covering my ass."

"I'm not judging, Joe. I've been sitting on some stuff, too." Though I had what I wanted from him, I switched to discussing some specifics of my banking observations, questioned how deeply I should go into the witchcraft situation in India and let him know I was going to be hounding the D.A.'s office about prosecuting the teenage girl as a robbery accomplice. He made some valuable suggestions.

I spent time putting one of Worthington's suggestions to work. I called a variety of furniture and appliance stores, car dealerships, nurseries, construction companies and such. I would describe large purchases or undertakings that I was interested in and ask what banks they dealt with along with terms available. Some places told me simply that they had in-house financing, while others suggested that I come in and discuss details. But there were those that named banks and described terms far too good to be true—which I was sure they were not.

Then, switching gears, I convinced the teenage girl's recently acquired lawyer to grant me an interview. After that I put out feelers to some OTU instructors I knew, asking for names of foreign students and instructors I could talk with. I called Thelonia Greenburg and got some valuable advice about where to get information on modern witchcraft beliefs.

Following a lunch of snack-machine items and coffee, I reentered my cubicle to find an email form Andrea. My presence was requested upstairs anytime this afternoon. Part of me wanted to make her wait awhile, but another part was too curious to stall.

Her carefully modulated voice and mild blue eyes didn't fool me. The boss lady was angry. She got right to the point. "I am still quite pleased that you beat out Nelda Cross Sunday, but she is scurrying around like bed of fire ants trying to bring down anyone who has disturbed her. She's threatening to sue the *Ledger* for permitting employees to participate in the orienteering race."

"That's ridiculous! It was a charity event. No awards were given to participants."

"I'm sure she knows that. And knows that no judge would permit such a suit to go forward. She's just being disruptive." Andrea shrugged as though deciding to shelve the anger. "I wanted to inform you so that you wouldn't be blindsided."

My mouth slightly dry, I said, "I've already been blindsided." She didn't interrupt me as I told her about the attacks on me and on Tamara's car. I included the aspersions delivered against the background of religious music, and noted how carefully they were worded to avoid slander charges.

"Why didn't you call in the police, as Ms. Gantt did?" The flint was back in her voice.

"I wasn't hurt, and at that moment I didn't want to involve the young girl or her mother in a police report. It's on the books now. And they've left themselves vulnerable by reporting it on the radio too soon."

"They?"

"I know that conspiracy theories are quite in vogue at the moment, but I believe a real one is being directed against the *Ledger*."

Andrea agreed. "Designed by Cross and my brother. Not just to take the paper away from me but to destroy its very nature—then recast it…" She gazed at the family portrait on her desk. "I don't think Andrew would have been concerned about details. His interest was money—and the freedom to maintain his lifestyle. I suppose a man like Cross would be able to hire people to—"

I interrupted and told her about the Light of Christ Church, along with my suppositions. I concluded, "The police are looking into them—as are some others." I hoped the Iron Maiden's cohorts would have something soon.

"And now so is the *Ledger*—despite Cross's twenty percent. Something else I plan to defuse." She paused. "Tell me, Lexy. Was your decision not to report the attack also a matter of walking a thin line due to your sexual orientation?"

"Yes." I straightened as tall as I could in the soft chair. "You yourself were asking about it recently."

Her eyes reflected surprise—and perhaps respect for my boldness. "I didn't get any answers. But I don't apologize for asking. When I plan to entrust someone with an undertaking, I like to know all about them."

I decided to settle for a draw.

I spent the core of the afternoon dealing with boring necessities. I attended a meeting on factual errors and editorializing in news copy over the past two weeks and contributed to the discussion on how to avoid such problems. I had a meeting with a photographer on pictures I wanted for developing stories. I fought dozing off during a pedantic young man's presentation of the new medical plan coverage going into effect in March.

I interviewed the fire chief on the cause of the apartment blaze, which was started by a man falling asleep with a lighted cigarette on the first floor and which left five other tenants without homes. On the way home I thought about the fact that Andrea had asked no questions about my progress concerning her brother's murder. A matter of not trusting me? Or assuming I was off bird-dogging in the wrong areas—as she desired?

At a stoplight I noted that I was about to cross the street listed as the address for the Light of Christ Church. I turned and began watching for a sign, slowing when I spotted it. The building was square and unpretentious, not at all churchlike. About to speed up, I stopped instead. Joe Worthington was leaving by a side door.

A man in the doorway called to him. He appeared to answer without turning back. What was going on now? If Joe had withdrawn from LCC, why return to the church itself? I muddled over that the rest of the way home.

The house was empty when I arrived. Sometimes I enjoyed that. But not now that Thea, the dark moth, was flitting about. Was this what Wren felt when I was off on assignment or—what had she called it—side-stepping others' expectations?

"Well, I'm not a paragon," I muttered to the serene goddess gracing the January page of the kitchen calendar.

I went to my desk and switched on the lamp. Light spilled onto the folder on Andrew Standish. On top was the clipping I had not yet read. Briefly it recounted the death of a African-American boy, age eleven, who had fallen from the top of a small roller coaster in an amusement park. The park was scheduled to be demolished and a shopping mall built. The date put it nearly thirty years ago. The mall had since been demolished to make way for a medical center.

A group of boys had tunneled under the barbed wire fence surrounding the decaying park. The group was a mix of black and white kids from a nearby elementary school and they all admitted to egging each other on to climb the tracks and stand on the top of the first rise. The only name in the article was that of the dead child—Luther Gantt.

SIXTEEN

The phone rang before I could formulate any theories on the connections between a long-dead Luther Gantt, Tamara, and her cousin, or to Andrew Standish.

Unexpectedly I recognized the gravelly voice of Schooner, bartender at the Billet. "Hey there, Lexy. Got a lady here who would like to meet with you—if it's not too late and you've got the time. She said to tell you she's been to church."

"On my way, Schooner. I trust you're still brewing that liquid mud. It's been a long day and I need a jolt."

I was amazed at the rapid pace of events. It was only yesterday morning that I had asked for the help of the Iron Maiden in getting inside information on the Light of Christ Church. I scribbled a note for Wren telling her where I was going. I started to add that it was on *Ledger* business—then I didn't. I wanted our life fluid—not hemmed in by unnecessary fences. Or was I being skittish? Maybe even stubborn?

I glared at the calendar goddess and blurted, "No I'm not! I'm just being me."

Just short of a half hour later I paused, as always, at the entrance to the Billet, a private club for women veterans. I always felt as though I were stepping onto the set of a bar for a World War II movie. Low yellow light brightened dark wooden booths, square tables and ladder-back chairs saved from old farmhouses. Mostly I enjoyed the display of women's military apparel going back to World War I hanging from tall, old-fashioned racks scattered about the room. I felt welcomed and privileged to share a time period I could never know, and touch lives with women whose experiences differed so from my own.

Schooner greeted me boisterously. She had come by her nickname while on her tour of duty in Germany, where she drank heavily. Sober now, she was involved in anti-drug-and-alcohol education for young people. She poured my coffee into a mug containing a picture of Eileen Collins, first female shuttle commander. "Found out who fragged your boss yet?"

"Who says I'm looking?" Her craggy face rearranged itself into amused skepticism. I added, "And he wasn't my boss. His sister is."

"So you're in the trenches this time. With Babs watching your back, I'll bet."

I would never get used to hearing the Iron Maiden referred to as "Babs." I sipped the strong coffee and scanned the room.

In a conspiratorial tone Schooner said, "Back booth...Major... nurse in Vietnam."

I observed the woman in question as I approached. Probably around my mother's age, she was beyond ideal weight but had an aura of physical well-being, skillfully touched-up silver blonde hair, and an alert expression.

"Major. I'm Lexy Hyatt."

The corner of her mouth lifted as she nodded for me to seat myself. "Ellen Landow. The Major part—Vietnam, a long time ago."

I said softly, "An uncle I never got to know died there."

She nodded understandingly and I saw a glimmer of acceptance. She began immediately. "Babs MacFadden called someone yesterday who called someone who called me. Things didn't need to go any further. By a fortunate, or maybe unfortunate, coincidence, I think I already have what you want."

She proceeded succinctly. "I attended a family gathering in Jacksonville at my sister's for Thanksgiving. She's widowed. My niece and nephew got me aside for a private talk. They were concerned about Irene, that's my sister, going overboard on a church she had gotten involved with."

"LCC?"

A curt nod. "Correct. She was planning to make them the beneficiary of her life insurance as well as sign for the house to go to them at her death. And she was already tithing twenty percent of her income. She's office manager for a construction company. Her children aren't concerned about the money. They're well-established in their own professions. They're concerned about their mother. Before this church business, Irene was considering retiring and doing some of the traveling she had always been interested in. Now that has been shelved."

She put an elbow on the table and massaged her temple. "I got her talking about the church. She showed me all the literature on their good works—helping the needy, saving the community from collapse. Irene even rattled off a memorized catalog of all that her twenty percent was accomplishing." Ellen Landow swept her hand across the table. "She was being guilt-tripped. Made to feel there was something wrong with being financially secure and splurging a bit."

She gave me a level look. "It isn't as though Irene has never done good in her life. She has and she still does. She's done things like tutor at Comfort Hall, where they house teenage girls removed from abusive homes. When those fires were raging all over Florida a couple of years ago, she spearheaded the drive to get lotions and powder and medicine out to the firefighters after the stores had all been cleaned out."

I asked, "So what did you do?"

"Her children and I mounted a quiet campaign—maybe even a sneaky one. Wouldn't have done to come at her head-on. But first I made certain it was right to interfere." She reached down and picked up a folder which she then pushed across the table to me. "I hired a private investigator—the kind who does most of his leg work through a computer. That's a copy of his report. Hope it's some help to you. It was to me—and Irene."

She shifted toward getting up. "Got a poker game waiting on me, but if you have questions give me the high sign."

"Do they ever raid this place?" I said impudently.

"To confiscate our toothpicks!" Her grin was smug. "Of course we do buy them from Schooner...and return them to get our money back."

I studied the contents of the folder carefully, not even noticing when my coffee mug was refilled or by whom. It was easy to spot the material that would have helped Ellen Landow encourage her sister's retreat from LCC. All the good-deed projects were for white Protestants only. All community problems were due to minorities. And they went after a lot of individuals—especially public school personnel. They had agitated for the removal of an African-American male teacher as the coach of a girls' track team, attacked the proposed adoption of an American history textbook written by an Asian-American, and secured the firing of a gay band director for including his partner as a chaperon to a competition trip—even though three husband/wife pairs went along.

There were several pages of financial charts. The Jacksonville P.I. pointed out the wide gap between the monies collected for charity and the amounts contributed. Instead, much went to fund publication and dispersal of hate literature, signs and transportation for picketing, and carefully orchestrated harassment of moderate and liberal public figures. He also included suppositions that he couldn't prove. He believed that LCC was behind a flood of anonymous notifications to the police department of supposed illegal immigrants and possible perverts—many of whom proved to be innocent of the charges but were trashed by the investigations. He listed individuals making legal contributions to far-right politicians and groups, but was certain the money came from LCC coffers. Also, he maintained that certain variations in names represented single individuals and that many of the common names were actually deceased persons.

I was most interested in his conclusion that LCC might be connected with a series of physical attacks on minority sailors while they were on shore leave in Jacksonville, graffiti scrawled on the cars provided for foreign participants in golf and tennis tournaments, and vandalism at two Latino dance clubs.

Toward the end of the report, I spotted the name Christopher Cross on a list of deacons who appeared to have profited greatly from their LCC positions in terms of salary and expenses. Also Cross had managed the campaign of a Young Turk conservative trying to uproot an older figurehead of his party in an election to the state legislature. Once election of the man had quickly sponsored legislation recommending the low-rent leasing of state land for communication towers. The investigator included rumors that Cross had been behind a smear campaign that cost a popular sports reporter and television personality his job. Nelda Cross's first husband?

I closed the folder and finished my coffee. Was politics the impetus for Cross's move to the Orlando area? The center of the state had been expanding in political importance for the last twenty years and, with it, interest in grabbing power from the old rural dynasties—lumber, citrus, phosphates. That could explain Cross's interest in the *Ledger*—and his manipulation of Andrew Standish. The paper had never endorsed political candidates—simply covered them thoroughly and urged people to make selections based on truth and facts.

I wouldn't expect Andrea to deviate from that course. But Andrew...I sighed. More reason for her to want her brother out of the business instead of suddenly meddling in it.

I went to the bar and twirled my empty mug toward Schooner. "Do me another favor, Schooner? Hold the poker table's drink tab for me to pay later."

"Roger that."

On the way home I tried to ignore my worries about Andrea's motives. I would much prefer to consider Chris Cross the potential villain but I couldn't see how to get around his need for Andrew Standish alive and functioning as co-owner of the *Ledger*. What about the tie-in with Nelda Cross? More Cross manipulation to control Andrew or more of Andrew's stretching the boundaries? Worthington did see Cross in the field near where Andrew died. At least he said he saw him.

I switched my attention to the foliage along the sides of the road moving in an erratic wind dance. The palm fronds of tall trees were streaming straight out. The fans of the lower trees beat upon each other. At a red light I took in the bumper stickers on the car in front of me, smiling at "Appease the easily offended—ban everything." Was that what LCC was after? A ban on everything but themselves and their beliefs?

My irritation ratcheted up several notches when I arrived home to find Thea's car in the driveway again. This time I had room to get by into the garage. Wren was in the kitchen slathering a mixture of cream cheese and nuts onto dark bread.

She said warmly, "Glad you're home. Hope you're hungry for these."

I pressed against her backside. "Maybe it's you I'm hungry for."

She twisted her head around for my kiss. I said, "How long will we be having company?"

Thea, her voice sonorous and mildly caustic, spoke from the doorway. "Long enough for me to share your food...and the company of your partner. Then this night owl has to go to work."

Still pressed against Wren, I felt her stiffen as I said, low and cold, "I caught your patter last night when I chanced on WDYK."

Thea lifted her chin emphasizing her long neck. "You should catch me tonight. I have a feeling I'll be in a Janice Ian mood again. The lady knows how to grab you in the crotch."

Wren moved from my embrace and thrust the plate of sandwiches into Thea's hands. To me she said, "Bring the wine glasses. I've already opened the bottle to breathe." She gave me a warning frown as I curled my lip to hiss.

I was hungry and I allowed the food and wine to dissipate my irritation. I listened with interest as Thea responded to Wren's questions about WDYK.

"Sure we're a pirate station. Right now the FCC is more concerned about the foul-language rappers than hunting for us. And we move around a lot. There are several places that let us mount our antenna. It's only eight feet. Our transmitter was the big cost and we've got it safely hidden."

I asked, "How do you get frequencies to broadcast on?"

"Not hard," Thea answered. "Mostly we use low frequencies of small stations that don't broadcast at night." She boasted with a grin, "Weekends we use a religious station's signal out of Tampa that's too weak to be picked up clearly here."

"What about the money end of things?" Wren asked.

"Contributions...people working for free...commercial time. C.K. Chen bought time for Leather Fever spots. So did that new herb and spice and tea place, the Root Cellar." She looked at me. "Tonight, along with Janice Ian, I'm going to rattle off makes of cars and license plate numbers."

Curiosity overrode my pique. "What's going on?"

"That bunch picketing Bound to be Read shifted to Rainbow Lane today. Got there early enough to take all the street parking. Bumper to bumper. Then they stayed in their cars and held signs up against the windows warning people not to shop at places that serviced..." She pulled a piece of paper from her pocket. "...fornicators, homosexuals, evolutionists, feminists, masturbators....You know the drill. But you should have seen some of the spellings. Tamara would shit a brick. I finally decided that 'lashavus' was lascivious. I took down the models and years of all the cars and their tag numbers. Going to broadcast them tonight."

"To what purpose?"

Thea heard the disapproval in my tone. She said harshly, "It's okay for them to take the tag numbers of people going to women's clinics and gay businesses and then find out where they live to harass them? But not for us to turn the tables?"

"I don't want to be like them, Thea." I tried to soften my criticism. "Bet your grandmother wouldn't like it."

"I do a lot my grandmother wouldn't like. But if it soothes your ruffled sensibilities any, I plan to suggest that if anyone spots them—out in public—to offer a rainbow decal to brighten their cars. Nothing mean or pushy."

I let it go at that and Wren skillfully steered the conversation into

134

neutral territory. When Thea refused a second glass of wine and made movements toward leaving, I asked abruptly, "Are you by any chance related to a Luther Gantt?"

Clearly surprised, she said, "Had a cousin by that name. Never knew him. He died as a little kid before I was born."

"Any relation to Tamara?"

"He would have been her oldest brother. But she never knew him either." Suddenly she stiffened. I had the feeling she was remembering something. "What's this about, Lexy?"

Did I hear irritation or apprehension in her tone, or was I just looking for something to hold against her? "I ran across a newspaper clipping about him falling from the top of a roller coaster. It was in a boarded-up amusement park scheduled for demolition. I noticed the name. That's all."

Her eyes narrowed and I thought she was going to say more, but all she said was, "Ancient family history. No big deal any more. But it'll be a big deal if I'm late for work."

Wren walked her out then returned to sit on the couch with me. I could feel her waiting for me to ask why Thea happened to be here. I bit the inside of my cheek to keep from doing so. Instead I asked, "Did you get that logo business tended to?"

She clenched a fist and pumped her arm. I laughed at the gesture so unlike her and drew her into my arms.

She nestled against my shoulder as she told me about her excursion. "I went down to the office where I had submitted my design. The secretary routed me to the business manager. He was one of those smarmy men that make you want to take a bath when you get away from them. He didn't want to return my design. Said it was among the top three being considered. He kept trying to pry reasons out of me. I had to get nasty."

I rubbed my cheek in her hair. "That means you iced his balls."

She pushed up and away from me, her green eyes flaunting her pride. "Yes!" Her expression became serious. "Something else, Lexy."

"What?"

"I heard Cross on the phone when I passed another office. I listened because I heard him use Worthington's name. I'm paraphrasing, but he said something like 'You work on that boss of yours to break with tradition. I want the *Ledger* endorsing Yount for re-election to the legislature. I'm sure you don't want me laying it out for her just how helpful you've been the last couple of months.' His voice gave me chills."

So Joe Worthington wasn't off the hook yet. Was his visit to the LCC building connected to that call?

Wren was continuing. "He finished the call with stuff that didn't mean enough for me to remember. Then I heard his wife's voice. I started to scoot because I didn't want another confrontation with her, but I thought I might hear something to help you."

"And?"

"She told Cross that he'd never get Andrea Standish to jump through hoops...especially with Andrew gone. Then she said in the most callously dismissive tone I've ever heard, 'I could have killed him myself for not stopping that dyke from catching up to me. I warned you that he was only good at looking out for himself. He'd have gigged you in the back instead of his sister just for the sport of it.' Then the phone rang and I did scoot."

I did the few dishes while Wren put away the rest of the sandwiches. Thea's presence hovered still. In my awareness only? Or Wren's, too? I turned out the kitchen light and pressed her against the counter. My mouth was hungry and hers responsive.

"You lost a commission because of me, Wren. I owe you. Maybe you'd like to take it out in trade—if you don't think I'm being smarmy."

She slipped away from me. "Not just because of you, Lexy. I won't let my work be used by people or organizations I object to. I'm of the school that believes you can't separate the art from the artist." It was too dark for me to see her expression but I heard the firmness in her voice as she said, "Now, as to your other suggestion, you're not going to add a Wednesday checkmark to that calendar in your head. Tonight we sleep."

"Wren!" My throat felt too raw for further speech.

"It's not sex you want right now, Lexy. It's aggression toward Thea. I won't let you use me like that." She touched fingers to my lips to stop any retort. "Besides, it's not me she wants. It's challenging you."

My stomach churned. Wren believed what she was saying. I didn't.

SEVENTEEN

On a whim I zipped into the side parking lot of the police station. The slick pamphlets I had gathered at nearby banks slid about on top of the two folders on Standish and Nelda Cross I had tossed into the car this morning. I skimmed through the pamphlets while deciding whether or not to see if Robbie Exline was at her desk.

I shook my head over the artful dodges of two of the banks represented by the paperwork in my hands. Both listed the user fees for those who did not maintain accounts under boldfaced headings, but the fees for the banks' own account holders were on a different page in small print. I felt ready to get all my bank research scrubbed and dressed for presentation in Monday's financial section.

I even had some insider info gleaned over lunch an hour ago from Pam Felder, the loan officer at Square One Bank with whom I had shared some high-school high jinks. She had spoken with me on the condition that I not use her name, her motivation being that she was the last surviving local employee since the takeover by a larger banking concern almost a year ago. Now that another takeover loomed, she did not expect to last much longer.

She had said, "There's no loyalty or consideration for customers or employees any more."

I glanced up as a figure walked by the front of my car and saw Warren Kessler. Quickly I opened my door and called a greeting.

He turned, his face blank. Then the skin around his eyes and over his nose crinkled as he smiled. "I recognize you but I don't remember your name."

"Lexy Hyatt." I swung my legs out of the car but remained seated. I was sure I was taller than Kessler and I didn't want that kind of edge at the moment.

He walked a couple of uneven steps, a cane against his pant leg, and leaned back against a truck. "Warren Kessler."

"I know. Peggy Thomas told me that you and she and the Standishes went to school together." His face went blank again and I hurried on. "She and I both work at the *Ledger*. She pointed you out before the orienteering event began Sunday."

"Have you been pulled in for another round of questioning, too?"

"No. A couple of guys tried to relieve me of my car Monday night. I have to look at mug shots." The glib lie came easily. One of these days I would let that bother me. "But they still have the water bottle I lost as evidence. What about you?"

Kessler stared back at the police building and I could see tension in his jaw and neck. Then he shrugged it off. "They rooted up an old problem between Andrew and me. Been buried too long to have meaning any more, but you know how the cops can be."

I chose to be blunt. "You thought he was the one who shot me with a paint gun, didn't you?"

He responded just as bluntly. "Yes. It was in character for him. I'll grant you Andrew was no coward. He'd take crazy risks to get a win— or whatever he wanted. Unfortunately he'd also risk other people's safety if they got in his way." The knuckles of the hand holding the cane were white.

"Did you find him?" I could tell by the stillness that settled about him he was getting ready to lie. I moved to forestall it. "Look, Warren. Whether you know it or not, I'm a reporter and I admit I'm looking into Andrew Standish's death. But not for a story. Partly it's personal and a bigger part is that I want to help Andrea protect the *Ledger*."

A softening of his stance told me I had played a card with value. Quickly I played another. "I know about the tower climb and what Standish cost you. I haven't passed that on to anyone. It will never appear under my byline. Play straight with me here."

He looked again at the police building, then back at me. "Okay. It was Andrew who shot you. I caught up with him and grabbed the paint gun out of his hands. Smacked it on a tree and threw it back at him. Got paint on me doing it. He was laughing. We started tussling. Andrea stopped us."

"What?!" That was not what I wanted to hear.

"We were at the edge of the woods. She drove up in a golf cart. We were all yelling at each other at once. I don't know what got said. Finally I said I had a race to finish and headed back toward the trail. Found a water bottle and tried to wash the paint off my shirt and hands. Yours, I gather."

"And Andrea?"

"She left, too. I heard the beeps of the cart backing up. We both left him alive."

His saying it, even with a clear gaze, didn't make it so, but I nodded as though accepting his version unquestioningly. "And then you finished the race."

He hesitated. "Not right away. I was angry and Andrew had spoiled the pleasure of the event for me. I kept to the woods and started back toward the front. Every now and then I could hear someone on the trail." He gave me a sheepish grin. "Eventually I cooled down and got over feeling sorry for myself. I decided to finish what I had started." Now it was a confident grin. "Bet there is something about that tower climb you don't know. No one does."

"Which is?"

"Two years later I went back and made it to the top." He pulled the cane away from his leg. "Made accepting this a little easier. I have to do things like that every once in awhile." He saluted with the cane and walked around to the driver's side of the truck.

I swiveled enough to reach the folder on Andrew Standish. I plucked the article on Luther Gantt from it, folded it once, and placed it carefully in a back pocket. Inside the building I exchanged pleasantries with some of the uniforms I had come to know slightly. Others eyed me suspiciously. I doubted that reporters would ever be accepted as allies by the cops.

Robbie was at her desk on the phone. I tapped on the glass of her door and she motioned me in. She hung up the receiver and got in the first question. "Have you and Tamara Gantt stepped on the same toes?"

"I assume you're referring to the trashing of her car. Not much gets by you, does it?"

"Everything relating to the *Ledger* is being passed my way very quickly." She widened her eyes and waited for me to answer her question.

I explained about the malicious early morning repartee on the radio and my belief that it was all LCC-connected. I also recited some of the info gathered by Ellen Landow's P.I. related to the Jacksonville branch of the church—though I omitted names. I omitted all of the references to Cross as well.

Robbie said, "I'll put some desk people onto monitoring the radio station. It's probably one bought out by Cross Communications."

So much for my avoiding his name. With what I hoped was a sufficiently casual tone, I asked, "What's the connection?"

She widened her brown eyes again and the gold flecks sparkled. "So we're going to pretend you don't know as much as I do? Okay. He's been a deacon in the Light of Christ Church, he recently bought into the *Ledger*, and the rumors indicate there were bigger deals to be arranged through Andrew Standish. Every bit of which I'm sure you know."

Of course I did, but it was what I was hearing between the lines that disturbed me. They were building a case against Andrea. "Maybe Andrew reneged on a deal. I've seen Cross. He didn't look like the kind who would take that well. And he was in the park Sunday."

Robbie's poker face told me she was fully aware of that. She shuffled some papers. "And what brings you here, Lexy? Not the pleasure of my company."

I no longer intended to show my detective friend the article on the Gantt boy. I didn't want her making the connection with Tamara. Again the lies came easily. "I'm planning a story on accidents and deaths at amusement and theme parks in the area. I'm thinking about starting with references to some that happened over the years. In fact, I've discovered there used to be a park where the Albert Medical Center is now. A little boy fell from the top of a roller coaster rise thirty years ago. What are my chances of seeing the files on that?"

"Slim...no, more like none. It's hard enough getting current stuff computerized. Old cases like that have probably fallen through the cracks. No telling where the paper file is. Station houses have been moved—some torn down, file boxes shuffled around. I know there's tons of old stuff stacked up at Central Warehousing waiting to be fed onto those hungry little disks." She threw up her hands.

"What about personnel from twenty, thirty years back?"

Robbie started to shake her head, then looked thoughtful. "We've got a night desk-sergeant who won't take retirement. Been a widower for ten years—likes the night shift. Talks a lot about the old days—keeps up with the retired guys. He might be able to give you something."

"Name and phone number?" I was reaching for a scrap of paper and a pen.

Robbie stopped me. "No. He's not very reporter friendly. Thinks you are all bottom feeders. I was in court this morning so I'll be here late catching up. I'll see what I can get from him for you." She smiled with obvious self-satisfaction. "That'll mean you owe me."

I grunted acceptance and we shook hands.

Forty-five minutes later I stood outside Andrea's office unable to distinguish the low murmur of voices from the other side of the closed door. I took a step back and two toward the stairs—then halted. The boss lady would just have to dismiss whoever was there. I needed information.

I rapped twice. Seconds later the door swung inward. I was unprepared for the sight of Fonda Allison, the warm browns of her hair and eyes and the bamboo yellow of her jacket, such a striking contrast to the cool tones of the room behind her.

"Lexy! We were just talking about you. Andrea was volunteering you as an escort and I was declining to take your time so unfairly."

As I entered the room Andrea turned from the large window. She said, "I was telling Fonda about the Hurston Festival and she expressed interest. I had a hunch, what with your teaching background, that you'd be spending some time there this weekend."

She made a small gesture with her fingers as if indicating that she expected me to agree. My back stiffened and I wanted to balk, but a small voice in my head reasoned that being agreeable might gain me the leverage I needed to pry answers from her about that last confrontation with her brother.

Andrea spoke again before I could. "Andrew's body will be released Monday and funeral arrangements will follow. I thought some separation from the situation before then would be good for Fonda. And I'd like her to return to Alaska with some positive images of our area."

I considered that Andrea may have wanted the separation for herself, but I said, "I do plan on taking in some of the Festival events this weekend." I turned to Fonda. "I'll let you know when I'm going later. If you check with Barbara MacFadden before she leaves, I'm sure she could provide you with some background on Zora Neale Hurston and Eatonville." And I glanced at my watch.

An amused twist of Fonda's lips and a stiffening of Andrea's shoulders told me that both women recognized my presumptive dismissal of Fonda.

The younger woman politely capitulated, saying, "I'll check with her now."

The door closed softly after her while Andrea and I stared at each other. She spoke first, a statement rather than a question. "You are upset about something, Lexy."

She was establishing the rules but I struck the first blow. "You knew exactly where to find your brother's body because you had stood in that spot and argued with him. And you must have known that he was the one who splattered me with paint." I let my anger show by the way I clipped and separated my words.

Andrea sat down in her executive chair and made a show of seeming unconcerned at my attitude. "So Warren gave me up."

She managed to make me feel awkward continuing to stand. I plopped into one of the arm chairs and fought the need to tap a heel. "Not to the police."

She dipped her head toward me. "You are proving every bit as capable as the Iron Maiden promised. Perhaps I wasn't so much hiding things from you as testing you."

"Do you think that wise considering the stakes?"

That stung her. "I know the stakes full well. And I need to win for more than just myself."

That barb hit me, but I continued to press. "May I know how you came to be in that section of the woods?"

She waited just long enough to assert her authority, then answered without contention. "If Andrew had been running a straightforward race, he should have already checked in at the finish. Since he hadn't, I knew he was out there doing something. Also, I had heard about the injured woman and the description of those assisting her was clearly of Tamara and her friend. So I decided to cover for them and find out what Andrew was doing, if possible."

She was far too practiced in self-control to allow either her voice or body language to reveal anything beyond her words. She continued, "I thought it feasible to skirt the woods rather than go down the trails. When I heard angry voices I checked it out. Warren and Andrew were going at it, not all that seriously. My brother was more taunting than belligerent. Warren stalked off, frustrated and angry, but Andrew had to keep jabbing. He yelled after Warren that he wasn't going to be able to win the race any more than he'd been able to get to the top of that tower when they were teenagers."

"Did Kessler reply to that?"

"No. He stopped, but then kept going."

"And you?"

"I left, too. There was never anything to be gained trying to argue with Andrew."

"Did he keep jabbing at you, too?"

Just as with Warren Kessler earlier, the stillness that settled about her prepared me to hear a lie. She said, "No. I drove off and left him to his games. His toy was broken. Most people had completed the course. There didn't seem to be any more trouble that he could cause."

Her skin rippled like a cat's. She was shedding that topic for one of her choosing. "Thank you, Lexy, for agreeing to take Fonda with you to the Hurston Festival." She was letting us be equals again. "I had thought I was going to be saddled with an emotionally overwrought female...but she's grown stronger each day. Filled out with an inner stature. Developed more exterior color and solidity, if that makes sense?"

"It does. I took her to lunch the other day and saw that happening. Has she ever explained her decision to marry your brother in the first place?"

Andrea shook her head. "Nor do I expect her to. Whatever was between them ended with his death. Or will be buried with him." Her strangely mild blue eyes said she would be burying emotional items of her own. "I've thought of offering her a position here—but I don't believe she would accept it." She touched a finger to a sweep of eyebrow. "She might have changed Andrew." A pause. "No. No one was going to do that."

The angst in her voice chilled me. I was engulfed by the desire to take her in my arms and warm the tension out of her. I was so startled by my response that I nearly jumped from my chair.

With an emphatic gesture, Andrea pointed me back into the chair. She said, "I hadn't planned to mention this yet, but maybe this is a good opportunity. And an opportunity to emphasize just how much is at stake here. When my parents died, my mother and I were in the midst of laying out plans for an evening edition of the paper, possibly with a different name. Florida is changing. Orlando is changing. What's immediate and local needs more in-depth coverage. Television news has declined into sound bites, entertainment and pompous talking heads. Internet coverage is either too general or too biased."

I was intrigued, excited. That meant expansion, more personnel, changes in assignments. It also meant more reasons for Andrea to resent, even fear, the meddling of Christopher Cross and Andrew.

She must have read the thought in my face. "It was a blow to discover that Cross had acquired the stock held by Media Acquisitions, but I don't intend to be permanently knocked off stride by it. Especially now."

It was a bit chilling to realize that "especially now" meant now that Andrew was no longer an obstacle, but I said, "Without the backing of your brother, Cross may be over-reaching." I got up. "I have a deadline to meet." I headed for the door.

"Lexy." I stopped. Andrea said, "I'm not unmindful of the position I've put you in."

That was as close to an apology as I was going to get. It pleased me nonetheless. I walked down the stairs thinking of Andrea Standish in her office so uncompromisingly alone. I stopped with my right foot poised to drop to the next step. The *Ledger* and the proposed new evening paper kept her from spending much time alone. How far would she go to protect them…? I hurried down the rest of the steps and to my cubicle—running from the thought.

EIGHTEEN

I plugged myself into my computer and let work crowd out the murder of Andrew Standish for the rest of the afternoon. Preparing to leave just short of five o'clock, I reached for the phone to call Wren to see if she wanted to meet me at the Cat after my martial arts class. The phone rang before I could lift the receiver.

It was Robbie. "Hey, Lexy. The night desk-sergeant came in early to cover for Bamforth, who's the latest to come down with the flu. That flu shot the Admiral coerced me into getting in October had better do the job." She dropped the banter. "I have his name, address, and phone number for you. I didn't mention they were for a reporter but only because he didn't ask."

I copied down the information. "Thanks, Robbie. Any advice on angle of approach?"

"My guess would be to shoot straight with him. Tillman retired about twelve years ago from a beat that included that amusement park area years ago. I checked a little. It seems that he was among the few cops to adjust well to the changes in race relations back in the sixties and seventies. But he wouldn't let them promote him out of uniform into Public Relations." She sighed loudly. "Those must have been the days when you could reason with the brass above you."

"You sound disgruntled, detective."

"I am. Ziegler and I have been taken off a case where we think they forced us to arrest the wrong person. Our reasons have been dismissed without really being heard." She laughed caustically. "So— what's a little overtime."

I knew that meant she and Glen Ziegler would continue the case on their own time. "Watch your back, Robbie." I hoped that also meant less time and attention being devoted to Andrea Standish.

"And you watch yours, my friend. You have class tonight, don't you? Park close to the building and walk out with other people."

I did not bristle at her advice. I remembered the weight of the tire iron as I wrapped it in my shirt. Why did I rate violence when Tamara's car rated only vandalism? Into the phone I said, "Sorry, Robbie. I didn't catch that last bit."

"I was just telling you that Lester Tillman is another night owl, so contacting him in the evening would be best. Will I see you and Wren at the Cat this weekend?"

"Not sure. We plan to spend some time at the Hurston Festival. And I've been asked to show..." I decided not to mention Fonda's name "...some visitors around."

Robbie chuckled. "You are one accommodating lady, Lexy. Stay out of trouble."

I chuckled myself. "Will do." I hung up thinking how impossible it would be for me to get in trouble with someone as mild as Fonda—a bird with a broken wing. It was good that Andrew Standish no longer existed to snap and crush the rest of those delicate bones.

The Iron Maiden appeared in my doorway. I waved her to a chair where she sat ramrod straight. She opened a padded notebook cover, and proceeded to run a pencil down the lines as she disseminated information.

"I believe you have worked with Tommy Chan, one of our photographers. A few days ago fliers were placed in doors in his neighborhood warning residents to watch their pets because Gooks likes to eat them. Be brief; I am on my way up stairs."

Where battle plans would be drawn up, I was sure. I gave her the information I had received from Ellen Landow at the Billet saying, "This should prove helpful."

She looked it over quickly and nodded. Her pencil moved down the page. "And I have information on Legislator Yount that may have connections here as well." She explained succinctly. "During the decades that the Democratic Party ran Florida there was a large group of wealthy conservatives, who wielded extensive power, sometimes overtly but more often behind the scenes. With the advent of Reagan they changed their affiliation to the Republican Party. Most of them are in their seventies now but clearly do not intend to relinquish power yet. It would appear they are working toward stacking the legislature with young conservatives like Yount who will advance their agenda."

I chimed in with, "The blatant attacks on groups like homosexuals and pro-choicers might be designed to keep attention away from other areas, such as immigration, gun control and unions. Smoke and mirrors stuff. And what if they were backing, even establishing churches like LCC as safer allies than the old KKK?"

"Ground a good reporter needs to be digging into."

"My foot's on the shovel." A lot of shovels, I thought. One in particular came to mind. I said, "The folder of information on Andrew Standish contained a clipping on the death of a little boy named Luther Gantt nearly thirty years ago. Why was it included?"

"When I was asked to compile the folder on Andrew, I was given the contents of a private file maintained by Rose Standish. It contained typical parent celebrations of a child—school activities, awards and, later, travel exploits. That clipping was there either as a mistake or for reasons known only to Rose. On a whim I included it in what I was compiling for you."

Her dark blue eyes challenged me to comment on the unusualness of her acting on a whim. I knew better than to do so.

With regret, I decided to forgo time with Wren at the Cat. Instead I punched in the number given to me by Robbie Exline. The phone was answered in the middle of the second ring. "Tillman here." It was a strong, no-nonsense voice.

I decided immediately to stick close to the truth. I identified myself as a *Ledger* reporter. I told him I was interested in the old amusement park that I had been told was once part of his beat. I asked if I could interview him as soon as was convenient for him.

He was cooperative. "Sure. And tonight would be good. Nothing on television I want to watch."

We settled on a short time after my class concluded, and I jotted down directions. I checked my email, making certain I was free to leave.

On my way out I was hailed by Peggy Thomas. "Just had a call about you, Lexy. Male—deep voice—sounded like he was used to giving orders and getting quick responses. Wanted to know if you were a reporter here."

I had been wrong to pat myself on the back at how easily Tillman had granted my request. He hadn't shed caution along with his uniform. I was looking forward to our meeting. I rested an arm on the counter. "How's the view from here lately, Peggy?"

Her mouth tightened and the softness of her face lengthened and hardened. "Heard a couple of the staff lawyers talking this morning. You know how the hard-hearted bastards think. Contingencies and scenarios—human individuals be damned. What little I caught made it sound like they were looking ahead to the 'what ifs' if Andrea is arrested for Andrew's murder!"

"And?"

"They were wondering who would run the paper while she was on trial."

The pitch of Peggy's voice rose a notch. "Or if she got convicted! As they were going out the door, I heard one say that Cross might have the standing he needs, on the basis of his clear twenty percent, to petition to run things until all wills were through probate and other legal proceedings concluded."

"I can't believe that would happen!" I exclaimed.

"Neither did I at first," Peggy replied. "But now I'm not so sure. Seems like the bad guys have more standing under the law nowadays than the good guys." Her face went slack. "Cross would kill the kind of paper the *Ledger* is. Andrew would have done it, too. And just to get back at Andrea."

"Get back at her for what?" Everywhere I turned, Andrea was getting a bad rap.

"For being what she is...disciplined, constructive, responsible. Andrew was none of that. He couldn't even understand my willingness to work all day Sunday at the park. Called me Miss Middle-Age Efficiency—as though we weren't the same age. Said he had a centerfold blonde ready to take over the front desk as soon as he dislodged his sister."

Fonda Allison appeared and placed her arm on the counter in a mirror image of my stance. She waved a sheaf of papers shoulder high and said, "You were right, Lexy. Miss MacFadden could and did provide me plenty of background."

I explained to Peggy, "The Hurston Festival."

"Oh, you'll enjoy that, Fonda. It's been going on about ten years now and keeps getting better—and bigger. This year they're adding a series of movies and performances covering the evolution of African-American dance in America." Peggy bent down and I could hear her rummaging through the contents of a low shelf. She handed Fonda and me each a bright yellow card. "Here's a listing of all the events and times, if you don't have one."

I thanked her and said to Fonda, "Wren and I will make some tentative choices and I'll check in with you sometime tomorrow. Okay?"

"That's fine. Wren?"

Peggy Thomas was fading away to answer the phone. I took a plunge. "My partner. We're a couple. I offer the information because I wouldn't want to put you in a compromising or uncomfortable position."

"Perhaps I should take offense at that." Her crooked smile erased any harshness in the words. "You're being considerate of sensibilities I'm not guilty of. A truly compromising situation was my foolish engagement to Andrew." The rise and fall of her breasts against the lapels of her jacket increased in rate and lift. "I wish it were possible to explain that to someone."

I may have been misreading the searching nature of her gaze, but I felt she was actually saying, "explain that to you." I decided to take a pass on the observation. I told her I needed to get to my class soon and we walked out together.

At the bottom of the steps Fonda said, "Peggy Thomas has been very nice to me—as have many of you. I wish I hadn't been standing there Sunday morning when Andrew was so brutal to her."

"In what way?"

"He was belittling her for working so hard on her day off. He said some really crude things about her being an overpaid flunky of Andrea the Great. I got away from him right after that and started my walk." She laughed, but with little humor. "I went off swinging those hand weights so hard I almost hit a little girl in the face. Her mother got her out of my way real fast." She brightened. "I burned off calories and anger."

Alone in my car, I checked the thick yellow card announcing lectures, forums, performances and arts and crafts offerings. All honored Zora Neale Hurston, now recognized as a major African-American writer of the 1920s and '30s. She died in poverty and obscurity in Fort Pierce in 1960. It would be 1973 before novelist Alice Walker found the grave and marked it with a stone declaring Hurston "Novelist, Folklorist, Anthropologist." During the decade of the 1990s the nearby Black community of Eatonville began to celebrate her as a favored daughter. To me, Hurston represented all the women whose achievements never received due recognition.

I shoved the card behind the visor and was soon at a nearby cafe, consuming a light supper of salad and coffee. In the rapidly diminishing light, I added to my notes on Standish's murder what Warren Kessler and Andrea had said about the three-way argument in the woods. It bothered me that neither could give the other an alibi. Not sure of the relevance, I scribbled in Standish's threat of replacing Peggy Thomas.

Arriving early at the Martial Arts Academy, I was able to park close to the entrance; I told myself I was appeasing Robbie. I retrieved my gi from the back seat and went in to change. The Major was conducting a class for what looked like pre-schoolers. Since all the seats were taken by adoring parents, I went back out and sat on a bench after I had changed.

A car pulled up to the curb, the brakes squealing. Three gi-clad youngsters spilled out the back and a teenager from the front. Kelleen O'Mara was one of the three. She approached me and said, "May I join you, Lexy? Mr. Diaz had to bring us early. My mother will pick us up. She's at a meeting with PETA about protesting the dog and cat show next week."

"Sounds like something the paper should be covering. I'll check tomorrow and see if it's already on someone's assignment sheet. Do you have a pet, Kell?"

"No. Mother said I could but I have decided I don't wish to own another being." Her pompous statement was followed by a lighter one. "Besides, dogs are always wanting something and cats act superior."

I was reclining with my back against the hard slats of the bench, long legs stretched out, toes tapping. Kelleen sat on the edge, her back as straight as the light pole rising above my car. Staring ahead, she said, "Why did those men attack you? Is it because you are a lesbian?"

The second question caught me with lips parted, the response I had started to give for the first frozen in my mouth. I shifted forward on the bench and looked down at her calm profile.

Kelleen turned her head up and toward me. "My mother answers all my questions. Or tells me where I can go for information."

"I'm not sure she would expect that of me. Or want it." I could see her pondering that thought.

She conceded, saying, "Maybe not. But I know about lesbians already. She explained it to me when there was so much on television and in the newspapers about Gay Pride Week last year. And I read the publicity releases in her office on the women comedians who appeared at the Center. I even met Suzanne Westenhoefer. I liked her. She knew how to talk to someone my age without being silly." She brushed her toes over the concrete, possibly an indication that she wasn't as self-assured as she sounded. "I thought you might be a lesbian because I've seen how you and your friend look at each other when she drops you off here. And because the water bottle she gave you was very special."

I thought of where that bottle was now and how much it had been handled. For the second time in a few hours I admitted, "Yes, Wren and I are a couple. As for the men who attacked me, it's more complicated than that. They were using me to attack the *Ledger*." Something else for her to ponder. It was time to turn the tables. "Where does your middle name, Cha, come from?"

The twitch of one corner of her mouth told me that she recognized my tactic. "When I was eight I heard some older girls in the bathroom at school talking about how women got babies. So I went home and asked my mother who the man was who helped her get me."

I put my elbows on my knees and braced my forehead against the hard ridge of my palms, thinking how unready Brie must have been at that moment.

Kelleen read my thought. "She was going to tell me when I was older so I guess right then I..."

It was the first time I had caught her hesitating for a word. I supplied it. "You blindsided her."

Kelleen actually smiled—and I glimpsed the stunning woman she would mature into. "Yes. But she told me. Not everything. She said that could wait until I was older. It happened when she was working at the U. S. Embassy in Korea. His name was Tok Cha. He was an interpreter and a cultural liaison. I had to look up that word later. She said they liked each other very much and spent time together but they knew it could never be a...a permanent relationship."

She looked up at me forthrightly. "I didn't understand all she said, but I am beginning to learn things that make it clear. She said it wasn't because they were different nationalities, but it was because of things connected with their nationalities—like religion, what you learn from your family, your beliefs about how life should be lived." Her toes brushed the concrete again. "She didn't know about me until she got back to the States."

I couldn't stop my retort, "Oh, my."

Kelleen's toes stopped moving. "I asked her how she felt about that. I believe she told me the truth. She said, 'First there was shock. Then there was pleasure.' I didn't have a middle name, so I asked her if I could take my father's. I think that pleased her."

"I'm sure it did, Kell. You two are a remarkable pair."

The stream of students arriving indicated it was time to enter for class. I stood and shivered. I had been so intent on my conversation with Kelleen that I hadn't noticed the dropping temperature. Kelleen paused in front of me, her face again solemn and unreadable. She bowed, then turned smartly on her heels and entered the building. I stood a moment smiling into the space she had left.

NINETEEN

Class began with wide-stance exercises for our thighs along with more stretching to strengthen our abdominal muscles. All the while the Major spoke gently, but with emphasis, urging us to follow our movements with our minds, then to intertwine them. I was beginning to understand, beginning to move without forcing it. Next we were put through breathing exercises paired with numerous body positions that for the first time felt natural to me.

The core of the night's lesson involved more practice in learning how to soften our bodies, to absorb or give way, so as to disrupt an opponent's movements and balance.

After class I changed into my street clothes and found Brie O'Mara leaning against her car, apparently waiting for me. She joined me near the door of the Academy.

Brie smiled. "I'm glad to see you're suffering no ill effects from the other night, Lexy. Have the police been able to track down those men?"

I answered, "A detective friend is looking into it. I wasn't able to give her much but she is following a lead." I added uncomfortably, "I've been worrying about what Kelleen did. I cringe when I think how she might have been harmed."

Brie shrugged. "My heart was in my throat, seeing her fly through the air like that. The truth is she prevented harm to you without being hurt herself." She glanced back at the car, where Kelleen sat primly in the front seat ignoring the by-play of the other kids in the backseat. "Kelleen and I would like to invite you and your friend to dinner one evening. It sounded like she called her Ren or Rin."

I spelled Wren's name and explained, "It was formed from the initials of her grandparents."

"How interesting!"

I cocked my head. "As interesting as the story Kell told me tonight about her middle name."

Again Brie darted a look toward her car, her face flushed with pleasure. "Oh, you can't know how much that means to me. It means she really is all right with it. I'm careful not to push or badger her about it."

"Ah...Brie...there's something else she seems all right about...the relationship between Wren and me."

Her warm laughter trilled into the chilly air. "A man I dated for a short time told me I had a precocious daughter. He made it sound like a mark of Cain for her and a burden for me. In actuality she is aware, quick, perceptive to the point of being intuitive. Took me a long time to stop being frightened by that. I learned to roll with it and you might as well do the same." Her face relaxed. "Kell and I wanted to suggest dinner the Friday night following your last Thursday class here. A kind of celebration."

"That would be great. I'll be looking forward to it...and so will Wren." I was thinking it would be a good time for Wren to give them signed copies of the *Bulletin* cover featuring Kelleen among the faces.

I walked to my car in the pinkish circle of light, sensing Brie O'Mara's eyes following me. The metallic thud of my door closing was echoed by hers. I re-checked the directions to Lester Tillman's house and estimated a twenty-minute drive. About three minutes beyond that I pulled into his driveway.

His was an old-fashioned, double-story frame house with a small inverted V-shaped roof shielding a front porch. Thick hibiscus bushes full of blooms obscured the porch railing. A yellow light spread a weak glow over the porch and steps. I climbed those steps while touching my back pocket to verify that it still contained the article on Luther Gantt.

The door opened as I touched my foot to the porch. A very tall, skinny man was silhouetted behind the screen. I held my ID to the screen. "Lexy Hyatt, Mr. Tillman."

He unhooked the screen door and ushered me in. "Lester will do—though there's not many to call me that since my wife died. Cop friends call me Tilly. Beat cops way back used to make that Tilly the Toiler." He grinned and years dropped off his unusually long, rectangular face. "Not a comic-strip reference I would expect you to understand. Try it on your parents sometime."

"I'll do that. And call me Lexy."

He waved me to a wide-armed sofa-chair as he settled into a high-backed rocker, which he inched closer to me. I was struck by the way his extremities moved as though manipulated by strings and only loosely connected to his torso. Though nearly bald, he sported a surprisingly black fringe circling from temple to temple. The backs of his hands had similar hairy patches.

"What is it you want from this long-retired cop, Lexy?" His intelligent eyes and frank tone warned me off modifying the truth.

For an answer I retrieved the clipping from my pocket and handed it across to him.

He read it carefully, pulling his lips in and out a couple of times. Continuing to look at the piece of paper in his hand, he mused, "This was a long time ago but it's one of those things I remember clearer than I would like. I still walked a beat in those days, even though I wasn't far from fifty. Most other cops didn't want it because the territory had become mixed." He explained hurriedly, "Oh, not together. There was a definite line down the middle of Pridemore Avenue. Middle-class colored, the term then, lived for a few blocks west of the avenue. Old-money whites were on the other side still living in modest in-town homes. Most of their kin later moved out to the fancy suburbs or to condos. But the kids did some mixing then."

"Did that make for trouble?" I asked.

"No. Oh, ordinary kid trouble—but not racial. That old amusement park had been at the edge of town but the growth of the 1960s changed all that. I tried to keep an eye on things even though the place was well-fenced off while bids came in for demolition and clearing. But kids have their ways of getting around whatever you set up to block them." His thumb played up and down the clipping. "When this bunch got inside and started climbing the scaffolding of that roller coaster, two of the little girls came running for me." His voice became hollow. "I was half a block away when I heard the screaming. Had to go over the fence." He looked at the palm of his right hand. "I still have the scars from the barbed wire."

I took the clipping from him. I was afraid he would work his thumb right through it. He continued, his hollow tone replaced by one of sadness. "There wasn't anything I could do. The roller coaster wasn't all that high but the Gantt boy came off it headfirst." He looked directly at me for the first time since I handed him the clipping. "I'll never forget how quiet his mother was when she got there and had to watch them put him in the ambulance. She just stood there with her hands on the child she was carrying in her belly. She was so big I was scared she was going to drop it right then and there. The only thing I heard her say was, 'Luther was my oldest. He always says someday he'd be taking care of me.'"

Tillman took a deep breath, then expelled it through tight lips. Slowly he relaxed and offered, "A cup of coffee...a beer...a sip of brandy? It's supposed to drop near freezing tonight. Course you'd have to do your sipping out of a shot glass."

"Brandy in a shot glass sounds like an adventure. I grew up on stories of my great-uncle's bootlegging exploits. Bathtub gin, slot machines in basements."

Tillman reminisced, "I had an uncle who would sail out from Hutchinson's Island to meet boats coming from the islands with British booze. Then he and some chums would run it up to Louisville, Kentucky. Later my dad downplayed all that, but I'm sure the money my Uncle Scott stashed away got the family through the rough times."

He unfolded himself from the rocking chair and went to the kitchen. I spent the wait checking out the room. He returned with shot glasses that proved to be double-sized and we both savored the warm bite in the first sip of good brandy.

I asked, "Do you remember the names of any of the other children who were there...at the roller coaster?" The Iron Maiden may have called it a whim but I had a stronger feeling about why Rose Standish had held on to that clipping.

Tillman's eyes were shrewd and calculating. "I do. Primarily because Standish's name has been in the papers lately. Are you trying to dig up dirt on your employer?"

I responded forthrightly. "No. My employer is Andrea Standish. If anything, I'm trying to keep her clean. The *Ledger* is important to me. It's her life. But Andrew Standish was one of those kids, wasn't he?"

Tillman nodded. "I had all their names in my report. Most of them agreed the Standish boy had led the expedition under the fence...had come up with the idea for the climb. Three or four of them were part way up when Luther fell."

"Was Standish one of those?"

"Yes. One of the girls on the ground said he had been telling Luther to shake his hands above his head the way boxers did on television. That's when the boy lost his balance."

I returned the clipping to my pocket and sipped more of the brandy. "I suppose his parents kept his name out of the paper."

"Not necessarily. It was an accident just like the one where kids tunneled into a mound of dirt at an excavation site and someone smothered before they could be dug out. Or there was a drowning during an unsupervised swim in a local lake. The media was willing to protect kids more then than now." He gulped brandy with a sour expression. "Of course they weren't doing their damage with automatic handguns then. Those kids that saw Luther die probably came away more cautious for the rest of their lives."

I shook my head inwardly. That wasn't true of Andrew Standish. He had devoted his life to risk...and had continued provoking others to extreme behavior.

We finished off our brandies while exchanging small talk about our professions. Then, walking me out onto the porch, he expressed a willingness to be contacted again if necessary.

I turned and stepped back to shake his hand. Just then the yellow bulb of the porch light shattered. Even when the pieces were drifting toward the floor, something seared my forehead at the hairline. Almost simultaneously, Tillman seized me by the neck, forcing me down behind the railing. The whistling sounds I heard could have been the wind, but not the dull explosions behind us. Next came the distinctive sound of tires squealing, burning rubber.

Tillman kept a hand firmly on my back as he peered over the railing. He removed his hand and we both stood. Exhaust hovered in the cold air. I turned from watching it dissipate slowly to see him digging into the wood near the doorframe with a pocketknife. Within seconds he displayed two chunks of metal about the size of pencil erases.

He said, "They're from a pellet gun. The fire power comes from a little gas cylinder. People use them to keep squirrels, raccoons or possums out of their yards. Or they let their kids target shoot cans with them. Have you stepped too hard on someone' s toes, Lexy?"

"How do you know they weren't aiming at you?"

"Any enemies I might have made are either dead or too old to shoot straight. And I don't believe in coincidences. First time you've been here—first time...." He jiggled the pellets in his palm. Then he pushed back my hair with his other hand. "Let's get something on that. Do you keep up on your tetanus shot?"

"I do." I heard the strain of delayed tension in my words—along with increasing anger. Violent acts directed at me were unnerving enough, but they rippled outward threatening others. Kelleen—and now Lester Tillman.

We returned to the living room and I sat in the rocking chair as

Tillman rubbed an antibiotic salve into the streak along my hairline which was beginning to sting. I felt as countless children must have felt in years past as he loomed over me and said with a quiet forcefulness, "Want to tell me what's going on here? I can see the wheels turning behind your eyes."

I gave him a very sketchy picture of Andrew Standish's death and the possible ramifications for the paper had he lived and also now that he was dead. Then I gave him a condensed version of Christopher Cross's interest in the paper and his probable employment of LCC members to cause disruption.

He perched on the wide arm of the sofa chair. "I told you I didn't believe much in coincidence." He tapped my knee with a bony finger. "But someone came at you with a tire iron." He looked toward the front door. "Someone else didn't care if they plugged you in the eye. That's malicious intent to do bodily harm—assault and battery."

I frowned, making the crease in my forehead sting again. The same thought had been hovering inside my head, but I wasn't ready to lay out any more facts or conjectures for this man just now. I thanked him for the info, the brandy and the first aid and left.

On my way home I thought more about what he had said. I still thought all the disturbances were Cross/LCC connected, but now I considered the possibility of two agendas in play—one aimed at discrediting the *Ledger* and dislodging minority employees, the other directed at me specifically. Why? Because I was nosing into Andrew Standish's murder? Another thought surfaced. Or because I beat out Nelda Cross in the orienteering event? There was serious venom in the woman.

I twirled the radio dial, skipping through country-western and rock oldies, seeking rhythm and blues while continuing to mull over what I had learned from Tillman. Though I was not as skeptical about coincidences as he, I was uncomfortable with Andrew Standish's involvement in the death of Tamara's brother. I reminded myself that, according to Thea, Tamara had never known Luther. Could Tamara possibly know that Andrew had been among the group of children that evening at the amusement park?

As though to mock me, coincidence flared like a shooting star as I caught and lost the dusky voice of Thea Gantt. As I drove I finally caught and held the fluctuating radio signal. Immediately I pulled over to the curb and idled. I turned off the lights and heater and my breath steamed the windows.

157

Thea was urging lesbians to visit Bound to be Read and the shops in Rainbow Lane in groups of twos, threes, or fours to show support. I was pleased to hear her suggest that people simply ignore the presence of any anti-gay protesters as though they weren't even there. She added that a lack of abrasive confrontation might defuse their intensity and frustrate their schemes. Apparently she had bought a little of what I had said the other night.

Suddenly she wiped my mild approbation from the slate. In a slow, undulating inflection she coaxed, "Now—let's turn to more satisfying images. The invitation of parted lips...tongues in a slow dance...arteries throbbing, veins sighing...the tortured straining before the flesh ripples with satisfaction." She took a deep breath. "Wear red for me, little bird..."

The last words were a husky whisper fading into a haunting, tremulous rendition of "The Lady in Red."

I gunned the motor and squealed away from the curb. I refused to touch the dial but I sped away from the signal, not slowing until there was only static.

TWENTY

I arrived home struggling to keep my mind blank and reduce the tension of my muscles, which were threatening to cramp. It didn't help that I found the house empty and dark except for some low lighting.

But Wren's car was in the garage. And I could hear the full-bodied tones of Krystal Kay's voice from the radio in Wren's workroom. She was completing a story about her experiences broadcasting from the bird sanctuary at a local wildlife refuge and trying to convince an aggressive crested myna that the microphone wasn't for roosting or eating. Her hearty chortle teased me into softening the hard line of my compressed lips.

Then I saw the silhouette of Wren's lithe form standing near the center of our backyard. I bumped my hip on the corner of one of her worktables and nearly toppled an easel as I hurried toward the door.

She turned at the sound of the door closing. "You're here. Good. It's almost time for the lunar eclipse to begin." She slipped an arm about my waist.

Putting my arm around her, I said, "I had a late interview that went longer than I planned." The truth was I had forgotten about the eclipse and our plans to watch it from our own yard. That rattled me. I didn't want all the stories I was covering or digging into interfering with my personal life. Or maybe I was letting Thea Gantt succeed in disturbing my rhythms, my confidence and my security. I would have to do a better job of guarding against all that. I punctuated the thought by pulling Wren tighter to my side.

Together we looked up at the moon poised above us as though bravely awaiting the invasion of the Earth's shadow. Directly overhead was the easily recognized Orion, and on the northern edge of the sky both dippers dangled. The small stars were washed out by the brilliance of the moonlight. It was clearly what Walt Whitman described as "night of the large few stars!"

Wren motioned with her free arm. "Can you see where I placed stakes for our trees?"

I could see strips of white cloth attached to stakes and whipped by the rising wind. I zipped my jacket against the cold. "What's going where?"

She pointed. "The magnolia there. A Florida maple over there for color in the fall. A dogwood nearby for spring color. Those three stakes closer together for crape myrtles—maybe a simple pink between two of those deep watermelon reds. And a kind of hedge of wax myrtle along the back line for privacy and to give the birds berries. Those two stakes are for the grapefruit tree and a lime." She squeezed my waist. "For your bourbon."

"I appreciate the thought, Wren, but no lime tree."

She was surprised. "Why not?!"

I began to explain as she took me by the hand and drew me toward two lounge chairs. "There's a line in a poem by Anne Bradstreet where she talks about her children as though they are birds leaving the nest and warns what disasters might lie in wait." I recited, "'Or lest by lime twigs they be foiled.' When I saw my first lime tree up close, I understood that line. Hidden among the leaves are long, needle-like thorns. A bird could easily fly in and impale itself on those terrible spines."

Wren tightened her grip on my hand. "No lime tree."

Her understanding and acceptance of my peculiarities washed over me. How could I be so foolish as to think that another woman's interest or teasing could interfere with us? To do that was to dispute our love, to dishonor Wren.

At that moment the first arc of the Earth's shadow began to nibble at the full moon. The primal nature of the event caused us to lower our voices, to nearly whisper our reactions. The cold intensified the experience. The only clouds anywhere were caused by our warm breath colliding with the chilly air. It took an hour for the moon, more white gold in color than silver, to be completely dulled to a dark, brick red.

Wren said reflectively, "How frightening this must have been to primitive peoples. It even challenges my certainties. We may not be as supreme as we think we are." Her tone brightened. "Do you know what causes the reddish color?"

"I do. A little bit of sunlight slips past the Earth and strikes the moon. But it has to filter through the Earth's atmosphere first and, because that scatters most of the blue light in the sun's rays, it's the red that gets through."

As the moon began to emerge slowly from the cloak of the shadow, I rose from the lounge chair and tugged Wren up from hers. I said, "It can work its way free without our help." I exaggerated a shiver. "And I need warming, woman."

Wren's low, knowing laugh made me shiver for real. Hand in hand we re-entered the house. The piquant voice of Selena, the Latin singer whose death was so senseless, filled the darkened room with the deceptively soft intensity and nearly painful musings of "I Could Fall in Love." I drew Wren to me and we slow-danced through the haphazard space. I felt complete and happy.

As the last of the song faded away, I turned off the radio. Then I imprisoned Wren's face in both my hands and kissed her ardently. I kept my hands in place as she leaned slightly back from me. I could see her wondering about my intensity.

I said, "Unlike what the song says, I did fall in love with you—and it is right."

I drew her face back to mine. We widened our mouths and our tongues slow-danced.

Wren snuggled her face into my neck and the only sound was our breathing. Then she stepped away from me and brushed at the hair on my forehead. I jumped as her fingers scraped across the wound. Immediately she questioned, "What's that?!"

As I tried to step back, she grabbed me by the elbow and pulled me to a worktable where she switched on a directional lamp. I squinted as she aimed the light at my face saying, "What did that, Lexy? Not a fall."

Though I often omitted information, I never lied to her. I sighed, "Over tea. Okay?"

She acquiesced but her "Okay" was spoken in a flat tone that said I would be permitted to waffle. In the kitchen she quickly and efficiently made our tea. I selected a licorice honey straw for mine and looked questioningly at her. She nodded. We sipped the hot tea in silence as she toasted bagels.

Hungrily I ate half a bagel. I explained that I had gone to interview a retired policeman concerning a story I was working on—omitting references to Andrew Standish and the Gantt family. I told myself I was protecting Wren from emotional involvement. I described Tillman, his home, and how much I had enjoyed the time with him.

I said, "More cops like him would be a big help."

Wren replied, "We've got Robbie and Glen Ziegler."

"But they're not in the trenches."

"And you're not getting to the point." She gestured to my forehead. I frowned but complied. I described leaving the house, the shattering of the light bulb, the burning sensation near my hairline and Tillman hauling us to safety behind the porch railing. I admitted that I had been the likely target but stressed that it had been only a pellet gun.

Like Tillman, Wren was angry at the potential harm. "It isn't just a matter of a pellet in your eye. One at the right point in your temple could have meant your life. This has to stop, Lexy! How do we make it stop?"

I ran a finger along the table edge. "I have an idea where it's coming from." That wasn't exactly a fib. Though I leaned toward Cross because of my interest in Andrew's death, or his wife because I had beaten her on the Sunday orienteering run, I wasn't satisfied with either possibility. I couldn't fathom a motive for Cross committing murder and I couldn't imagine even Nasty Nelda seeking satisfaction through life-threatening violence. Still, there was her viperish nature. She reminded me of the softball catcher on an opposing team in college who would risk being ejected from the game, or even risk harm to herself, to get even with a player who had stolen home. I added firmly, "Tomorrow I'm going to see about defusing the situation. Trust me, Wren."

"You're not giving me a choice, are you?"

I chose not to answer, and with a wry smile she reached across the table to stroke my cheek with the back of her fingers. As we finished our food, I changed the topic to the Hurston Festival and the inclusion of Fonda Allison in our plans. We made decisions about times and events. Also, I told her about Brie O'Mara's invitation and she wrote it on our calendar. All the while I was aware of Wren's concern and my own questions Standish's murder.

I rinsed our cups and saucers and placed them in the dishwasher, then tagged after Wren as she started down the hallway to our bedroom. At the wide arch entrance to the front room, I halted her with a light hand to her shoulder. Without a word I went to the large window facing the street and, tugging a chain, partially closed the vertical blinds with a rattling sound. Wren remained in the archway backlit by a spill of soft yellow from the kitchen nightlight.

I approached her. "You took us off course a little while ago." I drew her into my arms and danced her toward the couch.

"Lexy!" Surprise and excitement soared in her voice as I firmly forced her to the cushions. I held myself above her, then slowly settled my weight on the length of her. She lifted into me. I wove my fingers into her hair before gripping her head firmly with both hands. Her breathing deepened and she lifted more strongly against me, but I kept her head imprisoned against the pillow. She whimpered as I brushed my lips over her face and sucked lightly at the hollow of her throat.

"It's time we initiated this room," I whispered huskily.

Her whimper faded into a throaty hum. Her breasts rose hard into mine as I nibbled at her lips before covering them and stroking the licorice-scented recesses of her mouth. The humming became a moan of obvious desire. I increased the pressure of my thigh, delighting in her effort to open wider for me.

I moved away from her, settling back on my heels at the end of the long couch to remove her shoes.

"Come back," Wren complained, her hands reaching ineffectually for me.

"Yessss. But not until you're naked for me."

There was only the sound of her breathing for a long thirty seconds. Then she snapped open her corduroy slacks and the zipper sighed downward. She brought her knees up and flattened her feet on the couch so that she could shove the clothing past her hips. I grabbed the bottoms and she obligingly raised her legs for me to complete the removal. Her underwear came with the slacks and I dropped both to the floor.

"More," I commanded.

She didn't hesitate. She hauled the sweatshirt over her head and threw it toward the archway.

I laughed and reached to pull her up toward me by her neck. I took off her bra and tossed it after the sweatshirt. Back on my heels, I did my own undressing, slipping sideways to complete the task and tossing my clothes aside.

Thin strips of moonlight sliced across Wren's body catching an eye which flashed eerily. I felt as though I had captured an alien being.

Her voice low and breathy, Wren asked, "Why are you smiling?"

"I'm remembering a teenage daydream prompted by all the science fiction I have read." My own voice dropped low. "You fulfill my dreams, Wren."

"I want you to fill me."

I sucked in breath through my teeth and began stroking her legs with the tips of my fingers. Her thighs quivered and she rocked one foot against me. "You forgot my socks."

"No," I teased. "They make you seem more naked."

Her response was to curve her arms above her head, provocatively tightening her breasts, and to pin me with a hard stare to hide her passion. I nuzzled a knee against her crotch and bent down to tongue a nipple. Her sigh became a whimper as I clamped down hard with my lips and then tugged. I went back and forth between her breasts until her writhing demanded more. I shifted back and reached for a pillow. When I plunged a hand under her buttocks, she helped lift herself and I forced the pillow in place.

I ran my tongue along the edges of the plush triangle. "I want you wet, Wren. Wetter than you've ever been. Then it will be all my fingers filling you."

She gasped, "No...no, Lexy!"

"Yes. We've been moving toward that. You know you want it." I smoothed my cheek against her taut thigh. "But if you say no again, I'll mark it off the list." I stopped all movement and waited. Wren made no sound.

Slowly I parted her vaginal lips with probing fingers. Then I touched the tip of my tongue to the smooth warmth of her inner flesh. Her quiver came from within and I deepened my stroke arousing the fluid I wanted. I played along the opening and she spread wider for me. But I didn't enter her even though she pleaded and her hands fluttered in my hair trying to force me deeper.

"Not yet, Wren." I made my voice gruff. "I want you open. I want you wet. I want you hot for everything I can give you."

"I am!" she cried out.

I jerked my mouth away and began hurling away the back cushions from the couch. That gave me the room I needed to shift to her side. I put an arm under her waist and pressed my head on her abdomen. Pinning one of Wren's legs with mine, I lifted the other to rest on the back of the couch. Almost savagely I thrust two fingers into her, reveling in the quick easy slide and the way she thrust forward to receive me. She yelped her displeasure when I withdrew, but purred contentedly as I reentered her three strong.

I established a slow twisting rhythm, all the while coaxing, "Relax...widen...moisten my way."

As she became more aroused, I added my little finger to the mix, and she grunted my given name in guttural syllables, "A...lex... is." I withdrew only partially and grooved my thumb into the hollow at the base of my fingers. I raised my head and looked at Wren's face. Even with her head thrust back into the pillow, I could see her eyes shut tight and her lips parted. I had to say her name twice sharply before she opened her eyes and stared at me.

Then I said, "Now, my fine woman, receive all of me." I thrust deep and lifted her by the hard pubic arch completely away from the couch.

Her eyes grew wide, her face contorted in ecstasy. I lifted her again and again, driven by the raw moans that thrummed deep in her throat. When I felt the trembling that would vibrate into climax, I held her suspended through it. As the tense muscles of her lower body slackened, I let her down and withdrew my meld of fingers very carefully. Her long sigh of satisfaction floated over me. I stretched alongside her and breathed hard against the throbbing skin of her throat.

Moments later our bodies cooled. We shivered simultaneously and I challenged, "Race you to the bedroom."

She challenged in reply, "Just where do you think I'd find the strength for racing right now?"

Slowly we helped each other from the couch, but the coolness of the room prompted us to greater speed. I kicked aside a cushion in the center of the room.

Wren said, "Lexy! We've got to—"

"Tomorrow," I declared. "Do you want me to turn up the thermostat?"

"No," she relied. "I want to snuggle under the covers." She smacked my bare hip as we hurried down the hallway. "After I wash off all that you stirred up."

"I intend to have the pleasure of that." I said.

She read the reality of that in my tone and my eyes, and offered no dissent.

Silently she stretched out on the bed. In the bathroom I waited impatiently for the water to warm sufficiently. Thoroughly I washed my hands, then returned to Wren with a warm soapy cloth, another hotter one, and a fluffy towel. I could feel her watching my face as I slowly washed and rinsed and dried her.

When I returned again from the bathroom, she was under the covers holding them up for me to scramble in. I did so and into her arms and her impassioned kiss.

Wren whispered, her breath stirring my hair, "I don't know what I did to deserve that, but I hope I do it again."

All was right with my world and I drifted toward sleep smiling against the satiny swell of her breast.

TWENTY-ONE

I clicked on the overhead light and surveyed the scene of last night's passion. Cushions, Wren's clothes, my clothes—all were strewn about the room in a chaotic mosaic of sexual abandon. I bit my lower lip to keep from laughing out loud. I imagined Wren's amusement and chagrin when she later discovered I had left the picking up to her.

Slipping into my windbreaker in the chilly garage, I thought of the warm bed and luscious body I was deserting. Once outside I wasn't surprised to discover the dull winter green of the lawn hidden by a thin coating of frost. The cold-sensitive plants and shrubs of the neighborhood were a ragtag collection of strange shapes beneath protective sheets and blankets. A few houses down the way one front yard was a winter wonderland of ice forms created by a sprinkler system left running part of the night.

I decided that suffering the indignity of a pellet burn, oh-so-richly pleasuring Wren, and now braving the cold earned me a diner breakfast. I ate while glancing through a *Ledger* left behind by the last occupant of the booth. It contained a simple four-inch obituary for Andrew Standish, concluding with the announcement that a private, graveside service would be held Monday morning. Donations could be made in his name to the paper's scholarship fund for high school journalism students. Intentional irony on the part of his twin—or an attempt to salvage something good?

Another irony flared in the local section. A promotion for the first installment of my banking series appeared next to an ad for WCXC-AM. I could imagine the angry faces of Sarah Vitak and William Neville when noting that juxtaposition. The radio ad listed the address of the broadcast studio. Knowing my desk was clear, I considered detouring to confront Cross and see what thread I might pluck from the weave of his intrigues. A foolish decision? Or a way to end the vituperative attacks on *Ledger* personnel? And maybe the physical ones on me.

Putting down a tip, I muttered aloud, "Don't fuss, Wren. You wanted me to get them stopped. Talking to Cross might do it."

Slowed by heavy Friday morning traffic, it took me over thirty minutes to get to WCXC, but the timing couldn't have been better. Christopher Cross was getting out of his Lincoln in a small side parking area. I ignored the Employees Only sign and zipped in next to him, taking perverse pleasure in usurping the space reserved for N. Cross.

Cross frowned at my car, then rearranged his face into a semblance of good humor as I emerged. "Miss Hyatt, I believe. Are you deserting print journalism to check out the airwaves?"

"Not me. I just happened to see you getting out of your car and thought you might give me a minute." I settled against the trunk, hoping he would grant me the time right here and now. I didn't want to give him the edge of his own office setting. "I didn't realize you knew me, Mr. Cross."

His smile was patronizing. "I made a point of knowing all about the *Ledger* and her people before buying in. What can I do for you?"

On my way over I had formulated several oblique approaches. Now I scrapped them all. "You could tell me if you plan to keep your stock now that Andrew Standish's portion is beyond your reach."

His frown returned in a greater degree. "Isn't that more the concern of your employer?"

"You made it my concern when a tire iron was raised over my head and..." I lifted the hair back from my forehead "...a shot was fired across my bow."

Cross looked both startled and honestly puzzled—or he was a very good actor.

I continued, "And when someone shoveled shit in Tamara Gantt's car and maligned her, within legal bounds, of course, over your radio station."

The flesh of his heavy face hardened and this time I read awareness in his eyes, but still he said, "I have no idea what you're talking about." He started toward the building.

I wasn't about to be dismissed so easily. "Perhaps you should look into it. The circle of interested persons is widening. Andrea Standish...the detectives investigating her brother's murder..."

He stopped. "That bitch put you up to this! She's trying to divert attention from herself. Well, I'll give you something to take back to her. Her brother's forty percent was mine for a reasonable price only if Nelda managed to place at least third in the orienteering race. He

167

wanted to make a game of it. Otherwise he was going to offer it to the highest bidder after his marriage."

My mind flew to the possibilities. Had Andrea known that? Was that why I was sent out to beat Nelda Cross?

Cross was saying, "So Standish's death didn't benefit me."

I plunged on recklessly. "There's always a blow struck in anger. Or the desire for revenge of some sort. You were seen near where the body was found, you know."

He jerked his head and his jowls quivered, but he calmed quickly. "I don't care whether you're making that up or quoting a source. I didn't see Andrew but I did hear him—very much alive—and arguing with his sister. I was out in the open but they were hidden in the woods. And they were loud. At first they were yelling about some guy named Warren. Then Standish started taunting her with what might soon be happening to her precious newspaper."

When I made no response his sneering tone chilled the morning even more. "He told her that one way or another all the queers, niggers, and chinks were going to be disposed of...that bias in politics and religion was going to sell papers...that dead wood like Worthington was gone along with know-it-alls like that old bat MacFadden and boring blobs like the front-desk receptionist. I didn't hear her respond to all that because I was beginning to move away. I had been heading for the lake area to see if I could snap a picture of Nelda. But I don't doubt that Andrea was furious." He snarled, "Maybe mad enough to kill! So you had better play investigative reporter closer to home if you're trying to find an ass to tag for that braggart's murder."

Now I spoke. "Do you really expect me to believe you weren't involved in those plans? Or did it just upset you to hear them tossed out in the open like that since you manage to keep your hands clean technically?" I paused. "After all, there are always LCC zealots to do the dirty work. Right?"

Cross didn't blink but he clenched his right hand into a fist. "You may be a credit to your profession, Miss Hyatt, but my connection with the Light of Christ Church was in Jacksonville—not here."

I didn't blink either. "You didn't oil the way for Sarah Vitak and William Neville to gain employment at the paper?" I wanted him to learn how much I knew. I thought it might cause him to reassess his plans, if not beat a strategic retreat.

He embellished his answer with a smile of no warmth. "I

smoothed the way through Mr. Worthington for two old friends who happened also to move here from Jacksonville."

"And the religious broadcasts from this very station every morning?"

"The time was purchased. That's what a radio station does. Sell time. And now if you'll excuse me, the station has a claim on my time."

I let him go. Would he call a meeting and end the attacks on *Ledger* minority employees? Had I correctly read his puzzlement over the violence toward me? And what about his claim to be on the way to the lake to catch sight of his wife? Worthington claimed Cross was in that field to get the printout on personnel from him. Was it just chance Cross was in the right place to eavesdrop on Andrea and Andrew? I scuffed a question mark in the thick concrete dust.

Suddenly I was aware of sound and movement directly in front of me. I leaped to the side as a sporty yellow car skidded to a halt just inches from my bumper.

An indignant Nelda Cross flung open the door. "Are you making a career of being in my way?"

I enjoyed towering above her. "Actually I was just interviewing your husband."

"What about?" She glared reproachfully.

"The deal with Andrew Standish if you managed to place in the race. Guess I queered that." I judged her to be the kind who didn't recover quickly from someone else's first strike. "Why would Standish make a deal like that and then set out to help you win?"

Her desire to boast overrode her caution. "Because the fool thought he could arrange a more fun deal with me. He said that if I managed a first-place win he'd keep his bargain with Christopher but would put the stock in my name. That way I'd have a hoop to make my husband jump through."

"You didn't want that?" I tried not to sound as skeptical as I felt.

Nelda Cross continued brusquely, "Why would I? Christopher is a man—not an adolescent in a man's body. He doesn't play games. He wields real power. We do—together." Her ego carried her on. "I went along with Andrew because I wouldn't have minded winning." She sneered. "Any more than you would have. And because I knew the time would come when I could laugh in his face, especially after he suggested we'd celebrate my win in bed. He actually thought that would make me run my legs into the ground. His tag line was that he needed to store up some hot times before he married that icicle he brought back from Alaska."

I stared in disbelief.

"Don't doubt it," she added. "He was juvenile enough to think that would appeal to me—that I'd enjoy being used." She was boasting again. "But I was the one using him—keeping him focused on selling his stock—flattering him into swinging his weight with Joe Worthington."

A gust of wind lifted my hair. Nelda Cross's contentiousness faded. She actually gloated as she said, "That's quite a burn. Probably going to leave a lasting scar."

She was responsible for the attacks on me! I drew myself taller and bit the side of my tongue to keep from exploding. I kept my tone bland. "It took your LCC henchmen two tries to mark me." That startled her. "They were inefficient—inept. I wonder how well they'll stand up to the police investigation that's in progress." Whiteness highlighted the corners of her mouth. "And I wonder how Forum board members will react to knowledge of your—your skullduggery." I did my own gloating. "Great Gothic villain word, don't you think?"

Her nostrils flared and her voice was frigid. "Get out of my parking space! Stay away from me!"

I complied slowly. I savored the thudding sound as she rocketed forward into the space I had vacated and hit her own sign. I had put both Crosses on notice concerning their ties to the Light of Christ Church. I hoped that would diminish their activities rather than ratchet them up, and aid Andrea with whatever plans she had drawn up. But on the surface, neither of the Crosses appeared to stand to gain by the death of Andrew Standish. Still, that didn't mean they were exempt from exploding in deadly fashion at his crass and savage stratagems.

Morning rush hour was over, so I got to the *Ledger* about ten-thirty. I stayed in my car to jot down notes from my interview with Tillman and my encounters with the Crosses. Then I checked through everything on Joe Worthington. Both Crosses had emphasized Andrew's role in controlling the news editor, but Joe himself had mentioned Chris Cross more often in that respect.

I didn't believe Christopher Cross about being in the area of that thicket on his way to catch sight of his wife. He was there either to meet with Worthington or to check on Standish and his progress in assisting Nelda. Could he have heard something said by either Andrea or her brother to make him confront Andrew as soon as the coast was clear?

I jumped at a tap on my window. I got out of the car and greeted Peggy Thomas, who was bundled in a bulky jacket with a scarf around her head. I teased her, "Expecting snow, Peggy?"

She shook her head at my light windbreaker. "You and the boss never dress like you get cold. For all your calmness, I'll bet you both have hot blood."

"I don't know about Andrea, but mine flows warm now and then." I was thinking of last night with Wren. "Or maybe it just flows deep. You're not calling it a day at mid-morning, are you?"

"No, no. Andrea put Fonda to work covering for me." Peggy lifted a large folder. "And I get to play messenger. She didn't want these delivered by email or snail-mail. She's inviting some people to a summit conference but I hope they're going to be walking in on an arraignment in a Court of No Appeal."

"What's going on?" I didn't really expect an answer. Peggy motioned toward the building. "She had me put a for-your-information copy on your desk." She shivered despite the heavy clothing. "I sure hope it's warmer tomorrow."

"Going to the Hurston Festival?" I asked.

She looked both mildly embarrassed and yet eager to explain. "No. Maybe Sunday. Warren Kessler called last night. He's giving Paul Jared's son pointers on running hurdles. He asked me if I'd like to go to breakfast with him, then to the track. I've run into him a few times over the years, but last night on the phone he seemed different."

"How so?"

She hesitated. "At peace. Maybe Andrew's death has done that for him. It's kind of done it for me." Her stance exhibited defiance—as though warning me off from criticism. "Andrew doesn't warrant mourning. He ruined high school for me. Lied. Told the guys he'd had my virginity. Destroyed dating for me. I could never know if I was being asked out because of a reputation I didn't deserve or...." She shrugged.

"*Moon for the Misbegotten*."

"What?"

"A play by Eugene O'Neill. Dealt with a situation like that."

Peggy lifted her head. "Maybe I'll read it someday." Her smile was wan but she moved off with a determined tread.

As Peggy had said, Fonda Allison was at the front desk. Her smile was bright and welcoming. No hint of the grieving wife-to-be dulled her disposition. Had Andrew been privy to the knowledge of how his death would affect all who knew him, would he have lived a better life?

Fonda said, "That's a very serious expression, Lexy. What are you pondering?"

"A question best left to philosophers. Or poets."

Her brown eyes glowed. "I found a book at Andrea's with your Elinor Wylie in it. Her eagle and mole poem is something!"

"So which are you ready to be? The eagle who 'sails above the storm…stares into the sun' or the 'velvet mole' who can 'go burrow underground'?"

Her excitement was palpable. "Both! I'm going to accept Andrea's surprise offer to stay the rest of the winter here and burrow into every crevice of the *Ledger*. Then I'm going back to Alaska and sail above my father's attitudes and objections and make the *Nugget* mine."

"I have a friend, Charlie, who would say this calls for a high five." I held up my hand and Fonda slapped it with enthusiasm. Then we settled on the logistics of getting to the Hurston Festival the next day.

In my cubicle I sprawled in my battered but comfortable desk chair and pinched open the metal clasp of the envelope I assumed Peggy Thomas had placed on my desk. It contained a single-page, strongly-worded request for attendance at a conference of persons directly or indirectly concerned with developments at the newspaper. The meeting was scheduled for two o'clock Monday afternoon in the owner's suite.

I raised my eyebrows at the blunt statement that all the persons invited featured to some degree in the questions relating to Andrew Standish's death, the establishment of *Ledger* policies, and the structure of ownership and management. The names at the bottom of the sheet were Christopher Cross, Joseph Worthington, Vernon Yount, and three other males identified as deacons of the Light of Christ Church.

"You've been busy, boss lady," I mused in a low voice.

"Yes, I have."

Rapidly I straightened both my body and my chair at her sudden presence. Andrea, somewhat military in her dark maroon blazer and sharply creased gray slacks, took my side chair. Her fingers traced the letters of my et cetera paperweight.

To cover my discomfort at being overheard, I said, "I saw Peggy on her way to deliver these. Do you expect them all to attend?"

"They'll be afraid not to. Each will worry about what the others might say in his absence." She explained, "I met with Detective Ziegler yesterday evening. He will be interviewing members of LCC today concerning the attacks on staff here. I believe his partner is going to approach the morning show hosts at WCXC along with Mr. Cross himself." A devilish glitter sparked her eyes. "All that should provide impetus for attendance."

Inwardly, I breathed a sigh of relief that Robbie and I hadn't crossed paths in the radio station parking lot. Pointing to a name, I commented, "I don't understand the inclusion of Yount."

"Miss MacFadden did her usual thorough research—which I realize you requested. She passed it on to me along with the very pertinent information you secured from a friend of hers. The two of you make a good team. The kind of team our evening paper is going to need"

The "our" was a pleasure and a reward.

Andrea continued, "It should help me to pressure Cross—if not to sell his stock to me, at least to fade into the background. Legal donations to the Committee to Reelect Legislator Yount were on the books in the names of Cross husband and wife, members of LCC, and staff at Cross's holdings. The most valuable information is that if reelected, Yount is in line to head the Communications Licensing and Policy Committee."

"Sounds like you'll be going into the game with a pat hand." I thought this was another situation calling for a high five, but I wasn't bold enough to suggest it.

"The last few months have taught me not to assume victories will occur, but I do feel the pot will be mine this time." She went off on a tangent. "Andrew never played cards—or any games where his athleticism or brute cunning couldn't win the day. When I found him hiding in the woods, he boasted how he had marked Warren Kessler for life, and that he was going to scar my insides with changes here."

The cool reserve of her face hadn't slipped but I sensed her anger. Still, I risked a question. "Did you see Chris Cross in that area?"

The blankness of her pale eyes was unnerving. "No. Why do you ask?"

"He may have been near there." I couldn't bring myself to openly reveal what Cross claimed to have heard, but I wanted her forewarned before facing him in her suite Monday afternoon. Some detective I was turning out to be. Maybe the people who kept urging me to stick to reporting were right.

Andrea left without further comment. Almost immediately she was replaced by Joe Worthington.

"Good copy on the apartment fire, Lexy." He put a load of papers on my desk. "These are some of the reports from agencies looking into safety code violations. Keep at it."

"I am. Got time to sit down a minute, Joe?" Did I imagine that he looked wary as he took the chair just vacated by Andrea? This was my day for cutting to the chase. "I saw you coming out of the LCC church building Wednesday afternoon." I inserted into the uncomfortable silence, "It was just by chance. I had done an interview in that area."

Now he smiled. "Don't explain. A good reporter never apologizes for being in the right place at the right time to see things. I was trying to put a cap on breaking with them." The smile faded into irritation. "That's not right. I was trying to weasel concessions now that Cross couldn't force through his plans without Andrew. I told you how it was with that bunch, but I didn't tell you the complete truth about why I didn't leave when I found out what they were really all about."

I waited, sure that I was again going to hear something I didn't want to know.

"My youngest son is in the army. It's big-time serious to him. Officers Candidate School and all that. He got into some trouble the summer after he graduated from high school. A drug bust. He was just smoking pot but there was a lot of the hard stuff around." He scraped a thumbnail over his teeth. "Believe it or not, I was once a rookie reporter doing my time reviewing the police blotter every day. Things weren't so adversarial between cops and reporters in those days. I made some good friends—some connections. And I've kept them."

"Someone lost the paperwork on your son."

He looked relieved that he didn't have to say it. "That's it. I don't know how the LCC deacons found it out. Maybe Andrew stumbled on it or Cross dug it up. If it came out it would cost my son his career. When you saw me, I was coming from trying to reason with them that there was no longer anything to be gained from me and no percentage in destroying my son's life for nothing."

"Tell Andrea all this, Joe." I overrode his objections. "Nothing means more to her than the paper. And you're part of the paper. She'll understand the kind of hook you were snagged with." I hoped I was right. "Things getting ready to happen. She could use the information." That I was sure of.

I could see resolve building behind his eyes, but all he said was, "I'll think on it."

He left me to my own thoughts. The *Ledger* was more important to Andrea than anything else. And obviously Joe's son and his job was equally important to him.

174

TWENTY-TWO

Despite the difficult driving, I was conscious of Wren's fingers curving around my shoulder as she leaned forward from the back to converse with Fonda Allison. They talked easily—sharing experiences, asking and answering questions. Andrew Standish, the *Ledger*, and the orienteering run were all painstakingly avoided.

I turned onto the side road paralleling I-4. Ahead, only two structures rose high enough to disrupt the expanse of clear blue sky—Channel 2's super doppler tower brightened by a rainbow logo and the Eatonville water tower dulled by rust. They reminded me of pieces on a chessboard—each wary of the other's move but ready to engage.

Signs marked by bobbing balloons guided me to parking in the sparse grass of a schoolyard. Young people in jeans, white shirts, and colorful sashes, waved and pointed cars into orderly lines. Lettered in black down each sash was ZORA! We joined streams of people heading for the vendor booths along Kennedy Boulevard and the performance tents on the grounds of Hungerford High.

At the call of my name I dropped back to join two women I knew from my teaching days. We brought each other up to date and promised further contact. Before I could catch up to Wren and Fonda, I was hailed again. This time it was Thea standing alongside Tamara, who was talking into a small tape recorder.

As I approached them, I heard Tamara commenting on the satisfying sprinkle of white faces among the crowd. She was wearing a business woman's pinstriped power suit topped by a turban of tangerine and cream. Thea was stunning in a high-waisted pair of pants and a short jacket of brushed leather the color of burnished brass. Her hair was a mass of afro curls above a leopard skin head wrap. The crowd flowing around us exhibited a range from Florida casual to regal African. Zora Neale Hurston would have enjoyed it all.

Tamara clicked off the recorder and said, "Good day for getting away to something different."

I responded, "Wren and I brought Fonda Allison. I think this is going to be the kind of difference she could use right now."

Thea drawled derisively, "Checking out the bloods and pickaninnies."

Tamara snapped, "Stuff it, Thea. That's not what Lexy meant and you know it." To me she said, "Make sure you catch some of the step dancing competition. I've got a niece on a preteen squad and a nephew in a teen group. They'll wear you out just watching." She gave a hearty laugh. "They tried to teach me some steps and gave up. Said they were going to run me out of the black race if that's all the rhythm I had." She sobered. "It was good to hear them poke a little fun at their own stereotypes. I think that's a sign of progress."

"So do I. Even though I'm not a flaming redhead, I had to learn to make light of the teasing about having a temper. Which I didn't have—and don't."

"Maybe not—but things can get under your skin a bit." Tamara was looking to where Thea had drifted off to speak to others. Thea answered my glare with a broad grin.

I countered, "What's with Thea? She was a little sharp just now."

"Oh, she's like Davonne. Thinks my being assigned festival coverage is using my being African-American. I told her of course it is—and it makes good sense. I can look at things from the inside—and with more appreciative eyes." She grunted. "Actually, though, I made the mistake of telling her I had been removed from any coverage of Standish's death."

"I thought..."

"I know. The boss lady assigned me right off to dog the heels of the police and the detectives and then coordinate with you. But after my car was trashed, she pulled me off. Said it was for my own safety in case there was a connection somehow."

"Did you believe her?" I asked.

"Halfway."

"And the other half?"

Tamara tugged at her turban. "She might have heard about an exchange between her brother and me at their parents' viewing and thought I couldn't be objective. I was leaving the chapel as he was coming in, looking back and talking to someone. He bumped into me and knocked a flower out of my black armband. He picked it up and asked me if I'd taken it out of one of the floral arrangements inside."

"The bastard!" Another thought scuttled about below my anger. I was sure Tamara had let it be assumed a couple of weeks ago that she had not personally crossed paths with Andrew Standish.

"That's what I wanted to say. But I explained very politely it had come from a pot on my own window sill. You know, Lexy, it's always been a family tradition to wear a real flower in the band when viewing the deceased, but I don't know where the tradition came from or how far back it goes. All the way to slave days for all I know—maybe even further. I knew there wasn't any sense explaining that to him so I just held out my hand for the flower." Tamara's eyes clouded with bitterness. "He crushed it and tossed it aside." She shimmied as though throwing off repugnance. "Enough of that kind of darkness."

That comment, the return of Thea, and my own need to catch up with Wren and Fonda stifled any questions. I found the two admiring jewelry fashioned primarily from natural elements—polished stones, pieces of wood, woven vegetation. There was elegance in the simplicity. Slowly we moved from booth to booth, Wren and Fonda making occasional purchases from the offerings of clothing, folk art, carvings, blankets, dolls and toys and jars of honey and preserves. I bought a beeswax candle that made me think of a waterfall frozen in mid-plunge.

Eventually the rhythmic thumping of drums drew us to an outdoor stage where we perched precariously on rickety metal chairs. On stage were six young girls in white boots and flared red skirts below white tops. Their rapid-fire synchronized clapping, slapping, and stomping were exhilarating—the swirl and clicking of their beaded braids a counterpoint to the solid drum beats. They were followed by six older teens—two boys in black Ninja suits and four girls in pastels. All wore thick-soled, tall dark boots. They punctuated the traditional step dancing elements with exciting leaps and twirls, twists and turns.

We clapped long and hard. Fonda said, "That was marvelous! They've set my whole body to pounding."

Wren added, "They've exhausted me and I didn't do anything but watch!"

While Wren and Fonda chose to check out the puppet show and storytellers' tent, I made for the Writers' Pavilion. There were several authors at displays of their books, signing copies and answering questions. I recognized Tina McElroy Ansa whose *Baby of the Family* I had read, and Jereleen Miller from a picture and article in the paper covering her children's writing project.

I was surprised to see Thea leaving a display of *Soulfood Cook-book* by Fabriola Gaines and Roniece Weaver with a copy in her hand. Her head bent over the book, she was about to pass me when I said, "Didn't take you for a cook, Thea."

Her expression was more friendly this time. "And you'd be right. Got this for Grandma. Even got it signed. That's what'll make her like it. Gonna bring her tomorrow and take her up and down the street." She glanced around—looking for Wren, I was sure. Then her eyes came back to me and I could sense a hard question coming. "Is Tamara treated right at the paper?"

"Yes. Granted, she's had to be better and tougher to make her mark, but she's doing it. There's nothing out of line about her being assigned this festival, Thea."

She shrugged. "Maybe not. But what about being taken off the murder? Was that a matter of not trusting her to do the job right or because she knew Stan—" She couldn't bite the word off in time.

"Knew what about Andrew? That he was part of getting her brother to climb that roller coaster?" I remembered Thea's discomfort Wednesday evening when I had brought up Luther Gantt's name. I tried to subdue the icy flutterings in my mind. "How would she know that? He died before she was born, right?" I pushed through Thea's glaring silence. "I can easily ask Tamara."

Her long fingers gripped my arm as I turned to walk away. She answered grudgingly, "She found out awhile back."

The flutters solidified into a block of coldness. "How?"

"She was over to the house showing Grandma her two bylines in the front section. The Standishes had died and there was a picture of the whole family with their names. Grandma's mind is real sharp on old times." Thea wrinkled her nose and shook her head slowly. "She can tell me the name of every kid I ever got into it with. Told Tamara that was the name of one of the little boys with Luther when he died. Tamara asked her all sorts of questions. She always wanted to know stuff about Luther. Because she was born almost at the same time he died, I guess."

"What do you mean?" But I knew. I could hear Tillman describing Mrs. Gantt swollen with new life just as she was losing an older child.

"Tamara was born two hours after Luther fell and died. But I know my cousin, Lexy. She wouldn't let that get in the way of covering a story right. She's full-time professional. She is the most unemotional person I know when it comes to doing what has to be done—even if

178

it involves being African-American." She tossed her head and her curls flounced and quivered. "I used to try to get her riled up about it." A corner of Thea's mouth twitched. "But I also cut these knuckles on a bunch of teeth that called her an Oreo or Aunt Jemima. Course I hit harder when they called me an Uncle Tom."

Despite the tension between us, we laughed together—just as we had at Leather Fever. I was becoming used to the extremes of my reactions to her. Would we find the middle ground I walked with most people?

Trying to maintain the momentary lightness, I asked, "Did Tamara like you fighting her battles for her?"

"Of course not. But family's family."

I understood. How deep was the sense of family between Tamara and a brother who died almost as she was being born? Did I want to know?

Thea and I had sauntered outside and now I saw Wren approaching from the street. She handed me a paper plate with a circle of what looked like fried dough.

Thea exclaimed excitedly, "Funnel cake! Where'd you get that?"

Wren answered, "Way at the end of the food lines." She said to me, "I had them sprinkle sugar and cinnamon on yours. I had strawberry jam and Fonda tried hers with apple butter."

I sampled the pastry and mumbled through a mouthful, "This is great! Where's Fonda?"

"At the Hurston museum. I told her we'd catch up with her there. But we're going to have to spend some serious time around the food later. There are great big pots of chicken and black-eyed peas, pans of ribs and catfish, chitlins, pan-fried greens...and stuff I have no idea what it is." Wren smiled at Thea. "Would it be politically correct to ask you to come along and identify items?"

Thea's smile was all for Wren, but she shot me a look as she said, "At your service, my fair lady."

We crossed the street to the Zora Neale Hurston museum. Despite fresh paint and colorful flags, the square building still looked like the garage it had once been. The anthropologist part of Hurston would probably have liked that. Being familiar with the contents, I sat on a bench outside to finish my cake.

After awhile Thea joined me. Leaning back on the bench, she said, "You may be losing your friends later this afternoon." Clearly our discussion of Tamara and her long-dead brother was to be shelved for the time being.

Very carefully I asked, "How's that going to happen?"

"They're buying tickets to panel discussions and such. Wren said you had your share of such doings in another life and might prefer to stick with the outside activities.

"She's come to know me quite well." I hated sounding so stiff.

"But not completely."

I jerked my head around and stared up at her beautifully contoured face.

Thea's smug smile barely parted her lips. She said, "I offered to be your getting-home chauffeur. I'll be dropping Tamara off at the *Ledger* to do her write-up of today."

I was torn between two reactions. I chose one and blurted, "She's left her car there again!"

"She said sometimes it feels good to dare somebody to do it again." Thea frowned. "I sure hope they don't. Okay?" Clearly I didn't comprehend what she was asking, so she added, "Me giving you a ride? Or are you afraid to be alone with me?"

I refused to answer that. We both knew her intent was to stop me from questioning Tamara about Luther and Andrew. Instead I got up and went inside to clarify things with Wren. When I heard their enthusiasm about the discussions on minority contributions to modern-day art, a symposium on how to recognize and assist talented youngsters in all artistic areas, and a demonstration of dance techniques, I readily agreed to going our separate ways—especially since Wren would be paired with Fonda rather than Thea.

Returning outside, I said to Thea, "Shall we ease on down the road? If you think you can match my stride."

"I can match you at anything, Lexy Hyatt."

Not far down the street we spotted Tamara's turban. She was standing back away from clusters of young African-American girls and recording her impressions. The girls were waiting in line to be fitted with bright tissue-paper hats in the broad-brimmed style of those worn by Hurston in the thirties.

I said, "Suppose many of them will grow up to read Zora?"

Thea drawled. "Hope so. I have. Don't look so surprised. I read. Tamara saw to that." She looked admiringly toward her cousin. "She forced a bunch of us into it."

"Forced?"

"Tricked...bargained...whatever you want to call it. It was the price she demanded for help—help with homework, a loan, a ride somewhere...." She smacked a fist into her left palm, "... a brand new ball glove."

Tamara joined us for the rest of our tour before we met up with Wren and Fonda in the food lines. I was enjoying the day so much that even Thea's exaggerated gallantry with Wren didn't rankle. Fonda listened to Tamara's tapes and they shared their journalism backgrounds and differing individual battles with the status quo. I was content to listen and observe.

At mid-afternoon, Wren and Fonda went off to their seminars. Tamara continued her recording and did some interviews of celebrities. Thea and I wandered.

Tamara had just left the car when Thea said to me, "I wouldn't mind seeing the inside of the building." She added with clear meaning, "And I wouldn't mind being here to walk Tamara to her car later. Is that a problem for you? Or would you like me to run you home first?"

"I don't mind hanging around. I could check my voice mail and email. And I'd like to see Tamara safely to her car, too."

Tamara stopped and turned at the sound of our two car doors closing. Though she didn't move, it was as though she were tapping her foot as we approached. "I don't need bodyguards," she declared firmly.

Thea replied lightly, "Well, I need a bathroom and Lexy wants to check her messages. So lead on, Miss Toughie." She grinned at me as her cousin stomped up the steps and inserted a card in the lock slot.

Inside, I pointed Thea down a hallway to the VIP lounge while I checked the display board Peggy Thomas had so carefully arranged. Along with pictures and clippings there was an orienteering map slanted across an upper corner. In the tray at the bottom of the board were a number of push pins.

Putting aside the thought that I was defacing the map, I started inserting pins representing Andrew Standish and those of us near him at the approximate time of his death. Andrea and Warren Kessler admitted confronting Andrew in the thicket. Chris Cross was near enough to hear brother and sister arguing at the same time Joe Worthington drove down Garden Street spotting Cross in the field. Nelda Cross, Tamara, and I all came along the path. Nelda in front of me, Tamara behind.

I removed the blue pin representing me. Regretfully I pulled out the red for Nelda Cross. She was probably striking me with her canteen just as her co-conspirator was being struck down. I looked at the two pins in my palm. Fonda Allison and Peggy Thomas. Where were they?

I scrunched my eyelids and tried to visualize my notes on the two women. Fonda had said she started out on the walking track, then turned back to hunt for Andrea to tell her that she was calling off the marriage and returning to Alaska. Where and how long did she search before sitting down under that mimosa tree? Could she have been near enough to see or hear something pertinent? And Peggy Thomas? I couldn't visualize anything in my notebook pinpointing her movements after our early morning contact.

I tossed the two pins in the tray and went to the lounge. Meant more for the public and visiting dignitaries, the entry room was large and bright, mirrored and plushly furnished in blue and gold. A short corridor to the right led to the women's restroom where the floor tiles were a cafe-au-lait brown, the walls antique white, and the five sinks a serpentine pattern of dark and light tan. Despite the mirrored brightness, the colors were very soothing.

I bent over a sink to wash the stickiness caused by the second funnel cake I had snagged as we were leaving the festival. I heard a toilet flush and seconds later two black hands entwined with mine under the warming water. I watched as Thea worked her fingers over and about mine. She turned off the faucet and smoothed droplets from both our hands. I was acutely conscious of the pressure of her thighs against mine, her breasts against my back, her breath in my ear.

"Not a bad fit, am I."

The heat of her voice spread through me. I couldn't turn without first pressing against her. I didn't want to do that. I met her eyes in the mirror. "Back off, Thea. I'm not a 'little bird' or a 'fair maiden.'"

"Maybe you're what I really want to try on for size." The throb of her voice was more disturbing than the words.

I shoved back and gained enough room to step to the next sink. We continued to lock eyes in the mirror.

Thea sneered, "Unless the white lady is afraid the black will rub off."

I whirled to face her. "Don't you dare try to hang that on me!"

Her face reflected triumph at having pricked me. "Ah...maybe that isn't the case. Maybe you're just still stuck in honeymoon goo. That always passes, you know. When it does—I'll be around. We'd make a good time of it, Lexy. You may have everyone else fooled but I've spied the unruly cuss in you." Her voice flowed between a tease and a challenge. "You'll always have to step outside the group now and then—even if it's only a group of two. Let's make certain my smell is in your nostrils for when you do."

Before I could blink my eyes, she crossed the short space separating us. Her kiss was savage and I could dredge up no resistance. I was mentally battling with what she had said. Our teeth clicked against each other. I was aware of her muscled strength, despite her slimness. She pressed a thigh between my legs and I choked back a moan.

Just as suddenly she released me. One cool glance and she was gone, leaving my body vibrating to the force of her embrace and my mind scrambling to find a compartment in which to safely confine her.

I left the restroom and sprawled in one of the lounge chairs, defying the plushness to comfort me. I felt like an infielder fumbling every ball. No—not every one. Wren was as securely in my glove as I was in hers. Thea was wrong.

Appeased by that thought, I went to my desk and found no messages of any importance. I spent time reviewing notes and reports and updating my calendar for the next week. Seeing everything I had lined up was daunting but exciting. Then I roughed out an opening to an investigation into possible harassment of female firefighters under the guise of instituting old regulations. Recently the women had been ordered to have their hair cut in the near-military style of the men.

When I heard the voices of Thea and Tamara in the reception area, I joined them there at the display board. I was careful to look Thea in the eye but equally careful not to let my eyes drop to her lips. I pointed to the map. "Did either of you see Fonda or Peggy Thomas when you left the course?"

Thea shook her head. Tamara said, "No...wait...maybe I did see Peggy. After we handed the injured woman off, we stood awhile deciding whether or not to go back out on the course. A golf cart passed us going too fast and kind of rocked making the turn through the gate to get out on the course. That's why I noticed it. A clipboard bounced out and the woman had to back up and scoop it up. She was wearing a *Ledger* cap but her back was to us. That's why I'm not sure it was Peggy."

Tamara stepped toward the exit. "Okay, bodyguards. Do you flank me or go front and back?"

Thea declared suggestively, "I'd like Lexy in the front. I prefer the rear position."

Tamara arched an eyebrow. I strode toward the door, clamping on my lower lip to stop an expletive.

TWENTY-THREE

Thea and I exchanged no comments on the way to my house, but the interior of the car was charged. I felt bombarded from within and without. Now, standing at the foot of the short walkway to the front door, I watched her back out and drive away, hoping I had sufficiently reinforced the walls of the compartment to which I had relegated her.

Interior lights welcomed me home—to Wren, to the life we were weaving out of our two selves. I would permit no one to introduce knots into the pattern. I opened the door—and was annoyed to hear two voices emanating from the kitchen.

Fonda greeted me. "Lexy! I'm glad you got here in time for me to thank you for making this day possible. I don't know when I've enjoyed myself so much!"

Wren said, "I brought Fonda home so I could dress up the sketch I did."

At first I thought she meant the one done at the park the Sunday Standish was killed. Then I saw a very different sketch on the table where they sat. This was a radiant Fonda, obviously engaged in all she was encountering. Very lightly in the background Wren had sketched scenes from the Hurston Festival.

"And I thought," Wren continued, "that you might want to drive Fonda home."

It pleased me to know what she was really saying. She was itching to get to her studio for some serious work capturing impressions of the day. I didn't mind. I needed a little more space, too. Driving home alone would do it.

In the car Fonda chattered about the symposia and the dance exhibition. She fell silent as we neared Andrea's condo speaking again only after I pulled into a visitor's space.

Tracing the outline of a Hurston hat on a bag, she said, "I never played with a yoyo as a kid, but I feel like I'm one in my own hands right now. First I came here—then I wanted to go home to Alaska—now I've agreed to stay in a tutorial position at the *Ledger*."

I heard the hesitation in her voice. "But?"

Her smile was wistful. "But I need the white silence. And I can face it now. I need to face myself, too. I need to learn to live without..."

Without Andrew? Surely that couldn't be what she was thinking.

Her eyes were pleading. "Come in awhile, Lexy. Please. Andrea won't be home till after midnight."

Curiosity motivated me—and knowing Wren would be deep in her work. "All right."

The entry room was much like Andrea's office—furniture of strong, simple lines and cool colors. Fonda motioned me to follow her with the two bags I had carried in from the backseat. She pointed to a door as we passed it. "Bathroom." I shook my head. I hoped Thea hadn't made me permanently skittish about bathrooms.

The bedroom we entered was devoid of any personal touches. No toiletries or knickknacks on the chest or dresser—no clothes tossed anywhere.

Fonda saw my scrutiny and explained, "Everything is still in suitcases. Didn't seem sensible to really unpack." She pulled a smallish suitcase from under the bed, flipped it open, and began inserting her festival purchases. As I stepped forward to admire the Black doll, she said, "A shipmate of my grandfather returned to Alaska with him after the war—an African-American man. I think his youngest granddaughter will like this."

She placed it in the case next to the barbell hand weights I had seen her carrying at the park. A Women's Health Week headband was drooped over one. She added a cluster of brochures from the festival.

I thought of the orienteering map and the two push pins I had tossed back into the tray of the display board. "Fonda, did you see Peggy Thomas anywhere around when you came back from walking the track to look for Andrea?"

She stared at me an inordinately long time before answering. "No. I was concentrating on what I was going to say to Andrea when I found her—and later to Andrew. I was composing pretty speeches in my head." Her acrid tone was disconcerting. With obvious effort she soothed out her tone. "I did see Tamara and Thea though I didn't know their names then. Tamara was insisting that she had to finish the race and Thea was trying to argue her out of it. Said it was too far back to go. There were a couple of golf carts by the fence and Tamara took one. She said something about using it to get to the place where they had stopped and letting someone else bring it back."

The icy pricklings again. Tamara had not said anything about driving herself back out on the course. I was sure she had said a referee offered to give her and Thea a ride back. But I couldn't remember for sure her saying that's what she did. Why shouldn't she take a cart if one was available? Why was I working overtime being suspicious of everyone? Silently I ordered myself to put the detective to bed for the night.

Fonda said, her words gaining momentum, "I thought about taking the other cart to go look for Andrea. I knew it wasn't the right time or place, but I couldn't stand being in purgatory any more when it was Andrew who deserved to be there. I wanted to tell somebody that. I wanted to shout it at him!" She seized the case and dropped it to the floor, sitting down on the bed at the same time.

A barbell bounced out, dragging the headband with it. I bent to retrieve it. As soon as I held it, I realized I was testing its weight and balance in my hand. And then I knew something I didn't want to know—I had never put Fonda into the picture as a possible murderer. A mistake. I dropped the barbell back in the case but held on to the headband. Feeling drained, I sat down next to Fonda.

She reached over and touched the leaping woman logo, her hand resting on mine. "Were you running the race for someone special, Lexy?"

At a loss, I focused on her question and explained about my teacher, Miss Perry. I finished with, "I try to be happy about the lives she lived long enough to touch, instead of being sad about those she died too soon to influence."

"You keep saying things to make me like you. You did the day I met you and we talked poetry. Then at the bookstore I heard the manager indicate you were a lesbian. I almost talked to you then—back on our way to the *Ledger* in the car."

Not a welcome change of subject. I searched her face for clues to where this was going. I received none.

Fonda thrust her hands through her hair. "What would you have felt if you had been participating in Wren's name?"

Though I had faced that fear, I denied it. "I refuse to consider that."

Fonda's eyes were tortured. "It could happen. An Andrew Standish could make it happen. He made it happen to Brittany!"

The name was more a choking sound than a unity of letters. It grated on my ears. It scraped its way into my memory. Though I was not yet comfortable with computers, I had come to realize that I had always stored information like data bytes creating a myriad of files to be scrolled through for links. I did that now.

Brittany. One of the snowmobilers. A terrible gut-wrenching instinct told me which one—the one cut off by Andrew Standish only to be caught in the deadly snowfall—the one listed in the paper as Brit. I had assumed it to be a male name. I scarcely breathed the name aloud. "Brit—"

Fonda exhaled a shuddering sigh. "Yes." Her voice dropped into neutral. "I overheard Trooper Herron telling my grandfather that some observers below thought Standish forced her into the path of the avalanche." She gazed calmly at me, her emotions apparently on hold. "No one knew the truth about Brit and me. We were working toward that. I think my grandfather had an idea. My parents would have had a hard time with it." The small silence didn't last long enough. "They'll have a harder time knowing I killed because of it."

I felt as though a bubble encased us—shutting out all other reality. I wanted to push my way through the transparent wall and escape, but my heart swelled with pain and I couldn't desert her. "Don't tell me things I shouldn't hear, Fonda."

But I already knew things I didn't want to know. She must have taken the golf cart—the one with the green referee's vest. She must have come across Andrew right after all the rest of us had scattered away from the thicket. But she couldn't have come there intending to kill him....

She was reading my face, my eyes. "You know that I did it, don't you, Lexy?"

I couldn't stop the question. "Why? It wouldn't bring her back."

The remoteness in her tone emphasized her despair. "Brit and I quarreled about only two things. Snowmobiling was one. I thought they were okay for transportation and rescue, but recreational use was destructive of the environment. I even wrote an editorial on it. The other was Brit's need to continually test herself against men—to prove that she was every bit as capable as they were. I understood where that came from—a large family of mostly men who belittled women."

She fell silent and I prompted. "I can understand your feelings toward Standish, but what were you looking for in becoming engaged—in coming here?"

More life entered her voice. "I had to find out if he was really the kind of person who would so unfeelingly push someone into death just to win a contest. If he was—I wanted to find a way to punish him. Oh, Lexy, I know that was crazy! But I was stumbling around in a fog of shock and hatred and guilt."

"Why guilt?" The investigative reporter in me was awake again.

"Because I didn't try hard enough to wean her away from the snowmobiles and the risk-taking." She sighed. "But I didn't want to change her from being the woman I had fallen in love with. I knew I wouldn't accept her trying to stop me from challenging my father about how I thought the paper should be run. But she died. And it had to be in fear—and away from me." She hit the bed with her fist. "I had to do something!"

Fonda continued, more quietly but with a deeper anger. "It didn't take all that long to find out just how terrible Andrew Standish was. I rented a post office box here and hired a service to send me clippings on him." I thought of the contents of the folder that had been passed on to me. "And I saw firsthand the pleasure he took in manipulating people—in forcing them into situations that would maim them—and sometimes kill them."

She turned sideways and gripped my hand with both of hers. "But you have to believe me, Lexy! On the walk that morning, my head cleared. I just wanted to escape him and go home to mourn Brit properly—openly. I wanted to tell Andrea right away and Andrew in the evening. I took a cart but I felt conspicuous. I put on the vest that was in it so I'd look like I belonged. After I got pretty deep into the course I got asked some questions because people thought I was a referee. When two people asked me the shortest way back, I gave them the cart. They looked exhausted."

Her voice dropped lower. "I found Andrea—with Andrew. He was saying terrible things to her. She left and he stood there, his back to me, laughing after her."

Releasing my hand, she turned to stare at the wall. "He didn't hear me walk up behind him. I heard him say, 'You're going to eat dirt, sister dear. The best part is you're going to know it's me feeding it to you.' I must have made a sound because he started to turn. I was carrying one of the hand weights. I didn't make a decision; I just swung with all the strength I had. He grunted and crumpled up on the ground. I remember hearing the chatter of a squirrel."

I stared at the wall. Why had I failed to see her engagement to

188

Andrew as an inconsistency, a prelude to murder? How could I have missed the clues that she was a lesbian needing recognition?

Fonda let out another long sigh. "Then I heard voices. Someone said to watch for a referee. I took off the vest and threw it up in a tree." She turned back toward me. "I didn't know I had killed him. I walked along the edge of the woods not even sure where I'd end up. Somehow I got back to the front. I sat on a bench and waited for whatever would happen." Her voice trailed away.

We sat in a smothering silence, broken suddenly by an authoritative voice from the doorway. "Lexy...with me."

How long had Andrea been standing there? How much had she overheard? She disappeared but I stayed, watching Fonda's reaction.

Quietly, but not meekly, Fonda said, "I'm glad she heard. I put her in jeopardy—the police suspect her. I don't care what she does. Nothing matters without Brit. I've been pretending that my life could go on. That no one would have to pay. Time to give up the dreams and face the nightmares."

Not truly knowing what I intended, I pulled her gently into my arms. Keeping my cheek against hers, I murmured, "Your life will go on—and it may be a nightmare for a long time. I don't know Andrea very well but I know she'll stand with you."

I got up from the bed, but I couldn't leave her alone in that room without giving her something. I pulled her up and kissed her—on the lips—with warmth and caring. "Someday you'll wake to daylight. Someday another woman will kiss you—want you as Brit did. Be open to it, Fonda." I lifted her chin with a finger. "My kiss was not taken from Wren. Your acceptance of another woman will not negate Brit."

I followed the clacking sound of computer keys to where Andrea sat at a small desk. Without taking her eyes from the screen, she said, "There's a flight out of Orlando International at three a.m. for Chicago. She can make connections there for Alaska." Now she met my surprised stare. "You heard her. She didn't intend to kill Andrew. Didn't even know he was dead. Alaska is still a raw, independent state. The governor won't be likely to grant extradition even if it's requested—which I doubt. I rather imagine her grandfather is still a force to be reckoned with. The police here are juggling too many suspects. They won't arrest any of us without a witness or a weapon."

And just where, I wondered, would that miniature barbell end up? More important—what was I going to do about all this?

Andrea sensed the question. "You do what you have to. It would be convenient if you wrestled with the decision for at least twelve hours." After a long pause and my continued silence, she said, "Good night, Lexy."

As I left, I rolled down all the car windows, needing the rush of cold air. I hadn't been cajoled, pressured, or threatened; the decision was mine—and I had three blocks in which to make it. At that point a right turn would take me to Wren—a left to Detective Robbie Exline.

Andrew Standish had urged Tamara's brother toward his fall, crippled Warren Kessler, sullied the adolescence of Peggy Thomas. He had hoped to set Cross against Cross, had bullied Joe Worthington toward the loss of his career, schemed to destroy his sister. He had cost Fonda's Brit her life. And there had been others—faceless names in newspaper clippings. Had he lived...

I turned right.

Other Mysteries in the Lexy Hyatt series by Carlene Miller

MAYHEM AT THE MARINA

Lexy Hyatt goes to stay on a friend's boat where she meets a street-wise young woman named Charlie. All too soon people at the marina become suspects when a body is found floating in the lake. Lexy investigates, hoping to clear her new-found community, but is sorely challenged when she discovers that Charlie is hiding the murder weapon.

$11.95   ISBN 1-892281-05-8

KILLING AT THE CAT

Lexy gets a chance to prove herself as a reporter when a woman is found dead at The Cat, her favorite lesbian bar. When her own ex-lover looks like a prime suspect, she struggles to maintain her objectivity. A hot new love interest adds to her emotional quandary as she closes in on the killer.

$10.95   ISBN 0-934678-95-2

Order these and many more mysteries from:

NEW VICTORIA PUBLISHERS
PO Box 27 Norwich VT 05055
email—newvic@aol.com
Web—www.NewVictoria.com